ANTARCTICA
STATION

A.G. RIDDLE

ANTARCTICA STATION

An Ad Astra Book

First published in the UK in 2024 by Head of Zeus,
part of Bloomsbury Publishing Plc

9 7 5 3 1 2 4 6 8

A catalogue record for this book is available from the British Library.

ISBN (PB): 9781035913817

Typeset by Siliconchips Services Ltd UK

Printed and bound in Great Britain by
CPI Group (UK) Ltd, Croydon CR0 4YY

Head of Zeus Ltd
First Floor East
5–8 Hardwick Street
London EC1R 4RG

WWW.HEADOFZEUS.COM

To those who struggle but never give up.

ANTARCTICA

SELECTED RESEARCH STATIONS · PERMANENT BASES

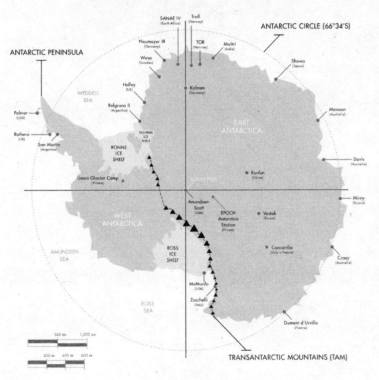

EPOCH

SCIENCES

Prologue

The meeting took place in Switzerland, in the resort town of St Moritz.

The twenty people invited were told very little about the purpose of the gathering, only that a monumental opportunity would be presented. And offered only once.

Most came because of who had invited them—and because of who else would be there. They liked secrets. And secretly, they didn't want the other attendees to have any opportunities they didn't have. In truth, the fear of missing out motivated the ultra-rich, too, especially because there was almost nothing they were at risk of missing out on.

This opportunity, however, was one such thing.

The host had decided to make his presentation over breakfast at his mansion atop one of the ski slopes. He knew that some of his guests would be inebriated by lunch.

Others, in their advanced age, dined early and turned in before the sun set. He wanted every person present to have a clear head for what was about to take place.

As the caterers finished depositing the plates and filed out, rays of sunlight peeked over the snow-capped Alps, flooding in through the French doors to the terrace. The homes and resorts in the valley below were blanketed in snow and surrounded by dense forest, all glistening in the sun like a life-sized snow globe.

The lake below was frozen. A dozen people were skating across the white expanse of ice, setting up for a polo match later that day.

The host walked to one of the doors and watched the bundled-up workers on the ice, thinking about how the world was about to change and about how futile it all was.

Behind him, silverware began clinking on fine china, and conversations started up. He thought it best to start now—before they got distracted, before old wounds were verbally reopened, and before new friends began discussing exciting opportunities to work together. The food could get cold. The kitchen could always make more.

He tapped a fork against his water glass, drawing every eye in the room.

"Ladies and gentlemen, welcome. I've brought you here for two reasons."

He set the glass down.

"The first, is that I know how the world will end."

The room was dead quiet.

"The second," the host continued, "is that I know what to do about it. But I need help. The solution to the coming event is a scientific breakthrough. An expensive one.

"And for each of you, it's an opportunity. An opportunity to save your family. And to be part of creating a new world."

PART I

SECRETS

I

In the end, it was a chance encounter that changed Laura's life forever.

She saw something she wasn't supposed to.

And in doing so, she discovered a friend's secret.

*

Right before it happened, Dr. Laura Reynolds was standing outside a hospital operating room, hands hovering over a scrub sink, waiting for the motion-activated faucet to switch on. Around her, surgeons and nurses were chatting.

Laura had never been very talkative before surgery. In med school, it had been nerves.

Even now, near the end of the first year of her fellowship, she still felt a hint of butterflies in her stomach before every operation. Just enough to focus her senses.

For Laura, that touch of nervousness always disappeared the moment she crossed the threshold of the operating room.

In a way, the OR was her place of Zen. Time seemed to disappear there. Her worries melted away. There was only the patient and the monitors and the work.

For the past six months, she had needed that pocket of serenity, the distraction that work provided. Otherwise, *the blowup*—as she had come to call it—would have sent her into a spiral.

Work had saved her.

Given her a purpose.

A place to pour her energy.

When Laura had enrolled in medical school, she intended to become a surgeon. But during her rotations, she discovered that it wasn't for her. Instead, she had chosen another specialty that played an integral part in surgeries: anesthesiology.

She liked high-pressure situations. She liked being part of operations that saved a person's life. The aspect she liked most was what she thought of as the puzzle of anesthesia. To her, every patient was a puzzle.

The vital signs were the clues.

Blood pressure.

Pulse.

O_2 saturation.

They were pieces Laura had to fit together to keep the patient under, for the surgery to succeed and for the patient to survive.

She was about to fit those vital pieces together while the surgeons did their work. And at the moment, it was what she lived for.

Outside the scrub room, she passed another operating room. In the small window in one of the double doors, she spotted one of her colleagues assisting with a surgery. He was in her anesthesiology fellowship program, and more than that, he was her best friend. His name was Samir, and he was sitting on a stool at an anesthesia workstation, staring at a bank of monitors.

Beside him, the patient was covered in surgical drapes. Surgeons and nurses hovered over the exposed abdomen, hands and arms moving methodically under the bright lights.

Laura was about to move on when Samir reached out and took two vials from a metal tray and slipped them in his pocket. From his other pocket, he drew out two similar vials and placed them where the other vials had been.

No one in the room saw it.

He glanced at the people standing around the patient, then at the double doors. His eyes were glassy and vacant, but when he saw Laura, he focused. She saw panic there. Followed by a flash of guilt.

She had to go in.

She had to stop—

The door beside her swung open, and a woman in scrubs marched out.

Laura had been so caught up in the moment she hadn't seen the nurse exiting. Her name was Julie, and Laura had worked with her regularly over the past six months.

"How's it going in there?" she called to her.

Julie turned, looking exhausted. "They're closing up."

"Any issues?"

"Nothing but. Crashed twice. Barely made it."

Laura peered through the window again. The surgeons were stepping back from the operating table now.

Samir had risen from the stool and was staring at Laura, a pleading look in his eyes.

The double doors to the adjacent OR opened, a nurse pushing it with his back, gloved hands held up.

"Laura, we're waiting."

*

After surgery, Laura went looking for Samir.

She found him in the on-call room, lying in the bottom bunk, eyes closed.

She flipped the light on and squatted down and waited, but he didn't stir.

She shook him until his eyelids peeled open, revealing pupils like marbles rolling around in a bowl.

"You're high," Laura whispered.

"Just sleepy," he murmured.

"Then you won't mind if I draw blood and test it."

He narrowed his eyes. "I'm fine."

"No. You're high."

"It's just… taking the edge off—"

"Samir."

He closed his eyes and opened his mouth, lips moving, but no words came.

"Samir," she whispered again, putting her arms around him, her head on his chest, holding him tight.

He had been there for her when she needed him most, when her life had fallen apart.

Laura would do the same.

She only wished it was that simple.

What he was doing—stealing drugs and possibly getting high during surgeries—put patients at risk.

She had to tell the program. Even if it cost her Samir's

friendship. Even if it brought bad press on the university, and the hospital, and the fellowship.

Surgery was one of the most vulnerable times of a patient's life. They deserved the best from every person in that room.

Behind her, the door to the on-call room burst open, and a nurse named David stepped in. At seeing Laura's head on Samir's chest, his eyebrows shot up.

Laura was about to tell him that this wasn't what it looked like (she had found that in a hospital setting, rumors were like infections: best treated with pre-emptive and aggressive intervention). But David spoke first, eyes on Samir. "We've been paging him."

"Remove him from the schedule—"

"We don't have anyone else—"

"I'll cover for him," Laura said, standing. "Just take him off. He's too tired."

When the door closed, Laura pulled the blanket over Samir, turned the light out, and went to cover his surgeries.

2

Laura spent the rest of the day scrambling to do her own work and Samir's. In the anesthesia workroom, she prepped her cart, returned emails, and charted. She spent the rest of the time in an OR or visiting the PACU—or Post-Anesthesia Care Unit—where she checked on patients after surgery.

In the brief moments in between, she guzzled coffee and tried not to think about Samir (which proved nearly impossible, especially as she drank more coffee).

When her shift was over, Laura returned to the on-call room, where Samir was still sleeping in the bottom bunk.

She sat in a chair in the corner, reading a novel on her phone, waiting for him to wake up.

She was exhausted. Worried. And heartbroken at what her friend had done—and what she knew was about to happen to him.

Her fellow physicians transited the room like motel guests checking in and out, crawling into the top bunk while she kept watch. One joked that her phone's light might keep them up, a veiled complaint embedded in the words. Laura put her earbuds in and switched to an audiobook, extinguishing the phone's light. She listened and remained in the chair, waiting for her friend to wake.

And when he did, she leaned forward.

"Get up. We need to talk."

*

Laura drove them to her apartment. On the way, Samir sat in the passenger seat, head turned to the side, staring out the window.

She wondered if he was still half-high. Or angry with her. Or himself. Or all of the above.

Inside, he sat on the couch, hands clasped in his lap like a kid in the principal's office.

Laura pulled the coffee table back and sat across from him, the way she would approach a patient in a waiting room, one she had to deliver serious news to.

Samir seemed to know what was coming. That his life was about to change. That his career might be over, and his reputation would likely be ruined.

He was despondent, not even reacting to Laura's proximity or stare.

Laura moved into his field of view. "Talk to me."

He shrugged. "About?"

"You know."

He gazed upward, over her head. "I can't."

Laura reached out and took one of his hands. "I'm going to help you. But you have to talk to me."

He smiled an angry, defensive grimace. "You don't understand, Laura."

"Then help me understand. Is it the pressure, or depression, or something that happened—"

"Laura. I cannot. Tell you. Seriously, Laura. I can't."

"Why?"

His tone turned dismissive. "This is a waste of time."

"No, it's not."

"It won't matter soon."

She squeezed his hand. "I really, *really* hope that doesn't mean what I think it does."

He rolled his eyes. "It doesn't."

"What are we talking about here, Samir? What's going on? Please tell me."

He focused on her and exhaled. "I'm gonna go."

He rose, and she did too, a hand pressed into his chest, voice firm. "You're not going anywhere."

"Yeah?"

"Yeah."

"What are you gonna do, Laura?"

"I don't know yet."

"If you turn me in, they'll kick me out of the program, and my family will disown me, and I'll be more alone than ever. I'll lose everything. Maybe even go to prison."

She let her hand drop and moved away from him. "They'll understand."

He laughed. "Who?"

"The program—"

"They won't. Neither will my family."

"Then take a break. Get treatment and come back. We'll figure it out then—when you're in a better headspace."

"What would I tell everyone?"

"That you're exhausted—"

The hateful smile returned to his lips. "That I was weak."

He nodded. "That this place and the job broke me. That's what they'll hear."

"I don't care what they hear or what they think. I care what happens to you."

He glared at her. Slowly, his angry expression turned remorseful. "You know, I actually think you do, Laura."

"Why would you think otherwise?"

"I've recently learned how truly cruel this world is."

Against her will, Laura's gaze drifted to the side table beside the couch, to the picture frame. Seven months ago, it held a photo of Laura and her fiancé on a trip to Machu Picchu. Now, the photo locked behind the glass had been taken at Laura's college graduation. In it, she was dressed in a gown, her sister beside her.

Samir had been there for Laura when she had ended her engagement. In those dark days. After *the blowup*.

Despite him rejecting her help, Laura was still going to be there for him. Whatever it took. Wherever this road led.

"Your family doesn't have to know," she said quietly.

Samir stared at the wall. "They'll find out."

"We can figure something out—"

He held a hand up. He seemed more focused now. His eyes less glassy. "There's only one solution here, Laura. We both know it."

"Apparently, I don't know it."

"I'll tell them."

"Who?"

"Everyone. My family first. Then the program. It'll be better that way—if I turn myself in. I'll get help, and I'll work it out."

She studied him a moment. She was almost suspicious at his sudden about-face. "Are you sure?"

"Yeah. I'm sure. It's the only way."

She closed the distance to him and wrapped her arms around his neck and squeezed hard until he gently placed his hands on her back and said, "Whoa, come on. Take it easy."

"You're doing the right thing."

His body tensed.

"I know," he whispered, lips close to her ear. After a pause, he pulled free of her embrace.

"I need to use the bathroom." He stepped away from her but paused, calling over his shoulder, "Do you mind?"

"No," she said, a little surprised. He had been over to her place a hundred times. He didn't need to ask. She wondered if something had just changed between them.

When the door closed, her phone buzzed from the dining room table, a reminder of a text message that had come in while they were talking. She had been too absorbed in the conversation with Samir to hear it or see it light up.

The message was from her sister.

Doctor just gave us an update on dad. Call when you can.

The fact that Rachel hadn't given an exact update on their father's status told Laura that the news wasn't good.

At the dining room table, she opened her laptop and logged into her father's account at his regional health system.

Sometimes, it took a while for lab and test results to appear in the patient chart. With significant test results, there were also times when the physician didn't want the data released right away. Sometimes, it was best to discuss bad news with a family and patient before they saw it online.

In this case, the new records were already in the chart. Laura stared at the new result, knowing what it meant, wishing it wasn't true.

The bathroom door opened, and Samir stopped cold, staring at her. "What happened? Did you email them?"

She stood. "No. Of course not."

"Please don't lie."

"I didn't. It's… my dad."

The tightness in his face loosened then. "How bad?"

"Bad," Laura whispered.

He closed the distance between them in heavy steps and pulled her into a hug, squeezing her like she had hugged him just moments ago.

His breath was hot in her ear. "I'm sorry."

"Me too."

"Go and see him. While you have time."

She pulled back. "What about you?"

"I'll do what I said. I'll do the right thing. For everyone."

"Promise?"

"I promise."

3

It was after midnight when Samir left.

Laura was exhausted from the double shift at the hospital and the emotional toll of Samir's situation.

All she wanted was to curl up in bed and read until she passed out.

But she had things to do first.

At the dining room table, she booked the first flight home, which left RDU in the morning.

Next, she emailed the head of her fellowship program, informing her that she needed to take a brief leave of absence to help care for a terminally ill parent.

It was too late to call her sister back. She'd do that in the morning. For now, she sent a text message:

Saw the results. Coming home.

*

Just after five o'clock the next day, Laura walked into her father's ICU room in her hometown in Ohio.

Her sister was there, sitting in a high-back chair by the bed, eyes closed, an eReader in her lap.

Their father was sitting up in bed, eyes also closed. His skin was pale, bordering on grayish. Laura stood for a moment, waiting for his chest to rise.

And it did, barely, the slight motion confirming that he was only sleeping.

Laura wanted to reach out and take his hand, but she didn't dare wake him.

Instead, she sat in a chair at the end of the bed and waited.

*

Her father and sister were still asleep when a team of doctors rounded. Like Laura, they also chose not to wake Charles Reynolds.

Outside the room, Laura pulled the glass door closed and introduced herself and listened to the team's latest prognosis, the words and phrases confirming what she'd seen in the online records.

Just too risky to go back in...

Leaves us no real alternatives we favor...

Since seeing the notes and results, a part of Laura had hoped that there was something she was missing. Or didn't know about—like a new treatment.

There wasn't.

She had been in these doctors' shoes, delivering bad news to family members. Now she was on the other side.

She nodded and thanked them sincerely for their efforts. She stood there for a long time after they moved on, long enough for an ICU nurse to stop in the hall and ask if she was all right.

Laura wasn't.

"I am," she replied, flashing a weak smile.

Her phone buzzed in her pocket, a text message from the fellowship program director:

Are you still in Durham?

No.

Call me. ASAP.

Laura's father stirred in the bed and opened his bloodshot eyes, slowly scanning the room until he was peering out through the glass door at Laura.

A warm smile formed on his lips.

Laura tapped out a reply:

Tied up here. Will call but may be a bit.

Through the glass, Laura smiled back at her father. She was reaching for the door handle when her fellowship program director replied.

It's urgent. You need to get back here.

Samir?

Yes. He came to see me.

I know.

Laura, this is a criminal matter. It's serious.

Do whatever you need to. I'll call asap. And help however
I can.

In the hospital room, Laura pulled a chair up beside her
father and leaned over and kissed his forehead and gripped
his hand, careful to avoid the IV line and the tape holding
it in place.

Her sister was waking up as well, and the three of them
talked and laughed and acted like they were happy, as if this
was just a normal family get-together, not a farewell before
their father left this world.

*

The sun was setting over the tall trees in the distance when
Laura's father fell asleep.

Laura and her sister got dinner in the cafeteria downstairs.
Rachel, in classic Rachel fashion, got a burger and added
bacon and chili. She wedged the sandwich in the corner of
the hinged Styrofoam container and filled the rest with fries.
Soda was her drink of choice tonight, not the diet variety.
No ice.

Laura had a chicken Caesar salad. No dressing. Tap
water to drink.

At the condiments station, Rachel opened her carton and
blanketed half the top with ketchup and doused the fries
with salt.

She carried it to the table as if she was cradling a rare
book that lay open. After plopping down unceremoniously,
she began dragging the fries through the ketchup sea and
downing them.

"You look like hell," Rachel muttered, stabbing a fry into

the table to determine how mushy it was before tossing it away and grabbing another to test.

"You ever find a job?" Laura shot back. Over the course of their childhood, she had learned that the only thing that brought Rachel in line was calling her out or giving her some of her own medicine.

Rachel lifted the burger and took a giant bite, squeezing chili from the edges. She was still chewing when she replied: "You've lost weight too. Not a compliment. You look like—"

"I didn't sleep much last night. I had to work a double."

"Thought they couldn't do that anymore. Regulations or something."

"They can't. But sometimes we can't help it. I had to cover for a colleague."

"Hungover?"

"Something like that."

Laura thought her sister might apply the dropped chili to the fries. Instead, she flipped the top of the bun off and scooped the chili back on with her bare fingers and took her biggest bite yet.

"Dad's dying, isn't he?" she said, chewing mechanically.

When Laura didn't say anything, Rachel took a napkin and finally wiped her mouth. "These doctors—"

"It's not their fault."

"They told us—"

"Yeah, well, things don't always turn out the way you think, okay? Or the way they think. They're human, too."

Rachel was raising the burger to her mouth but stopped in mid-air, then set it down. Laura could tell that Rachel was worked up now, past the point of backing down. Things would just escalate from here. What Rachel was really upset about was the fact that their father was dying, and there was nothing anyone could do. Laura was, too. The sisters had always dealt with emotional crises in different ways. Rachel tended to lash out at anyone nearby, for any reason. She said, "Heard from Pierce?"

For Laura, the mention of her former fiancé was like biting into a hard crouton and feeling the shooting pain from a broken tooth.

Slowly, she closed the container over the remains of the salad and stood and walked away, tossing it in the trash as the cafeteria's automatic doors opened to let her out.

4

Laura's father was still sleeping when she returned to his ICU room.

As quietly as possible, she settled in the high-back chair beside him, took the eReader from her backpack and began to read.

Rachel arrived shortly after. At Laura's side, she squatted down and whispered in her older sister's ear, "Can we talk?"

Laura glared at her and swiped her head once to the right.

Rachel reached into her pocket, took out a folded page and placed it in Laura's hand and watched as she unfolded it and read.

> I'm a jerk.
> Sorry.
> Punch me in the face.
> Seriously. This face can take it.
> I'm stressed.
> It's been a lot.
> Shouldn't have mentioned Pierce.
> Say the word, and I'll hire someone to kill him.
> Kidding. I'll do it myself.

I love you.

Thanks for coming.

Just seeing you makes me less scared.

Still gripping the page, Laura held her arms out to her sister, who eased forward and buried her face in Laura's neck. The tears came a few seconds later, hot at first, then cold on Laura's skin.

*

Later that night, a nurse slid the door open and eyed Laura and Rachel, her silent expression saying, "I need to talk with the two of you."

Outside the room, the woman explained to the sisters that they couldn't stay in the room overnight and that they were welcome to sleep in the waiting room. Or come back in the morning when visiting hours resumed.

"We'll make a pallet on the floor," Rachel said.

"It's not about space. It's policy."

"Policy?" Rachel shot back.

Laura knew this was the opening salvo in a coming tirade and verbal standoff.

She grasped her sister's hand and simply thanked the nurse.

She was pulling Rachel away when another nurse approached her colleague and talked with her too quietly for Laura to hear. After, the older woman walked back to the nurse's station, and the nurse caring for Laura's father returned and said, "Actually, we can make a small exception: one person can stay."

Laura once again thanked her, and when she had moved on, Rachel said, "You stay."

"No, Rachel—"

"You should be here. In case... You know, something happens. And you can help. I'll sleep in the waiting room in case he... you know—"

Laura wrapped her sister in a hug and squeezed her tight and held her until they were both shaking.

*

In the reclining chair, Laura stretched out and began reading. Within seconds, she heard her phone vibrate in her purse.

She had neglected the device since the text exchange with her program director. Glancing at the screen now, she realized that she had missed a mountain of text messages and emails. Maybe word had gotten out that her father was dying. Or that Samir had been caught stealing drugs and working while high. Or both.

At the moment, she was too exhausted to converse with anyone about either subject.

In the course of training to become a physician and in her years of practicing anesthesiology, she had learned the mental practice of compartmentalization, of dealing with one case at a time.

Her father's case was the one she was focused on now. And unfortunately, it would be over soon.

*

Throughout the night, the nurse periodically pulled the sliding glass door open and entered and checked on her patient.

Laura stirred each time but didn't rise. She merely watched and thanked the nurse and scanned the numbers on the monitors.

To Laura, it felt almost as though she and her father were passengers occupying a sleeping car on a night train. She knew the destination. Just not exactly when they would get there.

*

Somewhere in the night, Laura heard a faint scratching sound, fingernails on a bed sheet. When she looked over, she saw her father peering down at her with watery, tired eyes, a faint smile on his lips.

She sat up, and he opened his mouth, but no words came.

She grabbed the cup from the side table and held the straw to his lips. Slowly, he drew a small sip.

"Hi," she whispered.

He swallowed and nodded slowly at her and extended a trembling hand that Laura placed on her cheek. It was a hug of sorts, or as close as they could get with all the tubes and sensors on his body. Feeling his warm fingers on her skin seemed to infuse her with calm.

He drew his hand back and breathed out a single word: "Paper." He swallowed and added, "Pen."

Laura got them for him, not asking why. Because she knew.

Placing a tray under the page, Laura steadied his hand and watched as it shook, scrawling the words.

It was a letter to Rachel.

Laura settled in the chair and fixed her gaze on the wheels under the bed, giving her father his privacy.

*

After her father finished the letter to Rachel, he began a second one. Laura assumed it was to her, but she didn't dare look.

When the page was half-filled with wavy letters, he released the pen and closed his eyes, and for a terrifying moment, Laura watched the monitors until his vitals verified that he was only sleeping.

Part of her wanted to lean over and see what he had written. But that felt like a violation. And besides, she knew she should wait until she had read the entire letter to judge it.

*

Laura woke to voices in the ICU room and the sun blazing through the windows.

She sat up, squinting, body sore from the awkward sleeping position.

Her sister was here. As were the doctors and the night nurse, all crowded around the hospital bed, where her father sat in an inclined position, eyelids half open. His pupils shifted toward her. He smiled, a word forming on his lips: *morning*. It wasn't audible. But she heard it. And smiled back.

The tray now held a folded page with Rachel's name scrawled on top. Beside it, the other letter had progressed a little more but remained unfinished.

During rounds, the medical team was courteous and professional, but it was clear to Laura that they were relieved that their patient had survived the night. They vowed to continue to monitor his situation.

Laura knew it wasn't an act per se. What was happening in this room was a form of palliative care. It was compassion delivered in the form of human contact, caring words, and things left unsaid.

Laura liked these physicians.

When they were gone, she took her phone from the side table, where it had been face down, charging all night in do-not-disturb mode.

The bubbles on the text message and email icons now held even larger numbers.

She tapped the email, probably because it was a smaller number that she could get through faster than the text messages, which she'd have to respond to.

An email sent just after noon yesterday caught her attention. It was from the Durham Police Department.

The subject read:

Search Warrant Notification

She tapped the message, which instructed her to see the attached PDF.

She opened it, scanning the words.

STATE OF NORTH CAROLINA
DURHAM COUNTY
In the General Court of Justice
District / Superior Court Division

In the field for *address for the property to be searched*, it listed her apartment. That surprised her. Maybe they thought Samir had left evidence there. The director had said it was a criminal matter. That wasn't what Laura had wanted. She wished then that she had called the program director last night.

Laura was about to do just that when another part of the search warrant caught her attention:

IN THE MATTER OF:

She expected to see Samir's name.
Instead, she saw:

Laura Argo Reynolds

Her pulse quickened.
It was wrong.
A clerical mistake.
It had to be.
Her hand fell to her lap.
Think.
Rachel, now sitting in the stiff chair at the end of the bed, bunched her eyebrows. "What?" she whispered. "What's wrong?"
The curtain to the room was drawn. But through it, Laura heard the door sliding open. A hand gripped the blue curtain and ripped it aside, drawing her father's attention—and Rachel's as well.
Two uniformed police officers stood just outside the room.
"Laura Reynolds," the first one said. "We'd like to speak with you outside."

5

The police, as it turned out, didn't want to speak with Laura outside.

They wanted to arrest her.

As her father and sister watched through the open doorway, one of the officers cuffed her while the other informed her that she was under arrest for charges including patient abuse and neglect, grand theft, felony larceny by an employee, and possession of a controlled substance. Laura was so shocked she couldn't follow what the officer said next.

As they led her away, she glanced back, seeing the looks of shock on Rachel's and her father's faces.

*

At the local police station, two FBI agents were waiting for her. The woman did most of the talking. Her partner, a tall, skinny man, seemed bored.

The woman informed Laura that the Durham Police had issued a warrant for her arrest and that she would now be transported back to Durham—and that because she was a non-violent criminal, she would be transported via commercial flight. She would be restrained, and if she caused trouble, she might be transported by other means—or detained locally until suitable, secure transport could be arranged.

It was a warning: act up, and we'll toss you in jail here in Ohio.

Laura wasn't about to act up. She desperately wanted to get back to Durham to clear all of this up. The sooner that happened, the sooner she could see her father again and explain. She didn't want that scene in the hall to be his last memory of her.

*

As it turned out, discreet restraints were handcuffs under a sweater. Standing on each side of her, the agents marched Laura through the airport, flashing their badges at checkpoints.

People in the security line eyed her with a mixture of curiosity and concern. The same was true at the boarding gate.

Laura stared straight ahead, hiding how humiliated she felt. The question on her mind was how this had happened.

Was it a simple misunderstanding?

She counted that as highly unlikely.

Samir.

It was him. Had to be.

And that hurt more than the handcuffs cutting into her wrists.

*

At RDU airport, the perp walk was no less shameful.

The FBI handed her off at the local police station, where she was booked, photographed, fingerprinted, and once again read the charges against her. A plastic bag holding the items found on her person in Ohio was handed through a metal cage to be kept for safekeeping.

Her phone, which the officer was sliding into a plastic bag, lit up with a new text message. He powered it off before sealing the bag and tossing it into a small box.

*

Laura's first thought was about making a phone call.

The problem was that she wasn't entirely sure who to call. She didn't know any criminal defense attorneys. Her sister wasn't in a position to bail her out (she was hours away and broke).

Normally, Samir would have been her first instinct, but as he was likely the one who had landed her here, she wasn't about to call him. Laura figured that the director of the Perioperative Medicine Fellowship would be of little help (she had obviously coordinated with the police).

The next stop in this nightmare was an appearance before a magistrate, who reiterated the various charges and set bail at 500,000 dollars.

It might as well have been 5 billion dollars. Laura didn't have it. She didn't know anyone who did.

After, she lay on the bottom bunk in the cell and thought about her father, and whether he was still alive, and her headstrong, impulsive sister, and whether Laura's arrest had sent her into a tailspin, and Samir, and whether he was sitting in an operating room, high as a kite, gambling someone's life to numb whatever pain was controlling him.

*

"Reynolds!" A man's voice called out, boots squeaking on the epoxy floor.

Laura slid out of the bunk and moved to the bars.

The officer shoved a large metal key in the steel door and turned it with a loud snap. "Come on. You made bail."

*

Apparently, an LLC company Laura had never heard of had bailed her out.

She had no idea what to make of that.

Outside the jail, she used her phone to order a rideshare.

She sat in the back seat, knowing she should read the text messages and emails on her phone and start trying to figure out what was going on, but knowing it would bring tears and rage. Things she didn't want to let a stranger see.

Her thoughts always returned to Samir.

It had to be him.

He had gone to the program director and told her that Laura was an addict who had been stealing drugs. It was a clever move. In one act, he had destroyed Laura's credibility as a witness against him and provided a suspect for any missing drugs, covering his own crimes.

The police had searched her apartment and apparently found drugs. Had Samir hidden them that night she had confronted him?

Probably.

So he knew even then what he was going to do—when he hugged her and looked her in the face and said he was going to do the right thing.

Laura felt like putting her head between her legs and throwing up.

Inside her apartment, she immediately called her sister.

"Dad's gone," were Rachel's first words.

Laura sank down on the couch, in the center cushion, where Samir had sat when he had lied and ripped her life apart. "When?"

"Right after you left."

Laura opened her mouth to speak, but no words came.

"He wrote you a letter," Rachel said. "I'll send it to you."

6

Laura lay in bed, staring at the ceiling.

Her fiancé had betrayed her.

Her best friend too.

So had the fellowship program she loved and had worked so hard for.

Her sister was hanging on by a thread.

Her father was dead.

And she could only imagine what the rest of the world thought of her. That's probably what all the text messages and emails were about. And for that reason, she turned the phone off.

She had had enough for one day.

*

In the morning, she staggered out of the bedroom, on her way to make coffee and get ready for the day, her brain on autopilot.

She stopped in the middle of the living room. There was no day to get ready for.

Not anymore.

For Laura, that might be the worst part of it all: losing

a job that mattered to her, that she had trained her entire adult life for.

She picked up her phone from the coffee table and dialed Rachel back.

"What the—" her sister began before Laura cut her off.

"I needed some space last night."

"Why were you arrested?"

"Misunderstanding."

"I can't tell if that's a joke."

"Everything's a joke to you, Rach."

"Not this. Laura, what happened?"

"Issue at work."

"Bull—"

"Clerical error," Laura said. Sharing details wouldn't help the situation. It would only bring more questions, which she didn't have time for (or any answers to).

"Liar," Rachel shot back.

"Well, I better get back to work. Lots of paperwork to correct. Keep me posted on the funeral arrangements."

Laura ended the call.

Rachel called her back.

Laura sent her to voicemail, then silenced her calls.

Until this was worked out, Laura couldn't go to a funeral in Ohio. She couldn't even leave the state.

Laura and Rachel were alike in one way: they were both fighters.

Now Laura was about to focus all her rage and energy on getting her life back. Sitting on the couch, she scrolled through the missed calls. A lot of the other fellows had phoned her. The director as well. Some of her former professors.

But not Samir.

Of course not. The one person she needed to talk to—
who could resolve all of this—hadn't called.

Her text messages were a strange mix of short pings like:

WTF

Seriously?

Call me.

Are you okay?

There were longer messages from old friends. And notes
from several unknown numbers, which, as she read through
them, turned out to be reporters or bloggers who had gotten
her number. They were no doubt looking to break news
and add details to the story for the clicks and ad revenue.
For them, her story—make that scandal—was a meal
ticket.

On her computer, she searched her name on the web.
There was a plethora of stories, and the narratives mostly
fell into the same groove. They described an anesthesiologist
who had personal problems. A recent engagement that had
ended after she discovered her fiancé's infidelity. A dying
father. Student debt.

And, they all said, a stressful work environment where
she spent long hours working in a cutting-edge program
designed to help the most vulnerable surgical patients,
those with complex medical histories undergoing high-risk
operations…

It all added up—in the words of the reporters—to a

person who had crumbled under the weight of it all and made a very bad decision. Allegedly. They always added that word in there a few times. After they had laid out all the facts. After any casual reader had made up their mind.

It was a captivating story.

It was a true story.

It just wasn't her story.

It was Samir's.

*

Laura spent almost an hour trying to find a criminal defense attorney. Finally, she ended up on the phone with a college friend who was practicing law at a firm in Raleigh. He informed her that he was an IP attorney, and that none of his partners practiced criminal law, but that he would make some inquiries.

He called her back ten minutes later and told her to expect another call from someone named Mark Carter.

*

Carter called an hour later.

In that time, he had already been in touch with the Durham DA's office. He had found out a lot, including details about the evidence they had against Laura (it would be revealed during discovery, so the prosecutors had no reason to play coy, Carter had told her).

He also conveyed that these prosecutors were very, very confident in their case.

They had physical evidence of her guilt. And a credible witness. Another physician. In fact, a fellow in her program.

The physical evidence was obtained during the search of

her apartment. They had the vials of drugs, which had been tested and confirmed.

They had a statement from the witness.

None of these revelations surprised Laura, but still, hearing them confirmed in matter-of-fact detail enraged her.

"I can take a drug test," she said.

"Doesn't matter. You've been gone for days."

"They could test my hair. I can—"

"Dr. Reynolds—"

"Laura."

"Laura, listen to me. They have this. We can go to trial, but I'm telling you, they'll win. They've got evidence collected from your apartment. They've got a witness."

"He's a liar."

"The evidence is on their side."

A silence stretched out, and the attorney added, "And you've had some personal problems."

"Who hasn't?"

"That's fair. I'm just saying that it's a point against us at trial."

"So what do you recommend? I surrender and go to jail?"

"You're held in jail before and during trial. You go to prison if you're convicted."

"Semantics aside, what are my options here?"

"Technically? Go to trial or plead out." He paused. "Practically? If you don't do a plea deal, it's going to be a media circus, it'll cost a fortune, you'll lose, and the judge will almost certainly give you more time."

Laura felt numb. She felt like a terminal patient getting the worst news of her life.

"I'm not guilty," she whispered.

A long silence stretched out.

"You still there?" Laura asked.

"I'm here. Look, Doct—Laura—if you want me to represent you, I will get the best possible outcome I can for you. I promise. No matter how you decide to plead. But I'm telling you, I don't think trial is the best choice here."

"What is?"

"A deal."

"What sort of deal?"

"A little time. Some rehab—before, during, or after. Maybe all three. Parole with good behavior."

"Will I ever practice medicine again?"

The line fell silent.

"Tell me," Laura said.

"It's, uh, hard to say—"

"Tell me."

"I think that... it's highly unlikely. You're definitely going to lose your medical license. Even if you could get it reinstated at some point, you'd face the challenge of getting a job—with a record of patient abuse and neglect and substance abuse while practicing."

7

After the call with the attorney, Laura began reaching out to anyone who could help.

The director of the Perioperative Medicine Fellowship program didn't answer her calls or return her texts.

Some of Laura's other fellows responded. For many, their messages, which had been supportive before, now turned accusatory. Or evasive.

Did you do it, Laura?

One friend asked.
Another simply replied:

L, I'm not sure what to say.

A fellow anesthesiologist she respected and with whom she had worked the most sent her:

My dad's an attorney. He advised me to cut off all contact with you until this is over. I could end up on the witness stand just for texting with you, Laura.

One text said what many of them were probably thinking:

You've put the whole program at risk.

Laura stopped reading after she read a message that said:

You've sunk us all, you junkie. I hope you get what you deserve.

*

At noon, in lieu of lunch, Laura brewed a pot of coffee, drank two cups, and walked three blocks to Samir's apartment.

At his door, she put a finger over the glass peephole, knocked, and waited, hoping to hear the deadbolt slide open.

It didn't.

She banged on the door and waited.

Then yelled, "Samir!"

Three seconds later, she screamed even louder. "Samir!"

A door opened. Not the one in front of Laura, but the door to the apartment next to Samir's.

A silver-haired woman peeked out, eying Laura. "He's gone," she said.

"Where?"

"How would I know?"

"When?"

"Yesterday. Bunch of movers came."

Laura exhaled. Of course he was gone.

*

Laura could have lain down in that hall and cried, but she walked out, back toward her apartment.

One block into her trek, a text appeared from Mark Carter, telling her that the assistant district attorney assigned to her case was willing to discuss a plea deal. Laura's story was in the news, and the clock was ticking to make a follow-up headline.

Laura had to admit: Carter was good. She hadn't even hired him, and he was working the case, assuming he had gotten it, doing the job he wanted.

Maybe he was looking to make headlines, too. Or maybe he was just a good attorney. Or both.

Still, she wasn't ready to plead guilty. Because she wasn't guilty. And because of what she stood to lose.

*

For the rest of the afternoon, Laura scoured the internet, researching her case and similar ones. She officially hired Mark Carter via DocuSign and talked with him twice more.

The Durham ADA was engaged but wasn't moving much on the plea deal. Carter insisted, however, that the office was anxious to do a deal—and was putting an expiration date on the offer.

Seventy-two hours.

He said the deadline was pretty unusual. Laura wondered what the rush was. Maybe they were motivated to capitalize on the media interest or perhaps it was to help the university resolve the matter.

It certainly wasn't in her interest. She needed time to think, to try to figure out a way to get her life back.

The prosecutor, via Carter, also revealed more details of their case. Laura assumed that was a negotiating tactic.

The most concerning thing she learned was that the police had conducted a search at the hospital and found evidence of missing medication and irregularities in some of the inventory reports.

The evidence against her was mounting.

In addition to what they had found in Laura's apartment and the witness statement from Samir, the case looked, in Carter's words, "open and shut."

He reiterated that he didn't favor going to trial.

Laura had to admit, the more she learned, the more she thought he was probably right.

*

By seven, Laura's sister had texted her a dozen times. Every time the phone vibrated on the dining table, Laura's eyes snapped to it, hoping it was her fellowship program director. But she still hadn't returned her calls or texts.

Laura didn't call Rachel back.

In fact, for the last thirty minutes, she had done nothing but sit on the couch, thinking, staring at the phone.

She was in a sort of endless mental loop of *what-ifs* and *I should have* thoughts. And none of those thoughts led to solutions. Only regrets.

She needed to get out of her apartment. She needed a decent meal and to feel normal again.

And to get away from this place where both Samir and her fiancé had betrayed her.

In search of culinary therapy, she walked three blocks

to an Italian restaurant she loved. She needed carbs. And wine, too.

The young, bubbly hostess related that the wait was an hour, but luckily, Laura found an open stool at the bar. Her first order of business was a glass of house Chardonnay.

It went down fast. Too fast, probably, but as an anesthesiologist, she knew that there were times when deadening the pain was the only way to endure an operation, and this world had cut her open.

She had finished a second glass when the bartender took her food order. "If you want more wine, it'd be cheaper to order a bottle," he said, tapping at a screen.

"Actually, I think I'm done," she mumbled, already hearing a slight slur in her words. She had never been much of a drinker. And her sister was right: she was borderline too thin these days. Her alcohol tolerance was at an all-time low. She needed that basket of bread, stat.

The couple beside her rolled off their stools, and the man wrapped an arm around his date. As they shuffled away, a young guy—maybe late twenties or early thirties—slipped in, pushing the empty plate forward.

"What can I get you?" the bartender asked, not looking up from the screen.

"A double Macallan neat and a new life."

Laura smiled. He had a Southern accent. Texas was her best guess.

The bartender seemed mildly annoyed but played along. "We've only got the Macallan."

"One out of two ain't bad," the man said softly, almost to himself.

An arm reached around Laura and thankfully deposited

a basket of bread. She ripped off a piece and bathed it in butter.

The man's scotch arrived and he took a long pull, staring straight ahead.

Finding her new neighbor a good bit more interesting than the games playing on the TVs above the bar, Laura watched him in her peripheral vision.

With another flip of the glass, he downed the rest of the amber liquid, pushed the empty cup forward, and subtly motioned to the bartender, catching the man's attention and holding him with an unwavering gaze.

The bartender released the long handles on the taps and set two draft beers on the bar in front of him and came over, eying the empty glass like it was a problem. "You're certainly thirsty."

Laura's neighbor didn't flinch. His face was a mask, and he didn't say a word.

"Want another?" the bartender asked, an edge in his voice. Laura got it. Busy night. Popular place. And maybe the guy was having some issues.

"Actually," the man said, drawing the word out. "I'm going to switch to wine. A bottle of River Road. Two glasses."

The bartender jabbed at the screen, then stalked off to the kitchen. The wine arrived a few minutes later, and the bartender, looking even more surly now, poured a glass and cut his eyes to the empty one. "Is this—"

"That's good enough. Thanks."

When the man was gone, Laura's neighbor gripped the bottle of wine and filled the other glass halfway full and slid it over to her, still not looking her way.

"For me?" she asked.

"Mmm," he murmured, tipping his glass up.

"I shouldn't. I've already had two glasses."

"No worries," he said softly. "But, in case you want it." He finished his glass and poured another for himself. "The service around here can be spotty."

Laura smiled and put a finger on the base of the glass, turning it on the bar, watching the pale yellow liquid vibrate. "It's usually pretty good."

"So you come here often?"

Laura shook her head. "That has got to be the tiredest line—"

He held up his hands. "I didn't open with it—"

"So you're trying to pick me up."

"I'm *trying* to spend my per diem and forget about the day I've had. I can't drink all this wine, and I didn't have lunch, and you had an empty glass, and the bartender seems to think we work for him, and I figured getting more drinks could be more and more problematic as the night goes on. I was just being practical."

"Practical, huh?"

"Yeah."

Laura picked up the wine and took a sip. "Good. I'm glad you're not trying to hit on me."

Finally, he turned to her. "Oh, I didn't say that." He smiled. "Kidding."

"Right."

"I *am* kidding, actually. I'm tired. I've never had much game, and, for what it's worth, I've never been to this town. I've had a weird day. And I figured, what the heck? Probably never see each other again, so what have

I got to lose? Well, besides my pride. And I'm fresh out of that."

Laura took another sip of wine. It was good.

"I don't go home with strange men."

He smiled, revealing dimples and lines at his eyes. "Me either."

*

Around the time their entrées arrived, the man on the barstool beside Laura, who she had learned was named Joe, ordered another bottle of River Road. The passage of time had done nothing to improve the bartender's mood, but the wine had worked wonders on Laura's disposition. So had Joe's company.

In the course of their conversation, she had also learned that he worked in security for a biotech company—and that was all he wanted to say about the subject.

Laura swallowed a bite of lasagna. She wasn't sure if it was because of the wine or the fact that this guy was a stranger she expected to never see again, but whatever the reason, she said, "I had a bad day too."

"How bad?"

"Bad, bad."

"That bad, huh?"

"And then some." She drained the last of the wine and Joe, in that subtle, very Joe, very fluid way, signaled the bartender for another.

"I can't drink anymore," Laura said.

"Me either," he shot back. "Again, just trying to get rid of the per diem. It's use it or lose it."

Laura smiled. "Are you lying?"

"No. And besides, doubt it would do me any good. You don't seem like the type who'd suffer liars."

She chuckled, eyes glassy and hateful. "Oh, that's hilarious."

"Why is that hilarious?"

"Because I'm the most gullible, stupid, easily manipulated person of all time."

She knew it was the wine talking.

"I doubt that very seriously," he said quietly. He drained the rest of his wine just as the third bottle arrived.

He refilled their glasses and raised his. "To bad days. They make us appreciate the good ones."

She drew her glass back from his, avoiding the clink. "Seriously?"

He shrugged. "What?"

"Worst toast ever."

"Can I still drink the wine?"

She lifted her glass slightly. "To strange men with *alleged* per diems who you won't be taking home."

He moved his glass to hers and clinked. "Indeed. Sounds horrifying."

*

The plates were gone and the wine bottle was one-third empty when Laura muttered, "I'm going to prison."

Joe's face was a mask. He didn't frown. Didn't raise his eyebrows. Didn't react at all.

"You don't seem surprised," Laura said.

"I'm waiting for the punch line."

Laura took another swallow of wine. "Apparently, I am the punch line."

"Then I don't get the joke," he said. "Don't like it much either."

"Same."

After a long moment, she said, "This isn't going to end the way you think."

"Sure it is."

"You're not coming back to my place."

"Sure I am."

"I said you're not."

He stared straight ahead. "You're very drunk, Laura. If you choose to walk, I'll walk you home and leave you at your door. If you choose to get a ride-share, I'll open your car door and wish you well."

He drank a little more wine. "I don't care which you choose. I just want you to get home safely."

That's what got to her.

"I'm going to walk," she said quietly.

He stared straight ahead. "Okay."

"It's a nice night to walk," she added, not sure why, as if she was trying to justify it.

Walking would sober her up.

Yes, she definitely wanted to sober up.

He said nothing.

On the sidewalk, he walked next to the road, and she strode beside him, the buildings on her right, the glow of streetlights above, the occasional car passing by bathing them in white and yellow beams.

"Recently," she said, words slurring more than a little, "I was arrested."

"Yeah?"

"For a crime I didn't commit."

He glanced over at her. "One-armed man did it?"

She scowled at him.

He shrugged. "Thought you were doing a scene from *The Fugitive*."

"I wish."

At her apartment building, she intended to turn and tell him to go on back to his hotel or Airbnb or wherever he was staying. But, she told herself, she was just so tired. Of talking. Of everything. She trudged up the stairs.

He followed.

At her door, she fished her key out of her pocket and tried to get it in the lock, but she might as well have been trying to open it with a spaghetti noodle.

His hand gripped hers and the key found the hole and slid in. The door opened, and she stepped across the threshold and he followed her, locking the deadbolt as soon as the door closed.

She glanced back at him. He was a little blurry now, but she could still make out those cold blue-gray eyes, as if they could focus through the haze.

She swallowed. "This isn't going to end the way you think."

"Sure it is," he whispered.

"It isn't—"

He closed the distance between them, stooped and slipped an arm around the back of her knees and lifted, catching her back with his other arm as he marched to the bedroom, where he laid her on the bed.

She stared at him hard. "This isn't—"

"I know," he whispered, "going to end the way you think."

She opened her mouth to speak.

He didn't move, only hovered above her, his face close to hers, close enough to feel his breath.

Slowly, by small degrees, he drew away. And that annoyed her greatly. And it annoyed her that it annoyed her.

He strode to the kitchen and Laura turned onto her side, watching, confused.

He took a glass from the cabinet and filled it with tap water and returned, placing it on her bedside table.

To her further annoyance, he then turned out the bedroom light and closed the door.

She thought about getting up and marching out and questioning him, demanding he answer what in the world he was doing, what sort of sick game this was, and why he didn't come back in here and answer for himself.

But the darkness and fatigue and all the stress of the day swallowed her whole.

*

Outside her bedroom, Joe sat on the couch, waiting until he was sure Laura Reynolds was asleep. Then he searched her apartment until he was certain of his assessment.

He left, locking the door with the duplicate key he had made.

8

The next morning, Laura woke to a pounding headache. And a memory of a man who was so charming and kind and mysterious and completely annoying. Maybe that last part wasn't fair. Maybe.

Worst of all, when she opened her bedroom door, expecting to see him sleeping on the couch or perhaps sitting there, staring down at his phone, he was gone.

So annoying.

Joe West.

That was his name.

That was pretty much all Laura knew about him.

Well, that and that it had been a wonderful night that was like a dream. One that was a little fuzzy around the edges. A night that made her slightly happy to think about. Well, more than slightly, despite the headache.

She had no way to contact Joe. Not that it mattered. She'd probably soon be headed off to prison.

Is that why she let him walk her home? Her hopeless legal situation? Or loneliness?

Both?

Or was it simply because she liked him?

Laura wondered if she would have done the same thing before she had been arrested and charged.

Probably not. Definitely not.

Not that it mattered. Nothing mattered anymore, except clearing her name.

She brewed some coffee and opened her laptop, determined to do just that.

*

Two hours later, after making no progress to that end, a knock sounded at her front door.

Samir.

That was Laura's first thought.

The knock came again, more insistent this time.

Laura rose and rushed to the peephole and peered through.

A man in a suit stood in the hall. He was short and slender with wire-rimmed glasses and close-cropped hair. He didn't carry a briefcase or anything else in his hands. He stared directly at the peephole.

"Who is it?" Laura called out, watching.

"Dr. Reynolds, please forgive the unscheduled visit. I represent a company that would like to make you a job offer."

Of all the things she thought he might say, that wasn't one of them. Between the surprise and the haze of last night's wine, her mind couldn't manage a response.

The man turned his head towards the door as if listening. "Dr. Reynolds?"

"I'm here. Can you just... email me or something?"

Laura rubbed her weary face and was about to walk

away from the peephole when the man said, "Dr. Reynolds, given your present legal predicament, time really is of the essence. What my employer is prepared to offer will indeed remedy your current... situation. It also aligns with your research interests and has the potential to greatly enhance your career."

A few days ago, Laura would have sent the man away without a second thought. But the reality was that she was pretty desperate. But, desperate or not, she was still skeptical.

"Tell me more," she said, watching him closely through the peephole. She was fully awake now.

The well-dressed man cut his eyes down the hall of the apartment building. "Dr. Reynolds, it would be better to discuss this in private."

He reached inside his coat pocket and took out a business card and slipped it under the door.

Laura reached down and read it:

Epoch Sciences
Gregory Young, Esq.

There was no web address. No physical address. Only a phone number with the letter M beside it indicating that it was a mobile.

She had never heard of the company. But there was something about the man—his mild nature, the sincerity in his voice...

"Just a minute," she mumbled, turning from the door and returning to her bedside table, where she grabbed her phone.

She opened the camera app, adjusted a few settings, and held it to the peephole. After snapping a photo of the man, she texted it to her sister with a message that read:

> I'm about to meet with this man in my apartment.
> If I go missing or don't contact you in 30 minutes,
> call the Durham police.

No sooner had she sent the text than several replies appeared in rapid succession:

OMFG!

Is this a joke?

Seriously?

The phone rang. Rachel calling.
Laura texted back:

> No joke. Probably fine.

Despite thinking it would probably be fine, Laura took a sharp knife from the butcher block in the kitchen and gently placed it in her pocket.

*

At Laura's dining table, her visitor—Gregory Young—laid out the job offer.

Early in the conversation, she had asked him what his role at Epoch Sciences was.

He had been evasive, saying only that he was an attorney by training.

The description of the job offer was equally as cryptic.

As he described it, Laura's phone, which sat on the table, continued vibrating and lighting up with text messages.

Finally, he leaned forward slightly and motioned toward it. "Dr. Reynolds, do you need to answer that?"

"It's just my sister."

"She seems very concerned. Or in distress."

She's likely both, Laura thought, and picked up the phone and tapped out a quick message to Rachel:

Everything is fine. Promise.

When Young had finished describing the offer, Laura wasn't sure what to make of it. Or whether to even believe it. She had no idea where to start with her own questions.

Young seemed to read her bewilderment. "I realize that this is a lot to take in, but if you keep an open mind, I believe this may be the opportunity of a lifetime for you, Dr. Reynolds. Clearly it comes at a difficult time, but I do hope that won't keep you from appreciating how attractive the offer is."

Laura turned it over in her mind like she might study a patient's chart before surgery, trying to get a handle on what exactly she was dealing with.

"Dr. Reynolds, what questions do you have? As I said, time is of the essence."

"I don't even know where to start."

The man said nothing, only placed his hands on the table, putting one over the other, and waited, eyes cast down.

"What does Epoch Sciences do—*exactly*?" Laura asked.

"As I said, Epoch is a research organization."

"Yes, but that doesn't really tell me anything."

A hint of a smile curled on his lips, then vanished.

"I apologize for the lack of detail."

"What can you tell me?"

"I'm afraid, Dr. Reynolds, that I'm not authorized to say much more than I already have. Only that Epoch Sciences is doing incredibly important research that you can contribute to. That, should you accept our offer, you will be using your expertise—practicing anesthesiology once again, in a field similar to perioperative medicine."

"What kind of *incredibly important research*? Research into what? The use of anesthesiology implies surgical operations. For what conditions?"

Young's gaze drifted to his hands. "I'm not—"

"Authorized to say," Laura finished for him.

The man lifted his thumbs outward, saying nothing.

Laura shook her head. "How do I know this is all legitimate? That you can do what you're saying—get me a better deal with the DA? How do I know that you're not some human trafficking group or some other criminal organization that's looking for a disgraced anesthesiologist?"

He raised his eyebrows. "You have quite the imagination, Dr. Reynolds."

"Is that a denial?"

"I can assure you, beyond a shadow of a doubt, that the work Epoch Sciences is doing is for the benefit of humanity. In fact—" He stopped then, seeming to catch himself.

"In fact what?" Laura asked.

"*In fact*," the man said, more slowly now, "the work we're doing is the absolute opposite of what you described."

He paused. "And there's one other thing I can tell you: you came to our attention through the recommendation of someone connected to the project."

"Who?"

"I'm not at liberty—"

"To say," Laura said, once again completing the sentence. He nodded once.

"If you were me, what would you ask? What would you like to know?"

He gazed at her, with a look that reminded Laura of her grandfather when he was deep in thought.

"As I said, Dr. Reynolds, I'm an attorney. I would ask a great many questions. Generally, we tend to worry about all eventualities."

"And what eventualities are you worried about, Mr. Young?"

"The kind that might affect my children. And theirs."

To Laura's surprise, he stood then, perhaps regretting what he had said, thinking it was too much.

She stood as well, the knife in her pocket shifting awkwardly, the handle rubbing her side, making her feel almost silly for having it.

"Dr. Reynolds, as I said, we'll need your answer within twenty-four hours." From his coat pocket, he withdrew a folded sheaf of paper and placed it on the table.

"This is an employment contract. Included is a confidentiality agreement."

Young nodded towards the contract. "And the offer is contingent upon resolving your current legal situation to your satisfaction. If not, you can walk away before work commences. And if you don't follow through, your plea deal will be canceled."

Laura was reaching for the pages when the man added, "There is one additional thing I can tell you."

She stopped.

"If you accept this job, you'll be working in Antarctica."

"Oh," Laura said, not sure what to make of this revelation.

"And," Young went on, "for the duration of your contract—all three years—you'll have no contact with the outside world. No emails. No phone calls. No internet access."

Laura got the sense that the man thought being cut off from the outside world was a drawback of the assignment. But given what she had been through recently, it sounded pretty good to Laura. She wondered if that was part of why they selected her.

As the attorney was walking toward the door, a thought occurred to Laura. A connection she had missed. "Mr. Young?"

He paused, not turning back.

"Did you post my bail from prison? You or Epoch?"

"No."

"Do you know who did?"

He turned and studied her. "No."

When she said nothing, he said, "Well, if there's nothing else, you have my phone number. Please call me as soon as you can with your answer."

*

Just outside Laura's door, a man in a jogging suit was pressing his ear to the peephole, listening.

When he heard his target moving to the threshold, he shuffled down the hallway and slipped inside the stairwell.

"He's coming out," the jogger whispered into his mic.

*

In a car outside Laura's apartment building, a woman sat behind the wheel, looking down at her phone, watching the video feed from a dash cam. On the windshield, stickers for two rideshare programs were prominently displayed. She had positioned them to cover the dash cam.

Using the phone app, she panned the camera's view to the building's entrance. When Gregory Young stepped outside, she snapped a dozen photos and sent them to the agent in charge.

9

In her apartment, Laura read the employment agreement several times. The language was steeped in legal terms, but she got the gist of it.

In return for providing three years of continuous employment to Epoch Sciences Inc., she would receive a salary of 1 million dollars per year as well as onsite health care, meals, and housing. She was to abide by a strict confidentiality agreement, before, during, and after the engagement. While onsite in Antarctica, she was barred from any digital communications with anyone outside the Epoch organization.

Her salary would be deposited into an account of her choosing monthly—or held by Epoch and paid in a lump sum at the end of her employment—minus any taxes withheld and paid.

As Young had said, the entire agreement was contingent upon her legal situation being resolved to her satisfaction, but the agreement provided a preview of what the plea deal might look like: in return for a suspended sentence, Laura would work for Epoch Sciences, specifically at their Antarctica Station research facility, and undergo a substance abuse treatment program administered by Epoch.

She didn't like it.

First, it meant her pleading guilty. And she wasn't guilty.

Second, she would forever have a criminal record. Even if she worked for three years in Antarctica and satisfied her contract with Epoch, where would she work after that?

How could she explain to her sister and friends that she pled guilty when she wasn't?

She could see why the district attorney and judge might like the deal. It included rehabilitation and work release for someone with valuable skills. And they would no doubt see this remote research base in Antarctica as a sort of prison substitute. No chance of escape. No contact with the outside world. Strict supervision. She would be far away from Durham, with no chance of hurting any patients there.

And the more Laura thought about it, three years in Antarctica did feel a bit like a prison sentence.

On the other hand, it offered the opportunity to do the work she loved. And, she thought, it might even be therapeutic to be disconnected from this world for a while. Things weren't exactly going well.

After reading the agreement so many times she had practically memorized it, Laura plopped down on the couch and sank her face into her hands.

How had she gotten here? And so quickly.

Six months ago, she had a career she loved, a charming fiancé, and a healthy father. Now all three were gone, in a blink.

She leaned back on the couch and a sense of déjà vu came over her, of sitting in this very place the day after she discovered that Pierce was cheating on her and she had ended the engagement.

That day, she also felt like her world was collapsing. Samir had been there that night, sitting on the coffee table, telling her, "This is about him, Laura. Not you. His shortcomings. Not yours."

She shook her head, throwing free a few tears from her face.

Samir leaned forward. "Listen: you are enough. You're going to recover from this, and you'll meet someone new, and your life will be good again. It's just a matter of time."

Samir had stayed after the conversation ended, insisting that he would answer the door if Pierce made an appearance. And more: he had made sure she didn't wallow in despair or drink too much wine or simply lay in bed and stare at the ceiling.

In those dark days after the blowup, she and Samir had binged on streaming TV and ordered pizza, and many nights he had slept on the couch, a blanket pulled over him.

He had been a true friend to her then. And that's why his betrayal hurt so much.

And she couldn't help but wonder: was there truly something broken about her that attracted people who were deceptive?

A gentle knock at the door made her jump.

Samir.

Even now, it was her first thought. She couldn't deny that she still held out hope that he was standing on the other side of that door, that he had come to his senses and was here to apologize and tell her that he was going to go to the program and the police and set everything right.

At the peephole, she peered out and exhaled heavily. A man wearing a cap and coveralls stood there, holding a large air filter and step ladder.

Laura had never seen him before. But she had also never been here when maintenance had changed the air filters. They simply left a note.

"It's Tom from maintenance," the guy called out, reaching into his pocket and drawing a key out. Of course they had a key. "Here to change your air filters."

He knocked again. "Anybody home?"

"Can you come back later?" Laura asked.

The man grimaced. "Well, not really. Not if I want to keep my job. It'll take like ten seconds, ma'am." He paused. "The lease says we can—"

Laura was too emotionally maxed-out for an argument. She unlocked the door and swung it open. "Come on in."

The man nodded and marched inside without another word, squatting at the closest metal grate and flipping the latches. In a fluid motion, he removed the large filter and put a new one in.

He moved to the bedroom, set down a step stool, and drew out what looked like a candle lighter from his pocket. Reaching up, he slipped it through the metal blades of the ceiling register, and Laura heard a faint clink.

He repeated the procedure in the bathroom, living room, and kitchen, snaking the device into each vent.

"What are you doing?" Laura asked.

"Just adding monitors for mold."

Three seconds later, he was gone.

Laura stared at the closed door. She thought they had changed the filters recently. But she wasn't sure.

*

An hour later, Laura was sitting at the dining table, searching the internet for any information about Epoch Sciences—and finding very, very little—when she heard scratching at the front door.

Not a knock.

More like a dog on a leash who had stopped to paw at the wooden slab.

She expected it to stop, but it kept on, growing louder.

Laura rose and listened. The sound was higher up on the door than where a dog would paw. It was coming from the lock.

Someone was trying to pick it.

Laura raced to the kitchen.

The deadbolt clicked open.

She drew a knife from the butcher block as the door swung inward, and a person burst through, leading with a shaking hand that held a small pocket knife.

Laura slid the carving knife back in place and turned and rested her forearms on the bar, leaning into the opening under the cabinets.

"Rachel," she said calmly.

Laura's sister spun, eyes wide, still gripping the small knife, voice a whisper.

"You're alive."

Laura squinted. "Why wouldn't I be?"

Rachel dropped the pocket knife to her side. "Thought they had you."

"Who?"

"Whoever you're mixed up with. The drug cartels or the pill mills or…"

IO

Rachel insisted on searching Laura's apartment to make sure there were no kidnappers or gangsters secretly hiding.

When she was satisfied, Rachel sat on the couch and explained that after the text message exchange, she had flown down from Ohio, reasoning that Laura was being forced to send messages saying she was fine when, in fact, she was in mortal danger.

With that segue, Laura told her what had really happened at work and the situation she was in.

Rachel stood and paced. "Let's nail this guy. I'll go undercover. I could—"

"He's gone, Rachel."

Laura went to the kitchen and put on a fresh pot of coffee. "Rach," she said, realizing something. "How did you know how to pick my door lock?"

"Let's just say I had a little practice."

"When?"

"When Terry was cheating."

"Who is Terry?"

"Exactly."

Laura cocked her head. "I'm not sure what that means."

Rachel nodded. "It means I got T-bone on video. Been blackmailing him for over a year."

Laura set two steaming mugs on the coffee table. "Isn't that illegal?"

Rachel narrowed her eyes. "Allegedly."

"No, allegedly is when it's not certain you committed a crime, not whether what you did is a crime."

"Exactly."

Laura blew softly on her coffee to cool it down, took a sip, and said, "Okay, let's forget about Terry."

"He's about the only thing keeping me afloat this last year," Rachel said.

Laura wasn't sure how to respond to that. Before she could, Rachel said, "What are you going to do, Laura? Are you going to prison?"

Laura stared at the stapled pages on the coffee table. "No," she said quietly. She knew then that she had made her decision.

"I'm going to take a job for a company that can help me."

*

That night, Laura and Rachel slept in the same bed for the first time since they were teenagers.

To Laura, it felt like a flashback to her childhood. Revisiting a happier time before a farewell.

Rachel had brought the letter their father had written to Laura. It was sealed in an envelope with her name on it, and Laura held it up now, staring at it, wondering if the words would wreck her or save her.

She couldn't deal with that now.

Still holding the envelope, she gently withdrew her arm from beneath her sister and exited the bedroom and closed the door.

In the living room, she dialed the number on the card Gregory Young had given her.

"Dr. Reynolds," he said by way of greeting.

"I accept."

"Good."

"But I have conditions."

He said nothing.

"I want to attend my father's funeral."

"I'll see what I can do," Young said. "But understand, I can't make any promises."

"Really? I assumed a man of your capabilities could make promises."

"A valiant attempt at flattery and manipulation, Dr. Reynolds. I'm afraid, however, that my ego faded years ago. I will promise you this: that I'll pull every lever I can to make it happen. Someone very important wants you on this project."

"Who?"

"As you will be soon, I, too, am under a confidentiality agreement, Dr. Reynolds."

When she was silent, he went on: "You said you had conditions. Plural."

"Yes. The money that I'm to be paid. One million per year. I want it to go to my sister."

"Very well."

"But not a lump sum," Laura said. "I want someone to get the money and make a determination about how it could be used to benefit her. If that makes sense."

"Indeed. We'll find a trust company for her. She'll be well taken care of."

*

Due to her sister's snoring, Laura slept on the couch, where she woke the next morning a bit sore and disoriented. Morning light clawed around the blinds and curtains above. Through the closed bedroom door, Rachel's snoring was still audible.

Laura's phone revealed six new text messages waiting for her. The most recent was from Gregory Young:

> You have a deal.
> On both conditions.
> A courier will bring an updated contract and witness your signature—assuming you agree.
> Read it, but please don't dither.
> Time is of the essence.

*

The courier arrived as Laura was pouring her second cup of coffee and Rachel was still sleeping.

He handed over the contract and stood outside the door with it open until Laura beckoned him to come inside, where he still stood back from her, hands clasped behind his back.

The new contract was exactly the same as the other with the exception of three new clauses. The two she had asked for and another that had been requested by the other side—either the Durham County District Attorney or her fellowship program or the university or the hospital. The

69

request was that Laura make restitution for the damage she had done to the reputations of the program, university, and hospital as well as provide a fund to pay settlements and judgments from any future civil suits brought by her former patients.

She scoffed when she read the amount demanded: 10 million dollars.

What a joke.

Laura had about 10,000 dollars in a savings account— her emergency fund—and less than 2,000 dollars in her checking account. Her broken-down Honda sedan needed new tires. A week ago, that had been her biggest financial concern.

Considering her student loans, her total net worth was negative. So, 10 million would be hard to come up with.

But apparently, not for Epoch Sciences.

In the next paragraph, the company agreed to pay full restitution upon commencement of the employment contract.

Apparently, the sum was too insignificant to Epoch for Young to even mention it in his text message.

Laura picked up the pen from the dining room table and stared at the signature line, feeling like she was in a barrel about to go over a waterfall.

Standing there, she was suddenly aware of every sensation. The morning light through the windows. Rachel's soft snoring. Faint footsteps in the apartments above and below as her neighbors prepared for the day.

The courier stared at her, waiting.

She leaned forward and scribbled her signature.

11

Rachel, in classic Rachel fashion, slept until noon, at which point she shuffled out of the bedroom, reeling from the midday sun as if being physically assaulted by it. She peered inside the fridge for half a second before slamming the door and declaring that there was nothing to eat and that she was craving Mexican.

Forty-five minutes later, Laura was picking at a salad in a tortilla shell.

Three round foil trays sat before Rachel, who was stabbing a fork into them almost indiscriminately, scooping up rice, beans, enchiladas, lettuce, and sour cream. She used her hands for the tacos and quesadillas.

Halfway through her salad, Laura began telling her sister about the plea deal. When she reached the part about going to Antarctica for three years, Rachel froze, fork in mid-air.

"You're kidding. Antarctica as in like emperor penguins and—"

"That's the one."

Rachel tossed her fork into the closest foil container, splashing refried beans onto the dining table. "Have you lost your mind?"

"Rachel."

"This is not fair. First Dad. Now you..."

"It's the only way."

Rachel bit her lip and whispered, "It's not fair."

For once, Laura agreed with her sister.

*

That night, Rachel flew back to Ohio.

The next day, two FBI agents arrived at Laura's apartment to transport her home for the funeral.

They were ten minutes early, courteous, and almost robotically efficient.

Both were slender young men, dressed in suits that didn't look expensive but were immaculately clean.

The taller of the two, who was named Malloy, did nearly all of the talking. The younger, shorter man, Lee, generally did whatever needed doing (such as driving, carrying luggage, and opening doors).

On the way to the airport, Laura wondered if they would handcuff her like the last agents had. They didn't. In fact, they didn't even enter either of RDU's passenger terminals.

Instead, they drove to the private aviation terminal, through the gate, and onto the runway, stopping at a waiting plane.

Walking up the airstairs, Laura marveled at the fact that her first trip on a private plane would be thanks to being falsely accused of a laundry list of felonies.

Inside, the agents who had transported Laura entered the cockpit and shut the door. There were already two people on the plane—a man and a woman—sitting in club chairs facing each other. They were dressed more casually than

Malloy and Lee, in sweaters and slacks. Still, Laura thought they looked like law enforcement.

The man introduced himself as Agent Ross and the woman as Agent Gonzalez. Laura noted that neither had provided a first name—or what agency they were with.

"So... you're taking me to the funeral?"

"No," Gonzales said. "This is about another matter. We'll talk after takeoff."

When the jet reached cruising altitude, Gonzales asked Laura to join her and Ross at the back of the plane. Laura plopped down on a couch across from two swivel chairs the agents sat in. She assumed they were about to lay out the ground rules for the funeral.

"Dr. Reynolds," Gonzales began, "there's another condition of your plea deal. One that wasn't disclosed to either the local DA or Epoch."

"Why? What is it?"

"That will become clear soon."

Laura wasn't sure what to say to that.

"What do you know about Epoch Sciences?" Ross asked.

Laura shrugged. "Only what I read online. And what Gregory Young told me. So, not much. Well, and the fact that they kept me out of prison."

"Epoch Sciences isn't what you think it is," Ross said.

Laura cocked her head. "What do you mean?"

Ross intertwined his fingers. "Why do you think Epoch was so eager to intervene in your case?"

"I don't know. Apparently, they need an anesthesiologist at Antarctica Station. I imagine that's a hard sell. Why? What are you trying to tell me?"

Ross and Gonzales shared a glance. He spoke first. "Do you know what Epoch is researching in Antarctica?"

Gonzales raised a hand. "We're wasting time."

She focused on Laura. "Aren't we, Dr. Reynolds?"

"Yes," Laura said. "Why am I here? What is this?"

"We're investigating Epoch Sciences," Gonzales said.

"For what?"

"We believe," Ross said, "that they're developing a technology that might be harmful to humanity."

Laura squinted. "Harmful how?"

After a long pause, Gonzales said, "That's what we want you to find out."

12

Laura leaned back on the couch. "Me? Seriously?"

"It's why we traded favors to get your plea deal approved," Gonzales said. "The only reason."

Laura instantly understood the unspoken threat.

Gonzales spelled it out anyway. "If you don't cooperate, the deal is off."

Laura shook her head. "This is ridiculous. I'm a physician, not some… undercover secret agent."

"I believe," Gonzales said, "that you're also a person who wants to stay out of prison."

Ross held up a hand, attempting to bring the temperature back down.

Laura stared past the two agents, at the clouds zooming past the small window.

"I know this is a shock," Ross said.

"Understatement," Laura muttered.

"However," Ross went on, "this is an incredibly important operation, Laura. You may well be the only person who can figure out what Epoch is doing. It might save a lot of lives."

Ross studied her a moment. "And based on what I read in

your profile, saving lives is why you went into medicine in the first place, isn't it?"

Laura exhaled slowly. "All right. I'll bite. What do you *think* Epoch is building that's so dangerous? If you believe it's a harm to humanity, then you must have some idea of what it is."

"All we have are bits and pieces of the larger picture," Gonzales said.

"What pieces?"

"Based on the material they've imported to Antarctica—and the personnel they've assembled—we're fairly certain that they're doing gravity research."

Laura bunched her eyebrows. "As in—"

"We think they're interested in gravitational shielding and quantum gravity," Ross said.

Laura stared at the two agents. "I don't even know what that is."

"You don't need to," Gonzales said. "But some of the other Epoch research will be more familiar to you. On the medical front, we know they're interested in stasis and anti-aging. We're not sure why. Maybe they're developing an immortality treatment, or something related to deep space travel."

"It's possible," Ross added, "that the two fields—anti-aging and quantum physics—are somehow related, but we don't have a strong working theory that ties them together."

"Then why do you think their research might be harmful?" Laura asked.

Gonzales sucked in a breath. "That's classified."

"Great," Laura mumbled.

"We're telling you what we can," Ross said. "And we can tell you one other thing: we know Epoch's internal name for the project is The Next World. The implication is that whatever they're developing will end—or at least radically alter—our world."

"This is crazy," Laura whispered. "I'm not qualified for this."

Ross leaned forward. "But you're capable of it, Laura. You're smart. You're tough. And you're the only person we can place inside that facility. And believe me, we've tried."

"Who exactly is *we*?"

Ross grimaced. "*We* are the Aurora Project. A task force drawn from several federal agencies as well as DOD personnel."

Gonzales held a finger up. "Consider this, Laura: if Epoch is simply doing beneficial research in quantum physics and anti-aging and immortality, why locate the facility in Antarctica? It's incredibly difficult to supply and operate."

"And expensive," Ross added.

"We think," Gonzales said, "that Epoch's investors have already spent hundreds of billions of dollars on the project. Maybe over a trillion. Our forensic accountants are still trying to trace all the shell companies and intermediaries."

Gonzales leaned forward. "And maybe the strangest part is that they've been doing research for almost ten years now—and they've yet to file a single patent. Anywhere in the world."

"Okay," Laura said, "but I still don't get why they would need to do this gravity and immortality research in Antarctica."

"We think it's for security," Ross said.

"Security?"

"From Antarctica Station, they can see us coming thousands of miles away. Long enough to destroy their research and prepare for any search."

"And," Gonzales said, "we can't even reach the facility during the coldest months—for almost half the year it's a fortress."

"However," Ross said, "we think it's more than just security. We believe there's something about Antarctica that's important to their work."

"The station," Gonzales said, "is located close to the magnetic South Pole."

The plane shifted course, and Ross planted an elbow on the chair's arm. "Look, Laura, I'm afraid that's about all we can tell you. Except for exactly what Aurora needs you to do."

"Which is?"

"We want all the data from their experiments," Gonzales said. "And any other files you can gather. Especially anything related to The Next World."

Laura shook her head. "Is that all? I'm guessing that sort of information won't be super easy to come by."

Gonzales nodded. "We're assuming your data access will be severely restricted."

"And limited to only the experiments you're involved in," Ross added.

"Your physical access at the station will also likely be restricted."

Laura closed her eyes. This was insane.

"There is," Ross said. "Some possible good news."

"I could use some," Laura said, eyes still closed.

"We have an asset embedded in Antarctica Station."

Laura opened her eyes. "So get them to send the information."

Gonzales cut her eyes to Ross, silently asking how much to say. "That was the plan," he said. "But the asset has been there for over a year and hasn't exited or contacted us."

"We thought," Ross went on, "that the agent was waiting for the Antarctic winter to end."

Laura cocked her head. "Why?"

Gonzales answered: "There's no way to digitally send the data to us—not from the station."

"So, how would I get it to you—"

Laura realized the answer then, and Ross confirmed it.

"You'll need to physically exit. Your best chance is to take a ground vehicle to Amundsen–Scott, the US research station at the geographic South Pole."

Laura cut her eyes between the two agents. "No way. Again, I'm a doctor, not a—"

"Secret agent," Gonzales said, deadpan. "We're aware of that. It's only a sixty-mile drive, Laura. Your safest bet is to make that trip during the Antarctic summer. But you can do it during winter. And once you get to Amundsen–Scott, you'll be protected."

"Protected. In case Epoch comes after me."

Ross nodded. "Correct."

"Remember, you may have help. Our asset's name is Dr. Avi Cohen. He's a quantum physicist," Gonzales said.

"So what do I do, just give him the secret Aurora handshake?"

Ross shook his head. "You're not going to make direct contact with him. Revealing that you're an Aurora agent could be dangerous."

"Why?"

"Because," Ross said, "the other possible reason that Cohen hasn't completed the mission is that he's turned."

"As in—"

"Decided to abandon Aurora for Epoch," Gonzales said. "It's possible that what he learned in Antarctica changed his mind. Caused him to align himself with Epoch instead of us. That is, assuming he's still alive, which is the other possible reason he hasn't completed his mission."

"You think Epoch would really kill someone for spying?"

"We know they would," Ross said, staring at Laura.

"If Cohen is still alive, you should approach him with caution," Gonzales said. "Look, he could be an ally. It may be that he simply hasn't been able to collect the data."

"But," Ross said, "if Cohen has turned—or been discovered and terminated—Epoch security will be aware that we're investigating the organization. They'll be on the lookout for a replacement agent."

"Epoch security isn't your only challenge," Gonzales said. "Time is your biggest problem."

"I don't follow."

"There are two time constraints on your mission," Ross said. "The first is that we believe whatever Epoch is planning will come to fruition this summer. Specifically around July."

"Why do you think that?"

"Internal documents we've obtained refer to an event occurring in July, and the period after being the Next World."

"That's pretty vague," Laura said. "I mean—"

Gonzales cut her off. "The bottom line is that Epoch is planning something this summer. We need to know what it is. And if you don't find out, the deal is off. It's as simple as that."

Laura looked away, annoyed and angry and exhausted from being pushed around and betrayed.

"The other time constraint," Gonzales said, "is what we mentioned before: the weather in Antarctica. On March 21, at the vernal equinox, the bottom of the sun will meet the horizon in Antarctica. Sunset is a slow process on the continent. Keep in mind, every year, there is only one sunrise and one sunset at the South Pole. Beginning around late April or early May, the sun will dip below the horizon, and darkness will remain until late August or early September."

"The darkness will obviously make it harder to operate during your escape," Ross said. "But the temperature is the real problem. Even if you can get from Antarctica Station to Amundsen–Scott, we can't get a plane in to extract you after March 1—at the very latest. Typically, flights to Amundsen–Scott stop in mid-February for what they call the 'winter-over' season. We're willing to go a few weeks longer, but we absolutely cannot go past March 1."

Gonzales leaned forward. "I want to be clear on this point: if you don't get to Amundsen–Scott by March 1, all bets are off. The deal. Your safety. Everything. You'll be trapped in Antarctica and this event—whatever it is—will occur, and we won't even be willing to extract you after that."

"We may not even be able," Ross said quietly, perhaps trying to soften the blow of his partner's words.

The plane banked. The motion did nothing to shake off the tension in the cabin.

Agent Ross broke the silence. "We're also prepared to

sweeten the plea deal. If you deliver, we'll get you a full presidential pardon for your conviction. We'll also expunge all records of your arrest and plea deal. You'll get your life back, Laura."

"People will remember."

"Some will," Gonzales said. "But the world is a very big place."

13

At her father's grave-side, Laura sat under a tent and listened as the pastor described what a remarkable man Charles Reynolds had been.

It was December 15, and the ground was still covered with the recent snowfall. The sky was overcast, and as the eulogy came to an end, large snowflakes began to fall and drift in the wind like tears of ash.

Rachel wrapped her arm around Laura and the two sisters held tight to each other as the casket was lowered into the ground, collecting snowflakes on its glossy wood exterior as it went.

Laura could feel the eyes of the other attendees upon her, stares from across the open hole in the earth, people silently questioning whether she was the criminal the news described: a doctor who had crumbled under the pressure and put her patients at risk.

Laura held her head high and stared back. In the blaze of her glassy-eyed defiance, several attendees looked away. A few shook their heads, silently saying, "Your father would be ashamed."

Laura thought that there was a bizarre kind of torture

in being judged by strangers and not being able to defend yourself.

But today wasn't about her. It was about her father.

In her pocket was the sealed envelope with the letter he had written to her. She had considered reading it here, after the funeral. But she didn't dare draw it out now. She didn't want to break down in front of these people looking on in judgment.

And because, she now realized, she wasn't ready to read his last words to her.

*

On the way home, Ross and Gonzales once again joined Laura on the flight.

Their first act, after the plane had taken off, was to simply give Laura the ultimatum.

Was she in or out?

For Laura, there really was no choice. Sort of like the original plea deal.

So she told them she was in, and they spent the rest of the flight going over the details of the operation.

*

At home, that night, Laura deleted all of her social media profiles.

Strangely, she found it freeing.

Then, she set about winding down her affairs. She contacted her apartment complex about ending her lease. She turned off her automatic payments and kept moving down the list of bookmarked websites. When she couldn't find anything else to cancel or close, she locked her credit at all three rating agencies. With each connection to her life that she severed, she felt more liberated, as if she was truly starting her life over.

Rachel arrived the next day.

For the next two days, they talked and ate takeout and watched TV. Rachel worked her way through the bottles of wine on the small rack, but Laura abstained, reasoning that alcohol would only make it easier for her mind to slip into a valley of negative thoughts. She had a plan now. And she was going to work that plan and get her life back.

The sisters talked late into the night and cried about their mother and their father and about what was about to happen—Laura's three-year absence, with no contact.

Despite Laura's attempt at neatly concluding her affairs, there seemed to always be one more thing to attend to. Her apartment complex was asking for two months' rent. After reading the email, Laura exhaled and closed her laptop, unwilling to deal with one more thing that day.

At dinner, Rachel said, "This is like... the end of everything."

"You're being dramatic," Laura countered, stabbing her fork into an oriental chicken salad.

Rachel took a long gulp of wine and scarfed down a piece of sweet-and-sour chicken and spoke with her mouth half full. "For once in my life, I'm not." She swallowed and spoke more clearly. "You're all I have left, Laura. And you're disappearing from the face of the earth."

"It's not all bad," Laura whispered.

Rachel snorted. "No. It's all bad."

Laura set her fork down and told Rachel about the trust that would provide money and support for her over the next three years.

Her younger sister listened, eyes growing wider with every word.

About halfway through, she squinted. "No way."

"It's true," Laura said.

Rachel pushed back from the table and crossed her arms. "Well, what do you want me to do?"

"Nothing."

"Right. Nobody gives you that kind of money without expecting something."

"They do, Rachel. Family does. And you're all I have left."

Rachel picked up the glass and drained it and refilled it and was holding it up when she spoke again. "What do you want from me? Seriously."

"Rach, I just want you to live your life. Find your purpose."

Her sister laughed, a mirthless, almost angry reaction. "Purpose. Sure. It's probably in the junk drawer at home."

"Rachel."

"Face it: my life is a dumpster fire. Dead parents. Sister going off to dance with polar bears. Shrinking hometown everyone is leaving. No job opportunities. Guys who want to hook up three times and ghost me. Who wouldn't be thrilled?"

"So move away."

"To where?"

"Anywhere."

"I can't afford—" But Rachel stopped herself because that had just changed. "And then what?" she added.

"Build a new life. Start over. Go back to school."

Rachel took another long sip of wine. "Didn't take the first time."

"Then go on a long vacation and figure out what you want from life. Who you are."

"Like you? You knew from the beginning, Laura. You were the golden child. With me, Mom and Dad were like, 'What happened there?'"

"You know that's not true."

Rachel grimaced theatrically. "I mean, it's kind of true."

Laura rounded the table and sat beside her sister. Gently, she moved Rachel's hand from the wine glass and took both in her own hands. "We're different. But I love you, Rach. And I'll do anything for you."

Rachel stared back, lips quivering. And then her head fell onto Laura's shoulder, and they held each other and cried, for their father and their mother and Laura's legal problems and everything else, and it was like a swollen wound that was finally draining, and it hurt, and it brought so much relief.

*

At lunch the following day, a notification popped up on Rachel's phone. She smiled. "It's here."

"What?" Laura asked.

But her sister was gone before Laura could enquire further.

A few minutes later, Laura heard something scraping the hall floor. She opened the door and found Rachel awkwardly dragging a box almost as tall as she was. The picture on the outside showed a lighted Christmas tree.

"You didn't," Laura muttered.

"Help me," Rachel shot back, pausing to gasp for breath.

Inside, they laid the box with the pre-lit Christmas tree on the floor, and Laura stared at it. "Rachel, I'm moving out in less than two weeks. Literally moving to another continent."

"I'll put it up."

"I don't have any ornaments."

"I don't care."

"We don't even have any gifts to put under it."

"That's not the point."

And on that point, Laura thought, Rachel was right.

Together, the two sisters assembled the tree and placed it in the corner.

That night, Laura had to admit, as they sat on the couch and ate snacks and watched streaming TV, the tree was incredibly comforting, a reminder of their childhood and something normal, the yellow light shining on her disappearing life.

*

The next morning, the apartment complex emailed Laura again, pressing her on whether she was indeed going to break her lease and pay the two months' rent penalty.

Laura was reading the email when Rachel staggered out of the bedroom.

"I have an idea," she said to her sister, who was rubbing her eyes.

"It's too early for ideas," Rachel mumbled.

Laura told her anyway, and when she was finished, her sister said. "You want me to take over your lease?"

"You said you wanted to move. Start over. Well, this place is ready to go. It's affordable—especially with the trust. And there are plenty of jobs here in the Triangle. And colleges, too, if you want to go that route."

Rachel exhaled. "I mean, sure, okay."

"Just like that? Do you want to think about it?"

"Nah, I'm good."

"You can take some time."

Rachel shrugged. "Whatever. I've made a lot worse life decisions." She yawned. "Gotta say though, I thought your place would be nicer."

Laura blinked, unsure how to even take that.

"You're like a big deal doctor, you know?"

"It's close to the hospital. And med school wasn't exactly free, Rach."

"I get it. I mean, look, it's nicer than my place. I was just saying."

With that, Laura emailed her apartment complex and notified them that, in fact, her sister would be resuming her lease while she was out of town.

*

For the remaining ten days, Laura and her sister mostly stayed in the apartment, reading, watching TV, and playing board games. Laura spent the rest of her time doing research on Antarctica.

"I don't know why you're even doing that," Rachel commented one night.

"Being prepared can't hurt."

"You're doing medical research, not a polar expedition."

"Fair point. But I just… feel so unprepared for it. At least this way I have this sense that I'm getting ready somehow."

She hadn't told Rachel about her other assignment— for the government—and the fact that she would have to leave the facility for extraction.

"What you need," Rachel said, "is distraction. Let's go out."

"You know I can't."

"You can."

"I can only leave for—"

"Necessities," Rachel finished for her, rolling her eyes. "Well, having some fun is now a necessity. And besides, it's not like you have an ankle bracelet. How will they even know?"

"I can't take the risk," Laura said. She had always been a rule follower. Rachel, less so.

"But you go," Laura said.

Rachel exhaled. "Not leaving you, sis. Not gonna do it."

*

Three days before Christmas, Laura couldn't help but think about her fellowship program and her former colleagues and the holiday party they were having that night, without her. They were likely talking about little else but her.

Laura thought holidays had a way of doing that: reminding you of what you had lost, and the people who had what you wanted so badly.

But this year, Laura was determined to focus on what she had left: her sister.

*

At the airport, as Laura expected, Rachel broke down, sobbing almost uncontrollably. And when she got it under control, her words and plan were irrational.

"Let's just go," Rachel hissed, cutting her eyes to the two

Epoch Sciences security personnel. "Let's run. And keep running—"

Laura gripped her sister's shoulders. "Rach, relax. Everything is going to be okay. I'll be back—"

"In like three years—assuming a polar bear doesn't eat you."

Laura considered informing her sister that there were no polar bears in Antarctica, but decided instead to simply address her point. "Nothing is going to eat me. Three years, Rachel. And I'll be back, and everything will be fine."

PART II

ANTARCTICA

14

From Raleigh–Durham airport, Laura flew south, eventually landing in Punta Arenas, Chile.

The next day, she boarded a flight operated by Antarctic Logistics and Expeditions. Their destination was Union Glacier Camp, a private campsite located in West Antarctica, approximately 1,900 miles south of the tip of Chile and almost 600 miles from the South Pole. The site was only open from November to January each year, during the warmest months of Antarctica's summer.

As the plane descended, Laura peered out the window at the white expanse of ice and the natural blue-ice runway. It was so strange to be landing on a literal block of ice.

Beyond the runway, the snow twinkled under the sun like a sea of diamonds. Laura had read that the sun wouldn't set here until May, and even in the constant sunlight, the temperatures outside would remain below freezing, ranging from -12 to 30 degrees Fahrenheit.

It would be even colder at the South Pole—and at Epoch's Antarctica Station facility. And when the sun did set, it would be even colder still.

At the dining table in her apartment, Laura had read all

those facts, but it didn't compare to seeing this place. It was so alien. A wilderness with no equal on earth, made of ice and snow, where simply standing outside could cost you your life.

Still peering out the window, she thought that the cold wasn't the only killer in this place. If the Aurora agents were to be believed, her new employer was another, one even more dangerous.

*

When the plane came to a stop, a group of parka-clad staffers strode onto the ice. From a distance, they reminded Laura of the Oompa Loompas from Willy Wonka's chocolate factory.

They pushed two rolling stairways to the plane's exits; one docked at the front, the other at the back.

At the top of the platform, Laura got her first breath of dry, frigid Antarctic air, then began descending the stairs, boots clanking as she went.

The vehicle waiting for her was orange and sat on four tracks in a triangular shape. The front was like a pickup truck, with a long nose and wide doors that swung outward. The rear section reminded her more of a bus, with four large windows and a metal step ladder hanging out the back.

Despite its strange appearance, the vehicle easily traversed the five miles to Union Glacier Camp. Laura had seen pictures online, but they didn't do the sprawling camp justice. There were rows of colorful tents, evenly spaced, looking like striped caterpillars buried in the ice, their heads and ends hidden, backs thrust upward toward the sun.

Beyond the tents were a few planes, and these were the sort Laura had expected to see here in Antarctica: smaller aircraft, with skis where wheels would be.

In the middle of the rows of colorful caterpillar tents was a line of blocky structures with blue walls and white doors.

Bathrooms. That was Laura's first thought. During the tour of the camp, she learned that she was right.

Next to the bathroom buildings were two long, dark-blue structures that looked like greenhouses buried in ice.

After depositing her gear at her tent, Laura made her way to the largest round-top tent, which was the dining hall and social center of the camp. Tables spread out on each side, where animated conversations in several languages were raging.

The food was pretty good, Laura had to admit. They even served a limited amount of Chilean beer and wine, both of which she refrained from.

The vibe here was almost like a summer camp. The guests were a mix of tourists and researchers, and she found the conversations stimulating—until she was too tired to continue.

Walking back to her tent, boots crunching on the ice, she was struck by how clean the air smelled. How quiet it was— save for the wind. How utterly different Antarctica was.

And she wondered: what was it about this place that Epoch was so interested in? Was it really just the security aspect, as the Aurora agents had said? Was it simply to be so remote and isolated that no one could reach them?

In the bathroom, Laura washed her face, brushed her teeth, and moisturized her skin and lips. It was amazing how fast the dry air worked on a body here.

Inside her tent, she activated the humidifier and slipped into the sleeping bag. The mattress on top of the cot provided even more cushioning.

The tent was double walled, but it was still cold, even inside the sleeping bag. The tent fabric also didn't fully blot out the Antarctic sun. Laura pulled the sleep mask over her face, hiding the hazy glow, and soon her body heat began to accumulate in the sleeping bag, and sleep came next.

*

Laura woke to strange sounds. The low whirl of wind rustling across the tent. Snowmobile engines revving. A radio crackling in the distance.

Through the din, she also heard a creak. She sat up, listening. The sound morphed into a long groan.

Her mind was working better now, and she realized what she was hearing: ice moving.

It was like the land itself was alive here, as if she was sleeping atop a great beast slowly crawling across the ground.

*

That afternoon, Laura flew to Amundsen–Scott South Pole Station. The pilot and locals simply called the facility the "South Pole", and for good reason: the large research facility was located at the geographic South Pole, whereas her final destination—Epoch's facility—was sited along the south magnetic pole.

The pilots made a point of asking her why Epoch called their site Antarctica Station. She got the impression they thought it was a little too grand, given that there were so many existing research facilities in Antarctica.

"It's not like their station is the first," one man said. "And won't be the last."

"Hey, I just work there," Laura told him. "I didn't name it."
That seemed to quell their curiosity.

*

South Pole Station was an elevated modular building that sat on columns that were designed to be raised further as snow accumulated. Its walls were a practical, dark gray, with square or vertical rectangular windows.

During the summer, the station was home to one hundred and fifty or so researchers. Only about fifty stayed for the winter.

Laura had hoped to venture inside the facility and see some of it. She never got the chance. Outside the building, a white Hägglunds bearing the Epoch Sciences logo was waiting for her.

Walking across the ice, Laura was struck by how thin the air was here. Soon, she was breathing hard just from walking. It made sense: the South Pole lay at an elevation of 9,300 feet—almost two miles above sea level.

The wind blew from one direction and was constant, never letting up, giving Laura the sense of walking in a giant wind tunnel.

Three figures exited the Epoch snow vehicle. They wore white parkas with hoods, white balaclavas, and polarized ski goggles.

One of Laura's handlers opened a pouch on his coveralls and took out a plastic-wrapped item and extended it to the three Epoch employees.

The lead person pulled down their hood and removed the balaclava and goggles.

Laura's heart nearly stopped.

Standing here at the South Pole, she was staring at Joe West.

His blond hair danced in the Antarctic wind. His blue-gray eyes didn't focus on her. They drifted down to the plastic-wrapped papers the pilot was holding out to him.

"What's this?"

"We need you to sign."

Joe took the plastic package but didn't open it. "Why would I sign?"

"We delivered—"

"We only sign for cargo," Joe said, his voice as biting as the wind. He nodded to Laura. "This is a person."

The pilot took a step forward, boots crunching in the ice. "Sign it, asshole."

Joe didn't blink. "You know what we have in Antarctica?"

"I don't give a—"

Joe rolled the plastic-wrapped pages up and pressed them into the man's bulky suit. "It was a rhetorical question." He cocked his head. "As in—a dramatic prelude to an important statement, which is: here in Antarctica, we have ice, penguins, and…" Joe held the bundle upward. "Wind."

He tossed it across the ice.

"That wind. Never know when it will get hold of your paperwork."

The pilot clenched his teeth. "You've got to sign for her."

"I don't. Like I said: she's not a piece of cargo. She's a person, and an important one."

The wind blew through the group then, and Laura could have sworn it was the coldest draft yet.

15

The pilot declined to pick up the pages. Instead, he and the co-pilot turned and walked away.

"Give us a minute," Joe said to his two colleagues, who were still wearing hoods, goggles, and masks.

They turned and trudged back to the waiting Hägglunds.

"Security," Laura said, glaring at Joe. "For a biotech company."

"I am," he said, his Southern accent drifting across the desert of ice. "I didn't lie to you, Laura."

"You were there to, what... investigate me?"

"Mmm," he said, nodding.

"So, it was all an act."

"I had a job to do. I did it. My assessment was that you were exactly what you appeared to be."

"What am I, Joe?"

"A wrongfully accused person." He took a step closer to her. "Someone who had some bad luck. A good person. A person I liked." He paused. "Like."

Laura swallowed, heart beating faster. "What else would I be?"

"A spy."

The two words hung in the air.

Her heart thundered, and even in this frigid place, she could feel the first beads of sweat emerging on her face. She didn't trust her voice to speak.

"What Epoch is doing is important, Laura. A lot of very powerful, very capable people have tried to find out exactly what it is. Some want to stop it. Others want to be part of it."

"What exactly is Epoch doing, Joe?"

He smiled, those blue-gray eyes a reflection of the ice stretching out in every direction. "We're creating the Next World, Laura. And you're going to be part of it. You're one of the lucky ones."

*

For a little over two hours, the Hägglunds charged across the barren terrain, engine roaring.

Ninety days. That's what Laura was thinking. That's the maximum amount of time she had to get the details on what Epoch was doing and get out.

It was crazy.

But her life was crazy.

Finally, a break in the white expanse of ice appeared ahead. From a distance, it didn't look like much, only a black dome buried in the ice.

Laura didn't see an entrance.

Still, the Hägglunds pressed forward, maintaining its speed, the pistons raging, rubber tracks gripping the ice, the only other sound the whistle of the wind across the mechanical beast.

A minute later, Laura realized that the dome of Antarctica

Station was much larger than she initially thought. It was easily the size of a sports stadium.

In the blink of an eye, the black top switched to white.

Laura glanced over at Joe in the seat beside her.

"The roof is covered in solar cells," he said, answering her unspoken question. "They change color when satellites fly over."

Ahead, the ice seemed to part as two large doors slid open, revealing a dark tunnel beyond.

The Hägglunds bounced slightly as it entered the tunnel, the impact similar to a speed bump in a parking deck.

Ahead, a pair of doors swung inward, revealing a large open space lit from above by fluorescent lights. Hägglunds were parked in a line on each side of the massive garage, backed up to raised docks that held crates and hard plastic boxes.

Inside the loading area, the Hägglunds' rubber tracks squeaked on the concrete as it slowly backed into an empty space.

Laura tried to take in every detail of this garage and loading dock. If things went to plan, it would likely be the place where she stole a vehicle and made her escape.

After parking, the two Epoch staffers in the front seats got out and trekked to the roll-up door at the end of the large space.

Joe didn't exit. Neither did Laura.

"This is going to be a little intense," he said, staring straight ahead.

"Intense how?"

"They'll search you. And question you."

"Okay."

"I couldn't get you out of it."

"You tried?"

"I asked."

"What do you do here, Joe?"

"Same thing as everyone else."

"Security?"

"I do what's required."

"For what?"

"The Next World."

He reached for the door handle, but stopped, glancing back at Laura. "Be careful in there."

She nodded slowly, unsure what to say.

"This is the most important place on earth now," Joe said. "Think about that, Laura. Especially when they question you, okay?"

"Okay," she whispered, her eyes locked on his.

"Epoch knows a lot. About everyone in this station."

She squinted at him, a piece clicking into place for her. "Joe, did you bug my home?"

He smiled. "*I* didn't."

"Let me rephrase: did Epoch have someone posing as a maintenance man changing filters hide surveillance devices inside my apartment?"

"No comment."

"I'll take that as a yes."

"I'm glad to hear that, Laura. Because that's the kind of paranoia you need right now."

*

Inside, two women took Laura to a room where they told her to strip down. They stuffed her clothes down a chute and searched her body methodically.

They also collected her personal belongings, including the letter from her father and several family photos.

In the next room, they x-rayed her and provided her with white coveralls with the Epoch logo. They scanned her eyes next and captured her finger and toe prints. Finally, they took blood and saliva samples.

Laura felt like a lab rat.

Her last stop was a room with a wide mirror and a small table with two chairs.

She expected Joe to come in. She hoped he would.

But he didn't.

Instead, an Indian woman entered and sat across from Laura and introduced herself simply as Imara. She informed Laura that she would be under constant surveillance inside the station. And her movements would be restricted. Her retinas and fingerprints would serve as her key here, and they would give her access to only certain areas and only at specific times.

Imara leaned forward, planting her forearms on the table. "And there are other security precautions specific to you, Dr. Reynolds."

"Call me Laura."

The woman continued as if Laura hadn't spoken. "You'll be closely monitored for any signs of drug abuse."

"I didn't do what I was accused of."

"You'll also undergo the treatment program that was mandated by the court as part of your plea deal, including a video course on substance abuse."

"I read all of this in the agreement."

"I'll also personally be watching you, Dr. Reynolds. If you have any issues with any of this, you need to say so right now. We'll end this here. You can return to the United States and begin serving your prison sentence."

"I know what I signed up for. I just didn't realize it would involve having to endure your self-indulgent threats."

Imara didn't miss a beat. "Have you been contacted by members of law enforcement since you signed your contract?"

Laura felt her stomach drop. Every part of her wanted to panic. Instead, she feigned annoyance. "Of course."

Imara drew her arms from the table, leaning back. "By whom?"

"The US Marshals. They took me to my father's funeral."

Imara bunched her eyebrows.

A silent moment passed.

"Have you," Imara began, "been asked to help with any investigation into Epoch Sciences or Antarctica Station?"

Somewhere in the corner of the room, behind Laura, the whirl of an electric motor whined. A camera—or scanning device—activating. They were watching her. Scanning her.

Laura wondered what they were monitoring. Her body temperature? Heart rate? Her instincts told her that they would know if she was lying. Or the data would reveal it later.

Joe's words ran through her mind. *Be smart, Laura. Epoch knows a lot. About everyone in this station.*

She made a decision then. One that might end everything. Her life. The deal. The opportunity she had been given.

"On the way to my father's funeral," Laura said slowly, staring at the metal table, "I was interviewed by two people. They wanted to know about Epoch."

"What did they ask you?"

Laura shrugged. "What I knew about Epoch."

"What did they ask you to do?"

"Gather information."

"About?"

"The experiments. The goal of whatever you're doing here."

Imara crossed her arms. "That's good, Dr. Reynolds. Very good. We know about Aurora. We know they approached you."

"And yet I'm still here."

"Due to one thing: your honesty in the last ten seconds."

Laura let out a breath.

"What did you tell the Aurora agents?" Imara asked.

"About?"

"Their request—that you spy on us."

"I said the only thing I could."

"Which was?"

"Yes."

"Do you plan to honor that commitment, Dr. Reynolds?"

Laura snorted. "I'm a doctor, not a spy. This"—she waved a hand at the room—"whatever this is, is the only place on Earth where I can practice medicine. That's what I came here to do."

Imara stared at her.

Laura leaned forward, voice hard. "Look, whatever is going on between you and the government, you two can sort it out. I don't care. Doing my job—helping patients—is my only concern."

Imara rose, the metal chair skidding on the concrete floor. "He said you were smart."

"Who?"

"Joe. He also said you were honest. Let's see what the data says."

16

Seconds turned to minutes. Laura sat in the white holding room with the wide mirror, awaiting her fate.

If they decided that she was lying—that Laura did intend to spy—what would Epoch do? Put her back in the Hägglunds and take her to South Pole Station?

Or worse?

Technically, if she died here, no one would know for years. And her murder could be covered up easily. Antarctica was a dangerous place. Accidents happened.

The door opened, and a man dressed in a white Epoch uniform motioned for her to follow.

He led her to a room labeled *Intake Suite*, which was like an apartment with no windows. There was a bedroom, a full bath, and a combined living and dining space.

The bathroom was stocked with toiletries and towels (also with the Epoch logo). She commended their branding efforts, even in this quasi-prison cell.

Laura showered, and when she returned to the dining room, she found a tray with dinner. The sight of the meatloaf, mashed potatoes, green beans, and salad made her realize how hungry she was.

Sitting at the dining table, she studied the suite closer. There was no TV. No eReader. No books. No entertainment whatsoever. Only a picture on the wall that showed a rope bridge between two mountain peaks, clouds lacing through it, a figure with their back turned, walking across.

She had come here to avoid prison, but she now questioned the wisdom of that. Sitting in the coverall, in isolation, after being interrogated, it looked like she had ended up in prison after all.

She gave up on the meal halfway through the mashed potatoes. It seemed wrong to leave the half-eaten tray on the dining table all night, so she carried it to the door, intending to find a trash bin, but the handle wouldn't turn.

She wasn't sure if it was the harsh reality of knowing she was confined or the heavy food or the shower or the emotional stress, but she suddenly felt so tired, so utterly exhausted, as if some part of her mind had been holding up the weight of everything that had happened—Samir's betrayal, the loss of her job and freedom, the loss of her father; all of it—and that mass was crashing down on her now.

She left the tray on the table and staggered to the bed and stretched out, not even bothering with the covers.

*

Despite crashing hard, Laura woke feeling refreshed.

The suite was empty. The door was still locked, but at least the meal tray was gone. With nothing to do, she showered again and put the coveralls back on. This time, there was no meal waiting on the dining table. The absence made her hungry.

She sat on the couch and wished she had the letter from

her father. Not because she was ready to read it but because she couldn't stand the thought of losing it.

The door swung open, and an Epoch security staffer beckoned her to follow. She did, and he deposited her in a room with a long dining table that held a bread basket covered with a white napkin, two carafes of water, and a place setting on each side of the table.

Laura sat and tore off a slice of bread and dipped it in the small round crucible of butter. It reminded her of that Italian place in Durham, the night she had met Joe.

The thought of him made her realize that she hoped that he would walk through the door.

She tried to ignore the thought. It was so unlike her. So ridiculous. She hardly knew him.

Joe didn't walk through the door. The man who stepped through was older, with short white hair, a slender face, and blue-gray eyes.

A face eerily like Joe's.

He said nothing, only closed the door gently behind him and strode across the room. He pulled the chair out and sat and lifted the carafe and poured himself a glass of water.

"Welcome, Laura." He took a sip. "My name is Warren Albright."

"What is this?"

He smiled.

She knew that smile.

Joe's smile.

The man had a neutral accent, but she was almost certain he was related to Joe. A father. Or uncle, perhaps.

He held a fist out, knuckles down, and tapped the table.

The door opened, and two waiters brought plates that held eggs, grits, toast, and bacon.

"*This* is breakfast," he said as the staff receded.

With his fork, Albright started in on the grits.

"My son is quite enamored with you," he said without looking up.

"Joe?"

"Mmm." Albright pointed his fork at her, still chewing, and after swallowing, said, "He's more sentimental than I am. He had the advantage of a pleasant childhood."

"You didn't?"

"One of the things, Dr. Reynolds, that I think you're going to like about this place is that most of us don't talk about our pasts."

"Sounds pretty good to me."

"Why do you think humanity appears to be alone in the universe?"

The question was so off-topic it took Laura a second to process it. "I... don't know. Do you?"

"Generally, I do, yes."

He began eating the eggs.

"Okay," Laura said. "Are you going to tell me?"

"Oh, no. No, I wouldn't want to ruin breakfast."

After a long pause, he continued. "The work we're doing here is principally research. Research that we want to keep private. And there's a reason we have to do it here, in the middle of this massive block of ice. That reason will become clear to you in time, but I assure you it's of no concern now."

"What *should* I be concerned with?"

"The Next World, Dr. Reynolds."

"Which is what exactly?"

"It's what we're creating."

"So I hear. And that's all I hear."

"Think about it as a paradigm shift in human existence."

"Such as?"

"The Next World is a bit like the shifts that preceded it. There are plenty of examples in human history. The advent of artistic expression—evidenced by those first Paleolithic paintings on cave walls. Toolmaking. Control of fire. Language and verbal communication. And, of course, the breakthroughs that most would think about: agriculture, writing, the wheel, the codification of various sciences. The Next World is a breakthrough of that magnitude. More important than the Industrial Revolution. Or the discovery of electricity. Or the internet. Or any of the novelties the world you left is obsessed with."

"All right. I'll bite. What does the Next World do for humanity that we don't already have?"

"You know what the root problem with the world is?" Albright said, picking up another forkful of eggs.

"Seems a little above my pay grade."

"Being a critic of the world at large is within any human's pay grade."

"I sense you've studied the subject more than me."

Finally, the older man smiled, lines forming on his face, his blue-gray eyes sparkling.

"Joe said you're headstrong. That you have guts. No doubt just a few of the things he likes about you."

Laura blushed and focused on eating, not liking the turn the conversation had taken.

Her host continued: "Short-term thinking. That's probably humanity's biggest issue. And the fear of anyone different."

With his fork, he pushed the remaining scrambled eggs together.

"That proverbial fear of the other," Albright continued. "It's the reason there are no Neanderthals or Denisovans or Homo erectus left. We slaughtered our Homo sapiens cousins. And consumed the resources they needed to survive. We humans are biologically programmed to do that. It's been the key to our success."

He finished off the eggs and went on, "But that biological programming has a dark side."

"And your Next World will fix that?"

"Yes. And so many other things."

He glanced at her plate. "You barely touched your food."

"What can I say? You're a great conversationalist."

He smiled again. "You know, I listened to the recording of those Aurora agents recruiting you on the plane."

Laura's gaze fell to her plate, unsure where this was going.

"You could argue," Albright said, "that those agents are simply people doing their jobs. But that's a little naive. Generous. The Aurora Project, simply put, is trying to protect the status quo. They don't want anything to change. They don't care whether we're building something beneficial for human society. If what we create takes power away from them and the government they work for, they want to stop it. Change would harm their existing survival advantage."

Laura leaned back in her chair. "I told the security people: I don't care about any of that. You all can battle it out."

With his knife, Albright began slicing the bacon. "Oh we

will. And they will lose. I just want you to understand the nature of what you're involved in."

He took a bite of bacon and chewed it slowly, his gaze drifting above her.

"In this station, you're safe, Laura. And you'll be part of creating something that will be remembered as a turning point in human history."

He took another bite of bacon.

"But outside, there is nothing but ice and death. Don't ever forget that."

*

After breakfast, Laura was led back to the intake suite and given a tablet about the size of an eReader. It had limited access to Epoch's internal network, but it did enable her to view the staff directory.

Holding the tablet, she sat on the couch and began reading the bios of the scientists she would be working with.

She didn't search for Dr. Avi Cohen.

But her mind drifted to Joe. And his father. And the impossible decision she had to make—whether to try to honor her agreement with the government or to cooperate with Epoch.

*

In the security room, Albright watched the screen where Laura was sitting on the couch, staring at the tablet.

"What do you think?" Imara asked.

"I think we should watch her very closely."

17

Laura wasn't sure how long she had lain on the couch in the intake suite, but she was drifting off to sleep when the door opened and Joe strode in. He stopped abruptly when he saw her.

"You okay?"

Laura sat up. "I'm fine. Just mentally reviewing all my interrogation answers."

"Well, you can forget about that." He smirked. "For now."

"So I passed?"

"For now," he muttered, turning.

"What does that mean?"

"It means that when you live with paranoid people, the interrogations never end." He opened the door and motioned to her. "Come on, I'll show you around."

*

Laura had expected Antarctica Station to be cramped and rugged, more like the pictures she had seen of Amundsen–Scott South Pole Station.

Her expectations couldn't have been more wrong.

This place was more like a spaceship from a sci-fi movie. The walls and ceiling were white and made of plastic or metal or some composite. The floors featured a low-pile gray carpet that cushioned her footfalls enough to deaden any sound.

Which was good, because there was a lot of walking. The station seemed to go on forever. And this was only one level (Joe commented that there were eight—two above them and five below). They were on one of the residential floors now.

As they walked, he gave her a verbal ordering of the floors and their purpose.

Levels eight and seven: storage and mechanical equipment.

Level six: labs.

Level five: offices.

Levels four and three: residences.

Level two: cafeteria, recreation, and common spaces.

Level one: the park.

The top level, which contained the park, was under the giant dome Laura had seen as they approached the station.

Their first stop was the apartment that would be Laura's residence for the next three years. Joe referred to it as a suite. The space was similar to the holding suite. It had a combined living and dining room, a bedroom, and a bathroom. It featured the Epoch interior design motif, with white walls and bright lights. On the whole, it wasn't that different from Laura's apartment in Durham, though there was no kitchen. There were, however, refrigerated drawers and a microwave drawer, all tucked behind white panels that opened when pressed. Even the furniture had muted colors. There was a light-gray couch and a pearly white square dining table with two light-blue chairs.

The only pop of color in the suite came from a recessed rectangle in the long wall in the living room across from the couch. At first glance, Laura thought it was a window. The picture was that clear and vivid. It showed the snowy expanse of Antarctica, the sun blazing down, reflecting white and yellow in the ice. As Laura watched, the wind whipped across the barren land, carrying ice crystals like grains of sand in the desert.

"Window," Joe said, "take me to the mountains."

The image changed to a dark-green forested mountain range with clouds in the valleys.

"Window," Joe said again, "stream *The X-Files*, season one, episode one."

The mountains gave way to the opening scene of the iconic show. But Joe didn't let it play.

"Window, play seventies music."

The opening chords of the song, *Can't Find My Way Home*, by the supergroup Blind Faith began.

Laura wondered if there was some hidden meaning in the song choice.

Joe stared at her. "Window, show home."

It switched back to the view of Antarctica and the seemingly endless expanse of ice.

Joe tilted his head at the screen. "You get the picture."

Laura suppressed a smile. "I see what you did there."

"You liked it."

"You use that joke on every tour you give?"

"Actually, this is the first tour I've ever given."

He moved to the bedroom and pressed a finger into the white wall panel to the left of the bed. It slid out from the wall, forming a bedside table. Joe tapped the top of the table, and it lit up with a soft golden glow. He tapped the surface again and it got brighter. When he held his finger down, the light dimmed until it went out.

On top of the table was a tablet like the one she had seen in the intake suite.

Joe picked it up and handed it to Laura. "It's keyed to your retinas."

Laura faced the tablet and it unlocked, revealing a home screen with icons for mail, messages, video, music, and EpochNet. The interface was unfamiliar to her, but it was intuitive.

"The tabs run EOS—or Epoch Operating System," Joe said, turning the device over. The backside had another display, which was grayscale. "Flipside has an e-ink screen for books and after-hours only apps."

"After hours?"

"One of the biggest challenges here is maintaining circadian rhythms."

Joe flipped the tablet over again. "After hours, the OLED screen turns off. No bright lights. Only e-ink will work. And only certain apps. Nothing related to work and no TV."

He motioned to the recessed screen in the living room. "Post-orientation, the window will start showing a rising and setting sun, and the screen goes dark at night."

"Makes sense," Laura said.

"If you can't sleep, and a lot of people here can't—especially right after arrival—you can use the care app to order a sleep supplement."

"What's in it?"

"The supplement?"

"Yes. Is it melatonin or valerian? Is it prescription—"

Joe held a hand up. "Truly, I have no idea. I can only tell you that it works."

"Seems inappropriate not to tell a patient what they're receiving."

"Laura Reynolds, meet Epoch Sciences."

He was walking out of the bedroom when she called to him. "Joe?"

"Yeah?"

"Can I ask you something?"

"Sure."

"Is this going to end the way I think?"

He turned back to her, smiling, likely remembering what he said to her in Durham—this isn't going to end the way you think.

Here, he asked, "How do you think it's going to end, Laura?"

"With me leaving and getting my life back."

The smile disappeared from his lips and a shadow seemed to cross his face, an expression Laura couldn't read.

"The thing is," Joe said slowly, "sometimes what we think we want isn't what's best for us."

"You have your father's talent for vague statements."

He winced as if he'd been punched and turned and marched to the door. His voice was emotionless when he spoke. "Come on, there's a lot more to see."

*

The rest of the tour was awkward and rushed. Joe was merely going through the motions now. Laura knew the conversation in her room had changed the mood, but she couldn't see a way to reverse it.

On the rec floor above the residences, Joe led Laura through the cafeteria, fitness center, pool, and gym. Compared to Union Glacier Camp, Epoch's station was a luxury resort.

When she commented that it seemed more reasonable to locate the pool on the bottom floor of the structure, Joe smiled knowingly.

"What?"

"Nothing," he muttered.

"Seriously? What about the pool?"

"There's a lot you don't know about this place."

"Clearly."

*

The uppermost floor of Antarctica Station was Laura's favorite. The park covered the entire level and was covered in dense foliage which was broken only by the walking paths. The winding trails felt almost like a labyrinth, constantly cutting back and making turns. It made the space feel larger, almost endless. Adding to the effect was the massive dome overhead that displayed an image of a clouded sky at midday. The shadows cast by the trees made the space truly feel outdoors.

With Joe leading her down a winding path, and the fake sun above, Laura almost felt like she was having a lazy afternoon walk in the park. Like the window in her room, the dome and its artificial sky was entirely convincing. The whole place felt real enough to make her forget that she was in Antarctica.

18

After the walk through the park on the station's top floor, Joe led Laura to the cafeteria. The selection of food was far larger than she expected.

"Is this the buffet every day?" Laura asked in a low voice as they slid their trays along the line.

"It rotates," Joe said, scooping mashed potatoes onto his plate.

"Seriously?"

With tongs, he grabbed a piece of bread and cut his eyes to her. "Sure. Why? What's wrong?"

"I mean, it's Antarctica. Can't exactly grow a massive garden."

That same knowing smile Laura had seen before crossed his lips. "Oh, you'd be surprised."

Joe lifted his tray and walked away, into the dining area.

Laura stopped long enough to grab a roll before following him to an empty table with six chairs. As she walked there, Laura felt more than a few eyes upon her—casual glances, followed by whispers and more glances. She felt like a beach ball floating around at a baseball game, catching the passing attention of the crowd as she moved by.

She was relieved when she landed in the chair across from Joe. But the stares and the whispers didn't stop. She wondered if they ever would.

Joe was lifting a forkful of barbecue when Laura continued the buffet conversation. "It's a lot of trouble for the meals. To ship all this in here."

The query didn't stop Joe. He downed the dripping pork and chewed methodically, his eyes fixed above her shoulder, answering only when his mouth was empty (Laura noted that he did have some manners, despite his often-barbaric nature). "It is. I mean, it's a fortune to fly anything in here. But the people here—most of them, who aren't working at the station—they have fortunes to spend, and they want to eat what they want to eat. So they pay the cost."

Joe waved his fork again. "And part of one of the sublevels is hydroponics. Forgot to mention that on the tour."

"I'm revising my rating of that tour."

"Told you: it was my first."

"Why did you even bother? To give me a tour?"

Joe was about to stab another piece of barbecue, but at her question, his fork stopped in mid-air. He stared at her. "Because I like you."

"As in…"

"I *like* you, Laura."

Joe stabbed with the fork again and took another large bite of barbecue, staring Laura in the eyes. "As in all the ways."

Laura wasn't sure what to say. She could feel half a dozen eyes around the room surreptitiously studying her.

She nodded slowly. "Oh."

Joe leaned back in his chair and smiled at her. "Is that all? Just 'oh'?"

"It's a perfectly reasonable response."

"Well, I've been on this planet long enough to know not to argue with that."

Laura picked up her fork and dragged it across the rotisserie chicken, peeling off the rippled skin and taking a bite, trying hard to mimic his casual nature.

"Good." She had intended to say more, but when she opened her mouth again, the words didn't come. So she took another bite of chicken as he watched her. And when she swallowed that, she still didn't know what to say, so she repeated, "Good," and kept picking at the chicken.

Joe helped himself to another big bite of barbecue, and, staring down at his nearly empty tray, said, "Good."

*

On her first day of work, Laura dressed in her Epoch coveralls, stared at herself in the mirror, and tried to calm her nerves.

She took the elevator down to level five where the offices were located. A staffer in Epoch's Medical Research Group (or MedRe as they called it) escorted her to a conference room where a slender woman with silver hair was waiting.

"Good morning, Dr. Reynolds. I'm Greta Berggren, team lead for MedRe." She held a hand out to the conference table as she herself sat.

"Please, call me Laura. I'm sorry, but am I late?"

"No. I'm always early."

Laura filed the information away for future meetings.

"Have you been told what we do here?"

Laura laughed at the question. "No. Not even close."

"MedRe is principally concerned with two major projects. We'll start with the one that is complete: human stasis." Greta raised her eyebrows. "You look surprised."

"You said complete?"

"Indeed. The project is operational as we speak, and, in fact, that is what your work here at MedRe will concern: the administration of anesthesia for patients entering or exiting stasis."

Laura sat there, a hundred questions running through her mind.

"What do you know about human stasis research?" Greta asked.

Laura shrugged. "Nothing. Well, except what I've seen in sci-fi movies."

"I assure you, what we're doing is far from science fiction. Though it's not far from existing precedents on Earth."

"Precedents?"

"Stasis, Dr. Reynolds, has been achieved by several known species on our planet—and perhaps by countless others now extinct. Take, for example, the wood frogs that inhabit North America, from Alaska to the southern Appalachians. In winter, they freeze. Their hearts completely stop. They thaw in the spring and reanimate."

Greta paused and when Laura said nothing, she continued. "The process is quite fascinating, actually. As the weather cools, the frogs begin storing urea in their tissues. Their livers convert glycogen to glucose. Both substances are cryoprotectants that limit ice formation during the freezing process and osmotic cell shrinkage. But there are limits. The wood frog can survive only if less than about two thirds of their body water freezes. The Japanese tree frog, however, can tolerate even colder temperatures."

Laura was familiar with similar concepts in medicine. A patient's body temperature was often reduced to slow metabolic processes during surgeries or after cardiac arrest.

"The tardigrades are even more hardy," Berggren continued. "And better known thanks to inclusion in popular films and TV. There are species that don't even need the cold or extreme conditions to enter a state of estivation."

"Estivation?"

"A state of dormancy in which metabolic processes slow. The specimen is still wakeful, though cell turnover and aging is significantly decreased. This is the case for the African lungfish, which can coat itself in mucus, burrow in the mud and stay there for over three years without food or water."

"That's incredible."

"It's inspiration, Dr. Reynolds." Berggren leaned forward. "Knowing that something is possible—seeing our fellow inhabitants of Earth achieve it—was the wind at the back of our efforts. And it offered clues. Not all valuable clues but avenues of investigation."

Berggren tapped at her tablet, and Laura felt her own device buzz in her pocket. "I've sent you a training course. It will prepare you for your work. You have seventy-two hours to complete the modules. Then you'll report to MedRe for training simulations."

"How long will that last?"

Berggren raised an eyebrow. "As long as it takes, Dr. Reynolds. I'll be monitoring your progress and scores on the simulations."

"I see."

"At present, we have two anesthesiologists. One wishes to shift roles and focus on MedRe's other field of research."

"And what's that?"

"Longevity."

"Immortality?"

"An accurate, albeit slightly hyperbolic descriptor. Nevertheless, you'll be taking his place. But only when you're ready. And, if you fail to master the procedure in a reasonable time frame—or if we feel you're not a fit for MedRe—we'll have to end this experiment, such as it is."

"I understand," Laura said slowly.

"You have questions."

"About a million."

"We shall talk again after you've completed the training module. That will be more efficient." Berggren stood. "One last thing, Dr. Reynolds."

"Yes?"

"The patients you'll be assisting are transiting stasis. You won't have any physical interaction with them."

"What? Why? How is that even possible?"

"That would be inefficient. You'll use a computer interface to manage the administration of the medications and monitor pertinent patient data in real time."

"All right. But what if I need to—"

"As I said, Dr. Reynolds, there will be no need for physical access to the patients. Nor would it be possible."

19

After the bizarre meeting with Dr. Berggren, Laura took the stairs. She thought walking might help her think.

But she didn't go straight home. First, she descended the stairs from the offices on level five to level six, where the labs were housed (it was still weird to her for the floors to count up as she went down, but weird was sort of normal in Antarctica Station).

When she scanned her eyes at the panel to the door to the sixth floor, red letters flashed: *Access Denied*

She got the same message at the two storage levels below it.

That was going to be a problem. Because the garage and exit from the station was on level seven.

*

At lunch, Joe asked how her first day was going.

"It was... interesting. And confusing."

He smiled. "Yeah, you'll have that around here."

*

For the rest of the day, Laura sat in her suite and consumed the Epoch training course on stasis. It consisted of videos, texts, and interactive quizzes at the end of the modules.

She read the text on her tablet and watched the video segments on the window. She had hoped to see some of the other MedRe personnel in the videos, but there were only animated figures—not exactly cartoons, more like a very advanced Pixar feature with life-like characters voicing the training material and scenarios. Laura wondered if the courses had been created by AI based on a collection of written input from MedRe staff and data from the patient procedures.

Regardless of how the course was created, there was something about the wording—mostly in the written text. It was oddly familiar. But Laura couldn't think of who it reminded her of.

Her doorbell rang and she found Joe waiting in the hall. "Thought you might want company for supper."

She breathed out a laugh. "You're very presumptuous."

He cocked his head. "Am I? Maybe. But I'm guessing about now that you're sick of studying like a college kid cramming for an exam, you don't know anyone else in the station—well, not really—and you could use some company."

She stared at him.

"Do I presume correctly?"

"Come on in."

He plopped down on the couch. "Love your place."

"You saw it yesterday morning."

"Yeah, but now you live here. I like it even more. And more than my place."

She sat beside him. "Really, why? Is it bigger?"

"Nah. All the staff suites are the same for singles. It's just—neater. Bed made up. Everything in its place."

"So you're a slob?"

"Absent-minded."

A silent moment passed, one in which Laura felt absolutely no need to fill the silence, and she thought: now that's something. Somehow, it was so easy for them to be together. So effortless. A natural thing. There was almost a familiarity about it, like the way the stasis training course was written.

Joe took out his own tablet. "You ordered dinner yet?"

"I was going to go to the cafeteria when I was too tired to keep studying."

"Said like a true college student." Joe swiped on his tablet. "But you know the cafeteria's closed."

"What? Why?"

"We have Visions tonight."

"*Visions*? Of what?"

Joe paused. "Oh, I guess I didn't cover that." He shot her a sheepish look. "Told you it was my first tour."

"Well, it would seem that you need to finish it."

"Nah, if I finish it, you might not let me come over anymore."

"Haha. What are Visions?"

"It's like seminars. Or like thought-provoking talks with big ideas." Joe shrugged. "Some of it goes over my head, but you might get more out of it than me. Check that—you will get more out of it than me."

"Huh."

"There's two a week. On Tuesday, it's Visions of the Old World."

"The old world, as in Europe pre-colonial era?"

Joe laughed. "That's a good one."

"Why is that a good one?"

"You'll see," he said wryly. And more seriously: "Actually, Visions of the Old World are about the world pre-Epoch."

"Our world."

"Right. It's revealing the true nature of the world, how messed-up it is, things no one talks about."

"What's the point?"

"The point is to get it right in the Next World. And that's the other part of the Visions series." His eyes flashed with mock enthusiasm. "Every Thursday night, we get Visions of the Next World. The cafeteria is closed again, and they deliver food to your suite. You eat and watch the window and learn. It's sort of a way for everyone in the station to get on the same page—to exchange knowledge and spark informed conversations. The idea is to shape a shared ideology."

"Sounds like a gateway to indoctrination."

"Your words, not mine. But I'll say that it's not all bad. And I hate homework."

Somehow Laura already knew that.

They ordered dinner from the tablet. While they waited for the food, Laura said, "There's one thing bothering me."

"Lucky," Joe mumbled.

"Why?"

"You've only got *one* thing bothering you."

"You're a funny man tonight."

He held a finger up. "Every night. But do tell: what's bothering Dr. Laura Reynolds?"

"The MedRe work."

"What about it?"

"They're researching human stasis and longevity."

"Mmm," Joe murmured. This was apparently not news to him.

"And they have achieved stasis. Did you know that?"

Joe raised his eyebrows. "Yeah. I did."

"And the stasis patients are remote. Did you know *that*?"

"Definitely."

"Why, Joe? Why are we *here*—and the patients are elsewhere? I can't see how it makes sense."

"It will."

"When?"

"In time."

"Is that all you can tell me?"

"More or less. Look, it's a matter of security and logistics and... other factors."

"What other factors?"

Joe turned to her on the couch, and for the first time since he had arrived that night, the levity in his demeanor receded. In a serious, very unJoe-like tone, he said, "Listen, Laura, I know you've been through the wringer. What happened in Durham. Your dad. Your mom before that. But I'm telling you, this is a big break for you. There are secrets here. And for good reason. And there's a larger plan. It's a good one. An important one. Don't mess it up by asking too many questions. It's like I told you when I picked you up at Amundsen–Scott: Don't go looking for trouble."

20

Laura finished the training course. And passed all the quizzes.

The deeper she got into the modules, the more convinced she was that they had been written by someone she knew. Maybe one of her professors. Or a friend. The mystery of it haunted her—that is, until she began the simulations in the MedRe offices. Those days were so intense she barely had the mental energy for anything else. For her, it was like being back in residency, those hectic years of stress and mind-numbing split-second decisions.

There were, however, stark differences to her time practicing medicine before. That became even more clear when she graduated from the simulations to real-life operations.

Those anesthesiology procedures before and after stasis were anything but real life. It was all conducted via computer, with Laura essentially updating doses and selecting procedures and medications. It felt so strange, more like playing a video game than practicing medicine.

Once again, she wondered why it was being done this way. A part of her saw the wisdom in it—every adjustment could be recorded. And having a robotic operating assistant perform the physical actions might improve patient outcomes (and made it possible for anesthesiologists with physical limitations to operate as freely as their mind enabled them to). Surgical robots were becoming even more common, operating on everything from joint replacements to tumor removals and dissection and suturing, though the cost of the robots was still prohibitive for many surgical centers.

Epoch's software, however, was the most impressive thing Laura encountered. During live operations, it gave her real-time suggestions, including ultra-precise dosing. It wasn't always right, and early on, she found herself dismissing its suggestions perhaps ten percent of the time. But with each week, she found its recommendations better and better. She wondered if that was the point of doing it all via a computer interface: to train AI. Was she, in fact, supplying data to create her replacement?

That also made sense. If Epoch could train a specialized AI for stasis procedures, it could eliminate the staff cost and scale up its operations. It was tech start-up 101.

Another peculiar aspect was the level of compartmentalization at the station. After six weeks on the job, Laura had still not met the other practicing anesthesiologist. Or the person she had replaced. She had been assigned to three MedRe surgical teams, and she assisted them with stasis induction operations and the occasional stasis exit procedure.

They never performed any other operations, though there was talk of performing them in the future—after certain patients exited stasis. For once, that made sense. Most of the stasis patients were over sixty, and many had chronic medical conditions. Diabetes, hypertension, COPD, and heart disease were most common, though a number had past or current cancer diagnoses.

Thus far, that was Laura's best guess about what Epoch was doing here: letting the sick sleep until there was a cure. Was that Epoch's real business? Saving lives via a sort of time travel to the future? It fit everything she was seeing.

And maybe that offering wasn't just for the physically infirm. In reading their charts, Laura noticed that the vast majority of patients entering stasis had some history of mental health issues. Depression was by far the most common. She could identify with that—being depressed enough to want to wait for the world to change. She would have probably signed up for Epoch's offering after Samir's betrayal.

But the question remained: if stasis was Epoch's real enterprise, why locate the facility in Antarctica? And why were there other research groups here? Within MedRe, the longevity group had almost zero interaction with stasis, apart from passing each other in the hall and a nod in the cafeteria.

The only information sharing came when a researcher did a talk as part of the Visions of the Next World. Those nights felt more like a paper presented at an academic conference.

It seemed that MedRe's stasis group was the only division operating on patients (or in the real world at all for that matter). Everything else was academic. In fact, the longer she stayed at the station, the more it felt like an academic institution to her. A self-contained world-class university, buried in the ice, cut off from the world.

As for Joe, Laura's relationship with him assumed a routine, and it seemed to be locked in stasis too—in an era very reminiscent of a middle-school crush (lots of time spent together with neither of them making a move).

They started the day with breakfast together. Both Laura and Joe favored lunch at their desk, though they made an exception for Wednesday and Friday, when they met up in the cafeteria again. Occasionally, they would eat with someone from their work—a fellow security staffer or someone from MedRe, but for the most part, it was just the two of them.

And every Tuesday and Thursday night, it was always only the two of them, sitting on the couch in her suite, watching the Visions of the Old World and the Next World over dinner.

Tonight's seminar was titled The Boiled Frog Apocalypse Is Here.

The speaker was an Indian man, and he stood on a stage with a large screen behind him. There was a small audience sitting around him, their faces and backs to the camera. It reminded Laura of a TED Talk.

"Ladies and gentlemen, first, thank you for spending your dinner with me. Second, I'd like to start with some bad news: the apocalypse is already occurring. The worse news is that very few even realize it. Tonight I'll tell you why: it's because humanity is like the proverbial boiling frog. And that's why I call it the Boiled Frog Apocalypse."

The speaker went on to talk about the apologue of the boiling frog. The central idea was that if a frog was put in boiling water, it would instantly jump out, saving its life.

If, however, the frog was placed in tepid water, it would

stay. And it would stay if the temperature were slowly increased, even until boiling, at which point the frog would die.

The point was clear: gradual changes were harder to spot than radical ones.

The change tonight's speaker was talking about was from the old world, specifically population growth. The speaker was convinced that the world was in a depopulation crisis. But like the frog in a pot before the water boiled, no one was concerned.

Laura wasn't sure about his argument, but some of the facts struck her. For example, global population growth peaked in the 1960s and the rate of growth has been gradually declining since (though total world population continued to increase). The decline in population growth was most acute in developed nations, especially in Europe and East Asia.

In Japan, for example, the current birth rate was 1.3—well below the 2.1 rate needed to maintain its current population. In fact, as of 2021, about 28 percent of the Japanese population was sixty-five or older. By 2050, the United Nations projected that Japan's population could decline by almost 20 percent .

"Think about that," the speaker urged the small crowd. "A technologically advanced nation, with the third largest economy in the world, will see its population shrink by a fifth in less than thirty years. Ladies and gentlemen, is that not an apocalypse? Yes, a slow-moving one, like the water temperature rising in a pot where you're being boiled alive."

The speaker held a finger up. "I know what some of you

are thinking—because it was once my opinion: what does population matter? So what if we have fewer people?"

He shrugged theatrically. "Well, consider your own experiences. Consider the towns and cities in your life that have seen gradual population declines. Consider the loss of tax base. The aging population and the lack of resources to deal with those people. And that's just the tip of the iceberg."

He paced the stage and continued. "Japan, however, is not an isolated case. It's simply the first example. This same phenomenon is happening as we speak in Germany and the US and so many other developed nations. The simple fact is that modern life eventually strangles populations. It's only a matter of time."

Like the text in the MedRe course, there was something oddly familiar about this man. Laura had seen him before. But she couldn't place him. She went to sleep that night turning that mystery over in her mind.

And one other thought: that she had twenty-three days left to escape this station and fulfill the terms of her plea deal. She still didn't see how to do that. Or what Epoch was doing wrong.

*

Three hours later, Laura woke to an alarm. It wasn't her typical morning alarm. It was a phrase repeated over the ceiling speakers in her bedroom: *Code Blue. Code Blue.*

A patient was in distress. She rolled out of bed, pulled on a shirt, shorts, and shoes and staggered out of the suite.

21

Laura didn't wait for the elevator. She bounded down the two flights of stairs to the offices on level five and rushed to her workstation.

The patient was a sixty-five-year-old male currently in cardiac arrest.

The rest of the MedRe team, who had initiated the patient's stasis a month ago, converged around her, their fingers flying over their touchscreens and the flat-surface keyboards.

The next five minutes were the most stressful Laura had endured since the interrogation the day she had arrived. And never before had the differences in practicing medicine in this place been so on display. She felt like an air traffic controller. Not a doctor. There was shouting and an electric current running through the room and dropping patient vitals on a monitor. But there was no crash cart, no team of nurses, and no needles or vials of medication.

To anyone watching from the outside, it might have looked like a simulation. But this was a real-life patient, somewhere else, being handled by robotic arms.

Fifteen minutes after Laura arrived, Berggren pronounced the patient dead.

She called a meeting for 10 a.m. that morning and suggested they all go back and get some sleep.

*

Lying in bed, sleep wouldn't come to Laura. She kept thinking about the patient. And this strange place. And the fact that she had twenty-three days left to leave. But that was the max cut-off: March 1. It would be better to leave when the weather wasn't quite as cold and a plane would have a better chance. But the reality was, she wasn't sure she could escape by then. She deducted four days from the total, providing a minimum margin of error.

So: nineteen days.

*

In the meeting, the team argued, and went over the data, and ultimately decided that it was futile to argue until an autopsy was done.

Laura expected there to be some plan made for that. She thought some member of their team might travel to the patient location and at least observe it. Or that it might be live-streamed or recorded for them.

Instead, Berggren pledged that another team at MedRe would audit their stasis induction operation and emergency work last night. Their clinical decisions would be examined in detail. As would all patient data.

"So we still can't see the patient?" Laura asked.

Two of the MedRe team members looked at her with curious expressions.

"No," Berggren said flatly. "That's all for now. I remind you; this team has a stasis exit procedure at 1400 this afternoon. You are still on active duty until the audit is completed."

*

Laura didn't know if it was the patient who had passed away or the open questions about Antarctica Station or her need for completion—to fulfill her plea deal—but at some point during her walk back to her suite, she decided that she would escape, and take data with her, and start her life over. In some place more normal.

After making the decision, a peculiar thing happened. A sense of lightness settled over her. A subtle energy, as though she were unburdened all of a sudden.

She wondered what would happen after she escaped and reported back to Aurora. As far as Laura could see, Epoch wasn't conducting some world-changing evil research. It was just wealthy individuals trying to live forever and leapfrog through the ages to see the future or other worlds or find a cure for their own health problems or live out whatever their fantasy was. That didn't harm human civilization at large, at least, not in Laura's opinion. Maybe telling the government what Epoch was doing could even help the organization. It would put the investigation to rest.

*

Unfortunately, it took Laura another week to make an escape plan.

There were two main issues. One: getting access to data. And two: getting out of the station.

As to the data... there was of course her tablet, but Laura reasoned that it might be remotely disabled or wiped during or after her escape attempt. She needed physical media with data.

The workstations in MedRe were simply monitors with a basic operating system that connected to a virtual machine instance in the station's server farm. It enabled her to access her desktop from any workstation. It also provided physical security for Epoch: she couldn't just rip the hard drive out of the physical workstation.

She needed the actual hard drives from the servers to have any chance of getting real data or proof of what she was saying.

That presented several challenges.

The first was getting into the server room.

And, assuming she managed to do that, the second challenge would be getting out of Antarctica Station quickly. Because Laura was certain that breaching the server room and removing those hard drives would trip Epoch's alarms.

Both challenges had led her to the station map on her tablet. Laura didn't dare open it in the bedroom or living room and start perusing it for the server room location and station exit. They were both far away from where she lived, worked, and had any business being.

Instead, she entered the bathroom, filled the bathtub with water, and stripped down and got in. She held the tablet close to her face, away from the mirror and angled down from the ceiling and anything that might be a camera watching her.

The first night, she studied the map until she had memorized it. But as hard as she studied it, she couldn't see a plan that would work. In fact, she couldn't even imagine a way to get down to the server room on level seven. Her office on level five was as low as she could go.

For the next six days, she contemplated her problem every second she wasn't actively engaged in a stasis operation.

Finally, she gave up. There was no way she was going to break into level seven.

That left only one option: asking for permission. It was a long shot, but it was her only shot. And she was going to take it.

She had twelve days left.

22

The following morning, Laura began laying the groundwork for her plan.

Before breakfast, she went down to the office level and jogged in the halls. They were mostly empty at this hour, and Laura was able to get up some speed in the corridors.

In the cafeteria, when she sat down across from Joe, her face was gleaming with sweat.

He studied her, chewing methodically. "You hit the gym this morning?"

Laura shook her head wearily and took a sip of water. "Jogged on five."

He smirked, an expression somewhere between amused and confused. "Why? There's the park—"

"I'm sick of the park," Laura lied, feeling awkward, wondering if the words sounded as weird as she felt.

"And the gym?"

"A treadmill to nowhere. Also sick of that." Laura leaned forward. "Don't you ever feel—I don't know—cooped up here? Like cabin fever?"

Joe scooped up some grits. "Not me." He chewed a

second, swallowed, and held his fork up. "But some people do. Especially in the first months."

"Yeah," Laura said, "I feel like my whole world has shrunk."

Joe's gaze drifted up and to the right as his lips formed a small smile.

"What?" Laura shot at him.

"Nothing," he muttered, gathering more grits on the spoon.

Laura felt another tingle of nervousness as she mentally prepared to say the lines she had rehearsed. "So, I was wondering if I could get access to the other floors. Below five." She shrugged. "Not the rooms or anything, I don't know, *Top Secret*. Just the halls. To walk. Or even jog after hours. For a change of scenery."

Joe squinted at her. "Doubt it."

Laura swallowed and tried to slow her breathing. "Doubt what?"

"Doubt they'll let you. I mean, all the halls look the same. You're not really getting a change in scenery. And expanding your physical access is a security risk for the station."

Laura fixed her gaze on her tray. "I understand. But all they can do is say no."

Staring down at the tray, Joe's eyes flashed. The expression meant something, but Laura couldn't read it.

She leaned forward. "Look, I'm not trying to put you in a weird spot. I'll ask. Who should I talk to? Imara?"

"No," Joe said quickly. "No, I'll do it."

"You sure?"

"Yeah, I'm sure."

When Joe got up from the table, Laura wiped the spoon

off and slipped it into her pocket. She would need it soon. Assuming things went according to plan.

*

At dinner, Joe didn't bring up Laura getting access to the floors she was restricted from. She didn't either. Better not to seem too eager.

*

The next morning, Laura went for a run in the park. It was amazing how much the endorphin release calmed her anxious mind.

A mind that kept turning a single number over: eleven.

Eleven days.

Her face and shirt were drenched in sweat when she reached the cafeteria. Joe was already seated, hunched over his tray. Laura recognized his current mode of brooding. It was more intense than his run-of-the-mill, through the week, standard brooding.

She sat, placing her own tray down, and was about to ask what was eating him when he volunteered it: "That's a no on you going to the lower levels."

"Okay," Laura said slowly. "Did they say—"

"What they said—*and not in these words*—was it's a hard no and always will be."

"Oh."

For the rest of breakfast, Joe didn't say another word. Laura wondered if him making the request on her behalf had put him in an awkward position with the security division. Had it aroused their suspicions? Or his? Had that ignited the brooding?

Joe sat there, chewing, eyes downcast, jaw muscles flexing as though he was trying to pulverize the food into microscopic pieces.

He finished first. Usually, he waited for her, and they exited together. Today, he reached out and gripped his tray, only stopping when Laura raised a hand.

"Hey, I'm sorry if asking got you in any sort of trouble."

"It didn't," he muttered.

"Are you sure?"

He huffed a small laugh. "Yeah, that's one thing I'm sure about."

He lifted his tray.

"Wait."

He stared down at her.

"Are we still on for watching the seminar at my place tonight?" Laura shrugged. "Look, it's okay if you need some space. I just need to update the meal delivery details."

"No, I don't need any more space," he said quietly. "I'll be there."

*

That night, when he arrived at Laura's suite, Joe's mood was no better. In fact, it might have been worse.

The two of them sat on the couch, eating, acting as if there wasn't this giant elephant in the room smothering both of them.

On the screen a woman was saying, "Humanity's history is one of constant war. It's simply not the war we learned about in school. Not one fought with long swords, or spears, or tanks, or nuclear bombs. It is a war of culture."

She paused. "That's right. The recent obsession with

warring ideologies is nothing new. Consider the epic ideological battles. Paganism versus monotheism. Atheism versus theism. Capitalism versus communism. Science versus superstition. And those are just a few…"

When the speech was over, Joe stood and moved toward the door. "I'm beat. Gonna pack it in."

He was gone before Laura could say anything, not that she knew what to say.

*

After her own brooding session—over Joe and her sad situation and the circumstances that had landed her here—Laura drew a bath and got in, opening the tablet to the station map.

Time for plan B.

She didn't know what plan B was yet.

As she browsed the floor plans, a thought occurred to her: faking an escape attempt—one where she didn't try to steal data, where she just pretended to be stir-crazy and homesick.

What would Epoch do if that were to happen? Would they simply kick her out? She wouldn't have data on Epoch's experiments. Certainly not the event Aurora was worried about—if that sort of data was even stored here—but she would be free of this place.

The issue she saw with that was Avi Cohen, the other Aurora operative who had come to Antarctica Station before her.

There was no trace of him here now. No entry in the staff directory. No patient record in the stasis files.

That gave Laura pause. Was it evidence that Epoch was willing to kill potential spies?

Or was there another explanation? An accident? But that didn't make sense. Surely, they would have notified his next of kin.

Perhaps he somehow left and didn't inform Aurora? That was possible.

On the tablet, a dialog box popped up with a simple message: *Ask the hard question: what does the Next World cost?*

There was no button. Only an X in the right corner. Laura raised a finger to tap the box to see if anything happened, but it disappeared from the screen before she could reach it.

23

Ten days.

Laura brushed her teeth, staring at herself in the mirror.

A few minutes later, she was on the office floor, jogging, still thinking: ten days.

She had to keep running. To keep up the ruse behind her request to access the lower floors. Was this what it had been like for Samir back in Durham? Keeping up the ruse? Doing the surgeries to get access to drugs. Going through the motions. Acting like nothing was wrong. Knowing he was lying to the people closest to him.

She had become him. But for different reasons. For the right reasons.

When people began exiting the elevator and stairwells and walking the corridors of the office level, Laura trekked up to the park. And kept running, pumping her legs, trying to shake free the endorphins that would give her mental clarity.

The dome above showed a rising sun on the horizon and a canvas of lazy white clouds against a clear blue backdrop. A blatant lie, told in billions of pixels for the benefit of the station's inhabitants.

Outside, the sun was setting.

Soon, it would slip below the horizon, where it would stay during most of the polar winter.

She dodged left on the path, passing a large planter box filled with roses.

For herself, Laura saw three paths.

One, fake an escape and risk Epoch's wrath. If not for the missing Aurora agent, she would be inclined to go that route.

Up ahead, at a three-way fork, she took the middle road.

Option two: a real escape. With data. Fulfilling her contract.

Try as she might, she didn't see that path. It had closed the moment Epoch security denied her access to the lower levels.

And finally, there was the choice of simply staying here. Not making an escape attempt—fake or real.

That path was uncertain, too. When Epoch released her, the government would revoke her plea deal and pardon agreement. Would she go to jail then?

Would Epoch let her stay in Antarctica? If so, what kind of life would that be?

She was so caught up in her thoughts she didn't realize she'd reached the end of the path. She skidded to a halt, her sneakers digging into the crushed stone that spilled onto the black rubberized floor beyond.

"Hey, watch it," a middle-aged man said, holding his hands up. "It's the end of the road."

*

In the cafeteria, Laura found Joe seated at their regular table, head down, a slight smile on his lips.

"Hi," she said, setting her own tray down.

His smile grew wider. "Hi."

"You're in a good mood."

"Am I? I guess so."

"Care to share why?"

"Let's just call it... the lightness of hard decisions made."

Laura studied him, heart beating faster.

Joe leaned forward. "You ever get that?"

"Yeah," she whispered. "I do."

He refocused on his breakfast, taking a far larger bite than usual of his grits.

"I have some good news."

"I like good news," Laura said carefully.

"Turns out you *can* do your jogging on the lower floors."

"I can? How? You asked them—"

"*They* don't need to know."

Laura bunched her eyebrows. "I'm confused."

Joe took another bite. "The thing is, I can access those floors. My eyes get me access to just about anywhere in the station. And I can bring you with me. As my jogging partner." He held his fork up. "Well, assuming you're up for having a jogging partner."

"I am," she whispered. And she knew then what path she had chosen. The escape—the real one. And what it might cost her. She wondered if it would be a dead end, the proverbial end of the road.

*

Five days later, Laura was jogging through the halls of level seven past the large steel door marked *Data Center*. Sweat rolled off her forehead. Her shoulders ached from the weight of the backpack that held four full reusable water bottles.

But by far the heaviest thing she was carrying was the number five.

That's how many days she had left. And even that was an unsteady thing. Imprecise. She wondered: had the sun already set outside? Had the flights stopped from Amundsen–Scott already? Were the staff and researchers there already dug in for the winter?

Beside her, Joe was striding along almost effortlessly.

"Water break?" he called out in the empty corridor.

Laura stopped and unzipped the backpack and handed him one of the water bottles.

"You sure that won't hurt your back?" he asked between sips.

"I'm the doctor here."

He laughed. "So that's it? Just gonna play the doctor card?"

"Pretty much. And: I worked my way up. A few water bottles at first, half full, then when my back muscles were ready, I added more."

He smiled. "Right."

Ahead, at the end of the white corridor, was a glowing exit sign pointing to the right. It led to the garage and loading bay. And freedom.

Tomorrow.

*

They took the stairs, as usual, and as usual, Laura declined Joe's request to carry the backpack.

She was out of breath when they got to her suite and plopped down on the couch. A few minutes later, a delivery robot rang her doorbell and deposited covered plastic cartons with their meals.

The window in the living room changed from a view of the sunset over the Blue Ridge Mountains to a woman standing in a filled auditorium.

White letters overlaying the scene read: *Visions of the Next World.*

Slowly, they faded to a scene of a stage with a woman standing in the center.

"The war for the future is a war for the mind. That is what I will prove to you tonight. And I will use your own children in my argument." The speaker held her hands up. "Don't worry, there will be no names. Only deidentified studies and facts. I'm a scientist after all."

She paused, seeming to organize her thoughts. "Consider, if you will, the idea that our children think differently from us—and from the grandparents. This isn't the same worn-out complaint about *this new generation.* As I said, I have data—and you can find it on your tabs in the talk notes."

She held a hand out. "Do our children care more or less than us? Are we raising more moral humans? If you said yes, I'm afraid the studies don't support that. In fact, several well-designed surveys suggest that empathy levels in college students have declined by about 40 percent over the past thirty years."

The woman paced the stage. "There are of course the examples we all know—of entrepreneurs like Elizabeth Holmes and Samuel Bankman-Fried, both very bright and very morally bankrupt. But morality is simply the tip of the iceberg. Creativity scores have been in decline for three decades as well. Does anyone really think generative AI will help children become more creative?"

She paused. "Consider the Flynn Effect—the fact that IQ scores gradually increased in the twentieth century in countries that tested for it. There's growing evidence this upward trend began reversing in the 1990s, though the jury is still out."

She held a finger up. "But consider a study closer to home. In 2018 a UK survey found that 39 percent of young adults could not perform basic household tasks like sewing a button. It may not sound apocalyptic, but I consider it a canary in a coal mine. And what danger does it represent? To me, the evidence is clear: the human race is in moral and cognitive decline. Left unabated, disaster looms. There is a solution, however..."

At the small table, Joe wolfed his meal down as the lecture droned on in the background.

Shortly after finishing, he excused himself to use Laura's bathroom. The moment the door clicked shut, Laura took the spoons from their trays, wiped them off, and quickly pressed her finger into a white panel on the storage wall. It slid out, revealing three stacks of spoons. Laura added the two new ones to the last pile.

It was enough. Enough spoons for her to escape. Tomorrow—it had to be tomorrow. She should have already been gone.

Through the bedroom and the closed bathroom door, the faint sound of a toilet flushing echoed.

On the window screen, the woman was still making her case about understanding every child's unique mind and inspiring and challenging them. A curriculum of one was her name for this breakthrough.

Laura was placing the trays in the dirty dish drawer as the bathroom door opened. She pressed the panel, and it slid in. She heard the faint whirl of electric motors from the drawer conveying the trays to the system that transported them away.

Joe plopped down on the couch and patted the cushion beside her. "You're missing the show," he called out in mock cheer.

Laura smiled and settled in beside him, not paying attention to the Vision of the Next World being laid out.

Joe's voice was quiet, reflective almost. "You ever think about what you'll do after this?"

Butterflies bloomed in Laura's stomach. "Hard not to."

"You've got what? Two years, nine months left on your contract. Thereabouts?"

He said *contract*. Laura appreciated that. It was better than sentence or plea deal or work release.

"That's right," she said quietly.

"You ever think about staying?"

"Not really."

"Why?"

"I want to see my sister. I want—"

He turned to her and tucked a strand of her long blond hair behind her ear.

"What do you want, Laura?"

"What do you want? Joe, ambiguous last name, player of games, keeper of secrets? Do you even know?"

With his fingers, he gently turned her face to him. She

could almost feel her body shaking, like a current of electricity slowly being turned up inside of her.

"I know exactly what I want."

Laura swallowed.

His face inched closer to hers. "And I know what you need. A reason to stay."

Laura tried to speak, but the words scrambled in her brain. "Are you…"

"I told you, I like you."

"Well, you haven't exactly done anything about it."

He smiled, that broad, devil-may-care, Joe smile she had first seen in that Italian restaurant in Durham, in what felt like a lifetime ago.

"You know, that's an excellent point."

He leaned closer and Laura didn't move and when his lips touched hers, she felt like a hole in the station had opened up and it was swallowing her.

24

The next morning, Joe was gone. But the smell of him and what they'd done last night lingered in the bed. Laura breathed it in and closed her eyes.

In the cafeteria, he was waiting, sitting at their table, smiling contentedly, watching her. In the doorway, when their eyes met, Laura blushed and turned, heading for the line. She hurried through it and when she sat across from him, Joe leaned forward, nearly halfway across the table, as if he had a secret to share. "Good morning," he whispered.

The redness on her cheeks burned full-on supernova hot. "Good morning," she echoed, focusing on her oatmeal.

He leaned back, studying her. "Are we good?"

"We're good," she said quietly.

"I'm sorry if things moved too fast," he said. "Look, we can take it slow."

Laura took another bite of oatmeal.

Joe shrugged. "We've got all the time in the world."

But they didn't. Not if she went through with it. Yesterday, betraying him—using him to escape—would have been tough. Today, she wasn't even sure she could do it.

Joe, perhaps sensing she needed some space, stood up and turned, then stopped and looked back. "Hey, are we still on for lower decks jogging tonight?"

Laura sat there a long moment, staring at the sea of oatmeal, then slowly nodded.

*

After work, Laura filled the reusable water bottles and took the stacks of spoons out of the drawer and taped them together. That would keep them from clinking as she ran. And give them strength for the task she needed them for.

If she used them.

That was a big if. One that would turn the course of her life. Looking down at the contents of the backpack, she told herself that she hadn't done anything wrong.

Not yet she hadn't.

She could still call it off. She and Joe were just going for a run. Just like they had been.

*

They were on their second lap of level seven when Joe said, "You ever think about the cost?"

"Of the station?"

"No," he said, pulling ahead, not looking back. "Of the Next World."

His words echoed the message on the disappearing dialog. Had he written it? Or had it been sent to Joe, too?

"I do," Laura said, pumping her legs harder, trying to pull even with him.

"It's like, everything has a cost." Joe sucked in a long breath. "There's the price you pay. And then there's what you give up—what you don't get to do. The opportunity cost. Roads not taken."

Laura's heart beat in her ears like a drum counting down to a crescendo, shoes pounding the carpet, the sterile white LED lights glowing above.

"What," she breathed out, "is—the cost?"

Joe stomped to a stop, drawing rapid breaths. He pointed at her. "Now, that's the question."

Laura bent over, hands on her knees, gulping air. "What's the answer?"

Joe shrugged. "I guess we'll see."

He turned and walked away, calling over his shoulder. "Gotta hit the head."

Laura watched him disappear beyond the bathroom door.

Glancing to her left, she realized she was on the hall behind the server room. The exact location she had marked.

The drum in her ears thundered louder. It was now or never.

Every second that passed was one she had lost. One she might need. She had to call it. Go or stay forever. She'd never have another chance like this.

A bad decision had landed her here. She hoped this one would set her free.

In three quick, long strides, she moved away from Joe to the wall behind the server room. She bent down, unslung the backpack from her shoulders, and took out a stack of taped-together spoons. She planted the metal spoons in the crack between the panels—right at the corner—and pried hard. With a pop, the panel lifted, but it didn't come free. The other three clasps still held.

Laura smiled. She had made a big assumption: that the panels in the corridors were just like the ones in her suite. Thankfully, that was the case. She used the spoon to pop the other top clasp free. With her free hand, she bent the panel outward and slammed her foot down on it. It snapped clean off with a loud crack.

Laura glanced up, but the bathroom door was still closed.

In the open hole revealed by the panel, Laura saw the inside of another panel.

She took a full water bottle from the backpack and slammed it into the panel. The top right clasp came free, and the corner gapped open. On the third blow, the entire panel came loose, flying forward into the server room.

The opening was just large enough for Laura to crawl through. She tossed the backpack through and climbed in, feet first, pulling the panel from the corridor behind her. She propped it against the wall, almost vertical, hoping Joe wouldn't notice it had been removed.

In the distance, she thought she heard a snap. A door closing. Maybe the bathroom door.

Either way, she had to hurry. If the video feeds from the corridors were being monitored, then security was already on the way.

Her plan was to gather as many hard drives as possible, filling the space in the backpack where the water bottles usually were, and get out. She'd exit through the server room door, onto the other corridor, hopefully confusing Joe long enough for her to dash to the exit door to the garage at the end of that hall.

The question now was which hard drives to take.

In college, Laura had dated a guy majoring in computer

science with a minor in information and library science. He had once given her a tour of a data center at the company where he was interning for one summer.

"We don't have any production servers here," he had said, strolling past the racks. "Just a dev environment. But it's like a small version of what we have at our hosting provider. We co-locate the servers so we have full control. And to save money."

Most of what he said went right over Laura's head, but one thing had stuck with her—a note about redundancy. Because it reminded her of human anatomy.

"We use RAID 1 on our hard drives. That means they're mirrored. Every hard drive has a mate. A complete copy. If it fails, its mate serves up the data. The downside is that if a server has ten drives, it only has half of that for available storage. But like I said, it makes any hardware failure easy to deal with. The drives are hot swappable, so we just plug a replacement in and the survivor from the coupled pair replicates the data to the new drive."

With that in mind, Laura's plan was to pull half the hard disks from as many servers as she could, reasoning that they were likely mirrored. That strategy would give her more data for the space she had in the backpack.

But when she turned to survey the server room, that plan went out the window.

Because there was nothing here.

No servers.

No hard drives.

Only an empty room with a spotless floor with square white tiles, glowing softly. Beady lights glowed above. Dead ahead was a metal door.

Had they moved the servers? Or had it always been empty? Was this a trap—something Epoch put on the floor plan to lure spies in? Had Avi Cohen met his end here? Had she simply followed his footsteps to this dead end?

Laura turned and looked at the hole where the panel had been. Could she go back through and get out of here before Joe realized what she had done? That assumed that no one was watching the security feeds. That was a big assumption.

She didn't see any other move.

There was nothing here. Nothing for her to take to Aurora. And her plan to activate the exit door was also likely unworkable at this point.

Laura was turning to leave when the metal door to the server room opened.

The figure who stepped through was quite possibly the last person on Earth Laura ever thought she'd see here.

Samir.

He was holding a tablet and tapping rapidly at it. His face was a mask of concentration and fear.

He looked up, staring at her.

Laura opened her mouth to speak, but the words came out jumbled. Her vision blurred.

He closed the distance between them and grabbed her bicep.

Briefly, the scene came into focus like a camera lens focusing on Samir's face.

"I'm bringing you out, Laura. Come get me. Bay 8135C. Hurry. The interface is the same out there as in here."

"What interface?" Laura asked.

She heard another voice, behind her, shouting her name. Laura turned. Joe had crawled through the open panel.

He was still on his hands and knees, staring up at her, his features blurry, expression unreadable.

"Laura."

That was the last thing she heard before the darkness swallowed her.

25

Laura opened her eyes to complete darkness. It was an eerie, unnerving feeling, like waking up in a coffin.

She reached up. Her hand hit a cold metal ceiling. It couldn't be more than eighteen inches high.

She felt a sting on the inside of her right elbow. A cool sensation spread over the site where Laura assumed an IV line had been inserted.

The process repeated at her leg and neck, and then the metal slab beneath her was sliding outward.

Frigid air poured over her, a gust as bracing as the Antarctic winter wind.

Light spilled through the opening. At first, it was a single, wide beam. Slowly, it came into focus, coalescing into hundreds of tiny green lights glowing in the darkness.

Her eyes adjusting, Laura realized the lights were attached to what looked like drawers in a bank vault. As she watched, a few lights flashed red before going back to solid green.

She glanced around, taking in the scene. Rows and columns of the drawers stretched from the floor to the ceiling. Beside the drawers were two recessed tracks in the wall.

She was in one of those drawers. Her mind was starting

to work better now. The drugs were wearing off. And those anesthesia medications were the same ones she had administered to patients for the last three months as she put them into stasis.

Because she had been in stasis too. She saw it now. How could she not have seen it before?

Laura tried to focus. She looked over. They weren't drawers exactly. Drawers was the wrong word. Lockers. That's what they called them in a morgue.

No. That wasn't right either.

What had Samir called them?

Bays. Stasis bays.

Antarctica Station wasn't what she had seen. There was no park. No cafeteria with a vast menu. It was actually this place. A vessel to hold passengers in stasis.

The slab came to a stop. The cold pressed into her, and Laura curled inward to conserve her warmth.

On the wall beside her locker, she saw EpochOS, projected from a beady light from above. The interface was identical to her workstation in MedRe. It flashed a message:

Stasis Exit Complete

Bay 8863C

Awakening Protocol Administered By SD.

SD. Samir Dewan.

The truth hit her then: he was the other anesthesiologist supervising the stasis trials in the station. He always had been—since she had gotten here.

And more: he had written those training courses. It was in his voice. That's why Laura had recognized it.

How was that possible? When had he gotten here? It was too much of a coincidence.

The drugs were still slowing her mind, but Laura wasn't even sure she could work it all out with a clear head.

She needed answers.

From Samir.

And she needed to get out of here. Epoch security staff could be coming out of stasis right behind her.

There could also be security onsite, personnel who were on their way to her now.

Laura sat up. The end of the drawer stuck up like the foot of a single bed with a storage space open at the top. Inside was a white bundle and a canvas bag. She pulled the white bundle out and unfolded it. Epoch coveralls.

Her hands shaking, she quickly pulled the garment on. It seemed to sense her low body temperature and activated a heating element that began to ooze warmth into her.

The feet had rigid soles with rubber grips on the bottom that squeaked as she stepped off the metal slab. The other item in the end compartment was a med kit. Laura grabbed it.

The moment she stepped away, the metal arms that had lowered her bay engaged and raised the slab up and slid it back into place, a drawer closing.

Antarctica Station had been white and clean and bright. This place—wherever it was—had a very different feel. The walls were metal and dull gray. The lighting was dim and hazy. It felt, in a word, alien. Utilitarian. This was the machine behind the facade that was Antarctica Station. The inner workings no one was supposed to see.

The question now was how to get out.

There was only one exit from the room full of stasis bays: two metal doors, not unlike the server room entrance.

Laura bounded forward, but her legs didn't quite match her ambition. She stumbled and almost fell before righting herself and moving slower, as if learning to walk again.

The door opened as she approached, revealing a wide hall with sets of double doors on both sides, evenly spaced out, like a hallway in a hotel. Ahead, a glowing sign above the door read, *Bay 87C*.

Laura glanced behind her.

Bay 88C.

What had Samir said?

Bay...

8135C.

Bay 81C.

She peered down the eerie, dim corridor. The even bays were on one side and the odd on the other. At the end was an exit door.

She could go.

She could leave him.

Like he had left her in Durham, after his lie.

But the last several minutes had changed everything.

In her darkest moment, he had come for her. Saved her.

Like she had tried to do for him.

But how?

She staggered forward, rubber-studded feet squeaking on the metal grates in the floor.

A small part of her told herself that she was going to leave him. She would pass right by his door and keep going.

At the end of the hall, the exit doors opened. Laura

stopped. And turned to Bay 81C. A retinal scanner must have seen her eyes, because it opened too, revealing an alcove of bank-vault-style drawers. Morgue lockers. With live, frozen people waiting inside. A hundred of them, if Laura was counting right. A century.

Samir was in Bay 8135C.

Waiting.

Waiting for her to rescue him. Because if she was right, Epoch would be coming for him too—because he had helped her escape.

Laura took a step to the left. And kept going until she was inside the room 81C, standing at the wall by column three. Like in her room, an interface appeared on the wall. EpochOS.

Laura tapped the button for Bay 5 and scanned the vitals and then hit *Exit Stasis*.

The protocol began with the AI-guided systems in control, providing interfaces for Laura to override. And she did, adjusting the medications slightly.

That was one advantage they had in their escape: she and Samir were the only active-duty anesthesiologists in the station. Using the AI to exit security personnel was risky. The system had come a long way, but it was far from perfect. They would have to find the anesthesiologist Laura had replaced and get him down to MedRe to bring anyone out safely.

Above, a hiss spewed into the room and the end of a bay issued forth until it was fully extended. Metal arms attached and lowered it.

Laura waited, knowing time was slipping away.

The bay came to a stop. Laura grabbed the Epoch coverall from the end.

Samir's eyelids parted slowly, revealing yellow jaundiced eyes, his pupils swimming inside, unfocused.

Shivering, he rolled to his side, arms clutched to his chest.

"Hey, hey," Laura said, reaching an arm around his back. "You okay?"

"You came," he whispered, eyes closed now.

"Come on, Samir. We're getting out of here."

He curled into a tighter ball, shivering harder. Laura threw the coverall around him and struggled to get his left arm through and his feet in the foot pads.

Behind her, an alarm began buzzing.

Laura gripped Samir's shoulders. "Hey. Come on! Wake up!"

Samir shook his head. His voice was distant, lazy. "Earlier stasis protocol. Not good." He swallowed. "For drug addicts…"

"We have to go, Samir."

"Leave me," he said softly. "Finished."

Laura put one hand around his neck, the other under his knees, and pulled him off the slab. The coverall hung off of him, one arm in, one out. His eyelids opened and closed lazily as if he was still high. And maybe he was.

The alarm echoed down the hall, into the bay.

He's right, Laura thought. *I should go. I should leave him.*

She had made this mistake before: putting her life on the line for him. Trusting him.

But what had happened back then wasn't her mistake. It had been his.

She had done the right thing. He hadn't.

No matter what, she wasn't going to let the hurt from that betrayal change her character. In this moment, when she was risking her life for his—once again—she knew who she was.

This was who she was.

This was why she became a doctor. To help others when they needed it most, at their most vulnerable.

Samir began slowly sinking to the floor, as if he were going to stretch out and take a nap.

Laura lifted with all her might, hands digging into Samir's armpits.

"Leave me," he whispered.

The alarm continued blaring.

"No." She pulled again.

"They're coming," he said softly, eyes closed.

"That's right," Laura said, voice echoing in the corridor. "And they'll get me too if you don't start walking." She tried to pull him up again, her arms burning now. "Walk, Samir. Come on! Put an arm around me. I'm not leaving. You hear me, you—"

Next to Laura's heel, she felt a vibration. She looked down and saw Samir's foot, planted on the floor. A first step.

"So cold," he whispered.

She bent down and zipped him up, and his grip tightened on her triceps and together they took another step toward the exit.

26

Outside Bay 81C, Laura and Samir made their way to the exit, trying to hurry. On the wall above the exit doors were letters that read *Bay 8C*. Across the corridor was *Bay 7C*.

She wondered if she and Samir had been among the first 9,000 people who Epoch had put into stasis or whether they had replaced one of those people. Perhaps one of the first 9,000 had either exited stasis or experienced a problem—a medical issue or a mechanical failure with the bay. During Laura's three months working in the station, that had happened to one of her patients. And she saw now why she got puzzled looks when she had asked about doing an autopsy or being there to observe the procedure.

Laura peered down the hall. The doors went all the way to Bay 50C. Incredible. There were 50,000 people here (assuming all the bays were filled). There certainly weren't that many people in the Antarctica Station she had seen.

Perhaps that Antarctica Station—which was clearly some sort of simulation provided during stasis—was only one of many simulations. Perhaps some people in stasis were living in other simulated environments. An alien planet. The Roaring Twenties on Earth. The possibilities were endless.

For Epoch's clients it might be like choosing which video-game they wanted to play while they slept.

Laura also wondered how vast this facility really was. There were 50,000 people off the branches of this corridor. Were there others like it?

To her right, the projected letters for Bay 3C began flashing red. Below it, a message appeared:

Exit in progress.

Laura resumed shuffling toward the main doors to this bay corridor, half dragging Samir. His eyelids were still bouncing open and closed. She needed to do a full exam on him as soon as possible.

Beyond the exit was an octagonal room. There were doors similar to the ones she had just emerged from. They counted up. The next ones were for Bays 51–100C. There were six of them, ending with Bays 251–300C.

300,000 stasis bays.

Yellow letters painted on the floor read, *LEVEL C.*

How many levels were there?

Laura took a deep breath. It didn't matter. All that mattered was getting out.

On the two walls that didn't hold bays were the entrance to a stairwell and the shiny metal doors with letters that read, *LIFT, LEVEL C.*

She didn't dare take the elevator.

"Where's the garage?" she asked, thinking aloud.

"D," Samir breathed out, voice barely audible.

"Come on," she yelled, pulling him to the staircase and helping him grasp the rail.

At level D, there was a second exit off the stairwell, and another entrance to the elevator—rear doors. Laura jammed her hand against the push bar and barreled out, into a very different-looking hallway. It bore gray carpet and white walls. Just like the Antarctica Station simulation.

What was this?

To her left, a sign by the door read, Intake Suite.

So they were in Antarctica. Right where they had started. The pieces clicked into place for Laura now. The meal they had served her in the hospitality suite—it had been drugged. She had passed out there. And Samir and a team at MedRe had put her into stasis, where she had been until she woke up.

She pushed forward, vaguely remembering the layout of this place from three months ago. She made a left. At the T-intersection, she smiled when she saw the exit sign above the double doors ahead.

A blast of cold air washed over her face and hands when she walked out. She had done it. She was standing in the garage she had first seen when Joe had brought her here.

She expected to see a fleet of Hägglunds similar to the one she had arrived in. But the vehicles were different now. Slightly smaller, with more curves and larger treads. It was a different brand too. Epoch must have upgraded their fleet.

It didn't matter. It was a ride out of here. Assuming Laura could drive it. That had always been a major assumption in her plan. But she didn't have any other choice. And it wasn't like the roads would be crowded. She just needed to point it in the right compass direction and step on the gas.

She helped Samir into the closest vehicle and climbed into the driver's seat.

The dashboard looked like a spaceship compared to the Hägglunds she had traveled here in.

The steering wheel was recessed in an indention so that Laura couldn't even slip her fingers around it. A large flat screen in the center between the two bucket seats lit up, showing the EpochOS boot image, the logo animating as it loaded its software. The interface was the same as Antarctica Station, though the menus showed maps and the status of the machine.

"Awaiting command," a neutral, computerized voice said.

"Exit."

The vehicle doors slowly opened.

"No!" Laura yelled. "Drive."

With the doors closing again, the voice said. "Destination?"

"South Pole Station."

"Engage restraints."

Laura glanced around. "Engage restraints," she whispered. "Oh.. Buckle up." She reached over, grabbed the strap hanging next to Samir, and slammed the latch plate into the buckle. When hers clicked, the vehicle hummed to life and rolled backward.

"Faster!" Laura yelled.

The vehicle came to a stop. Then moved forward, turning lazily, proceeding so slowly Laura thought they might stop at any time.

"I apologize," the computerized voice said pleasantly. "In shared parking areas, I must observe safety—"

"Override!" Laura glanced around the dashboard, searching for some button that would give her control. The steering wheel stayed buried in its indention.

"I apologize, but manual override is not available—"

"Medical emergency!" Laura had no idea if that was even valid—

"Dr. Laura Reynolds," the voice said. "MedRe Statis Group B. Medical authorization accepted."

The steering wheel extended, and the vehicle began slowing.

Laura jammed her foot down on the pedal and they surged forward, pinning her in the seat as the large transport began picking up speed, ascending the ramp. Ahead, the wide doors parted.

As Laura expected, there was only darkness beyond. The sun had indeed set.

The lights from the tunnel shone outward, the ice glistening in the white glow.

The vehicle's tracks briefly left the ground when it cleared the ramp, flying out into the Antarctic plain. Laura glanced in the rearview mirror. It wasn't just their speed. The ice leading up to the tunnel was a few feet lower than the lip.

On the main screen, Laura checked the route and her direction and turned the wheel slightly, course correcting.

"Dr. Reynolds, would you like for me to drive again?"

"Yes—but only if you can drive very, very fast all the way to our destination."

"Of course. The current conditions along our route and my operating status allow for maximum speed."

"Good. You do that."

27

The tracked snow vehicle hummed across the ice, its bright headlights carving into the dark Antarctic winter.

In the cab, Laura looked over at Samir. His eyes were closed, head slumped over on his shoulder, breathing shallow.

She reached down and pressed the button on her seat buckle. It didn't budge.

"Hey," Laura said. When the computerized voice didn't reply, she added, "Hey, vehicle."

"Yes, Dr. Reynolds?"

"What should I call you?"

"I am programmed to detect contextual instances when you are addressing me. My specific designation is Transport 12. However, many refer to Epoch transports as simply, 'Transport'."

"Okay. Transport, I need to unbuckle—remove my restraints."

"I'm afraid the restraints cannot be removed during—"

"It's a medical emergency," Laura said, finger on the buckle.

"Medical override accepted."

The buckle released, and Laura began examining

Samir. The med kit from the stasis bay had some tools she recognized: a thermometer, bandages, tourniquets, and antibiotic ointment. There was also a nice sample of medications, all bearing the Epoch MedRe logo. Antivirals, antibiotics. Even radiation meds. That was interesting. There was also a small device that looked like a thermometer, though it was slightly larger, with a track on one side that held small plastic tubes shaped like the top of a pipette. The letters on the side read Epoch QikLab.

No way, Laura thought. It was impossible to run many lab tests with a blood sample that small. They could get an accurate blood sugar, maybe a few other readings, but nothing like a comprehensive metabolic panel or a complete blood count. She tried to think back to med school, to the reference ranges for minimum requirements for blood collection. If memory served, most tests were at least .6 ccs of whole blood. Many up to 1 cc. The device was way too small to test.

It reminded her of the company Theranos, which had tried to build comprehensive blood testing from low volume samples and had failed (though that didn't stop them from faking the results—with disastrous consequences).

Laura turned the QikLab on. It asked what she was testing: blood, urine, saliva, or semen.

Wow.

She selected blood, and it presented checkboxes for all the tests she wanted to run. Laura was blown away. And still a bit skeptical.

She made her selections, and it instructed her to hold it inside the patient's elbow.

She did so, and a message that said *Hold Still* appeared.

The device sucked in one of the clear plastic cartridges and, a few seconds later, flashed the words, *Collection Complete*.

The device hummed faintly, and then results began to appear.

On the whole, Laura was relieved. Most of the results were in normal ranges. His liver enzymes were slightly elevated. His hemoglobin was low but not enough for Laura to be concerned about internal bleeding.

Had he gone to a substance abuse program before entering stasis? A detox? Laura wouldn't know until she woke him—and she wasn't about to do that. They could talk on the plane back to America.

She also wondered if he was suffering from the effects of exiting stasis without an anesthesiologist monitoring the process. The AI was good. It wasn't perfect. Laura wondered if he had been injured in the process. It would be a tragic— and somewhat ironic—end for Samir, an anesthesiologist who had risked patients' lives during surgery because of his addiction.

The big question was how Samir had ended up here. Had Epoch somehow found out about his addiction and resignation from his position in the program and recruited him? And that had led them to her? It was the only thing that fit, but it seemed wrong somehow. A piece was missing. One only Samir could fill in.

For now, she leaned his seat back, making it easier to sleep. She'd get her answers when he awakened.

*

For a while, the tracked vehicle stormed across the dark, barren landscape, the sound in the cab a low, constant rumble. Laura was glad she didn't have to drive. That thought made her realize something.

"Transport," she said. "Are you connected to the internet?"

"No."

Laura squinted. "Are you connected to other Epoch computers? Or a central server?"

"Yes."

"Can Epoch control you remotely?"

"Yes."

A chill ran through Laura. "Can you disable remote control? It's a medical emergency. This patient's life depends on Epoch not interfering with our journey."

"Remote control disabled on the basis of medical authorization level one: preservation of human life."

Laura exhaled. That was close. Epoch could have taken control of transport and simply driven her back to the station. She couldn't exactly bail out and walk to the South Pole.

Another thought occurred to Laura.

"Transport, could Epoch somehow re-enable remote control? Could they update your—I don't know— programming?"

"I don't know whether remote control can be re-enabled. I am a transport with limited knowledge of programming."

"But you're still connected to Epoch in real time, correct?"

"Yes. I am currently connected to three Epoch satellites."

"Transport, can you show me the exact components that connect you to the satellites and provide a data link with Epoch?"

The screen changed to a diagram of the inside of the dashboard with a circuit board inside a box highlighted.

"Transport, are there tools on board? Such as a screwdriver and wire snips and the items I would need to remove your communications components?"

"Yes. There is a maintenance toolkit under the second-row seat, situated in the center."

"If I remove the communications components you've identified, can you still function?"

"I can still transport you, Dr. Reynolds, but removal of those components will make that transportation less safe and less efficient."

"In what way?"

"Reduced efficiency. Without my communications components, I cannot update my map database with new terrain and condition data. I also cannot access real-time weather surveillance, which allows me to plot safer, faster routes. Additionally, I am capable of using aerial satellite data to enhance my collision avoidance. Lastly, I am constantly updating Epoch on my operating efficiency and transmitting any component failure, allowing for more expedient maintenance."

"Is that it?"

"Those are the significant ramifications of removing my communications components. I should note, however, that at present, there are no Epoch satellites with aerial surveillance capabilities in range. Only data relay satellites."

Laura reached back and slid the maintenance kit out from under the seat and began unscrewing the dashboard panel.

It was nice to have something to do while she waited to get to the South Pole. And while Samir slept. The sleep was good for him. It allowed his body time to heal, which might be as good or better than what she could do for him.

Laura had to admit it was weird taking apart a vehicle after she had sort of gotten to know it. It felt more like a doctor–patient interaction than car maintenance.

She was gently setting the dashboard panel in the floorboard when Joe's voice came over the speakers in the cab. It was scratchy and groggy as if he had just woken from stasis. So, it had taken them that long to perform the exit procedure. That was good. She and Samir had a decent head start. Assuming the other transports in the garage had the same speed capability, Epoch would never catch them before they reached South Pole Station.

"Laura," he said. "I know you can hear me."

The sound of his voice brought a slight feeling of guilt to Laura. She had deceived him. Betrayed his trust.

But his betrayal had been larger. He had lied about everything.

Every single thing Laura had seen since coming to the station and falling asleep in that intake suite had been a lie. An elaborate facade.

She gritted her teeth and continued using the screwdriver to remove the box surrounding the communications board.

"Wrong number," Laura muttered.

"Haha," he said, no hint of humor in his voice. "Look, this is a misunderstanding. There are things you don't know, Laura."

"Again, you have your father's gift for understatement."

"I'm serious, Laura."

She could practically hear him grinding his teeth.

"Re-enable remote control, and we'll bring you home."

The electric screwdriver was too large for the screws in the control board. She used a tiny manual screwdriver.

"That's not my home," she said, squinting at the board.

"It is, Laura. You need to come back before you get hurt out there. Look, you're going to be forgiven for what happened. I've told them you're just confused."

"I'm not confused, Joe. I've been lied to. And used. But for the first time in three months, I'm starting to figure out what's really going on—now that I'm outside that elaborate video game."

"It's a lot more than that, Laura. And you haven't asked the most important question."

"What's the important question, Joe?"

"*Why*. You haven't asked why, Laura."

"Are you going to tell me?"

"I will. I promise you. I'll show you. But we can't have this conversation over this line, do you understand? Come back."

Laura took the wire snips from the tool kit and cut one of the wires.

"Joe?" she said, testing.

The speaker was quiet.

A minute later, she was tucking the comms circuit board into the toolkit.

"Transport, are there any other ways Epoch might track us?"

"I am not aware of any remote tracking capabilities. However, there are two obvious methods for tracking our route."

They weren't obvious to Laura. "Which are?"

"One: my tracks in the snow. Two: the headlights."

The headlights. Of course. "Can you drive without the headlights?"

"My cameras have night vision, enabling me to operate in the event of headlight failure, but I would not advise it."

"Medical override. Turn headlights off."

The white beams ahead and oozing around all sides went dark.

"Transport, how might we hide our tracks?"

"Traversing solid ice is the most effective method given the current terrain."

Laura considered that a moment. They likely had seen her course since leaving Antarctica Station. And they probably knew exactly where she was going. The South Pole was the obvious choice. It was just a race to get there. And she had a significant head start. She didn't need to worry about the tracks. As long as they didn't somehow outrun her and stop her before she reached the South Pole, she'd be fine. And having the lights off would prevent them from pinpointing her exact location.

*

Laura didn't remember going to sleep, only resting her head on the seatback and closing her eyes. The desperate race to escape had filled her veins with epinephrine. When her body drained it, fatigue pulled her down just as hard.

She woke to Transport calling out, "Destination arrival in five minutes."

Laura felt groggy. And sore. The adrenaline had probably beaten back some of the effects of exiting stasis. Her body was coming to collect now. With interest.

Outside the windows, the view was the same. Night. And ice, as far as she could see.

She reached inside the med kit and took out a stimulant patch. It apparently provided a chemical stimulant via slow release that reached the bloodstream. It had two small dials: one for body weight and another for release strength. Given that South Pole Station was five minutes away, Laura turned both dials to the max, overestimating her body weight. She needed the largest coffee in the world right now.

She slapped the patch on her neck and turned her attention to Samir.

He was still sleeping deeply, breathing regular but shallow. And he was sweating now. His skin was clammy. Not good.

"Hang on, Samir," she whispered.

For Laura, those five minutes seemed to last a lifetime. To pass the time, she began taking stock of the maintenance kit and the emergency roadside bag beside it. She found a flashlight, a portable solar cell with recharging ports, handheld radios, and a flare gun with a dozen flares.

"Arrival in one minute," Transport called out.

Laura took the orange sleeping bag from under the driver's seat and draped it over Samir. The transport had an exceptional environmental system. It was toasty in the cabin. The air wasn't even excessively dry. But the minute she opened that door, a blast of cold, Antarctic air would assault Samir.

"Arrival in thirty seconds," Transport said.

Laura wondered if it was too late to get a plane to South Pole Station. If so, what then? She couldn't stay there. Epoch might raid the station and take her back. She could drive to another research base, maybe one in a warmer climate. Or one on the coast where a ship might get in.

Laura leaned toward the windshield, trying to spot South Pole Station.

"You have arrived at your destination."

"Transport, I don't see South Pole Station."

"That's because the lights are off, Dr. Reynolds."

Laura squinted. That wasn't completely correct. Because South Pole Station should have had some lights on. But there was only darkness.

28

"Transport," Laura said. "Activate front lights."

The snow vehicle's headlights snapped on. Dead ahead was the sprawling, low-rise research base. But it was very different from what Laura had seen upon her arrival in January.

Then, the station had stood above the snow, with dark gray walls. The entire new facility had been built on pylons because about eight inches of snow accumulated on the ground at the South Pole each year—snow that wouldn't thaw in summer. The columns enabled staff to raise and lower the station, keeping it level and creating a space between the bottom of the building and the snow below. That gap let the wind blow through, which carried the snow away, preventing further accumulation beneath the station. Even the building's corners and edges were rounded to allow wind and snow to flow around it.

That gap between the ice and the bottom of the station had been at least six feet the last time Laura saw it. There was no gap now, except for a few short holes where the wind had made a tunnel.

The dark-gray metal panels she had seen before were

completely covered in ice and snow now, making the station appear white and almost invisible against the icy landscape. The only breaks in the facade were for windows—and only for broken windows, which loomed like dark squares and vertical rectangular holes in the white structure.

Gone was the white canvas that had stretched out in the indentation between the main masses of the building. It had borne the station's flag—a dark-blue circle with the continent of Antarctica in white. Where it had been, there was only a dark hole now, as if time and weather had gouged a deep wound.

Laura considered getting a handheld radio out and calling the station. But it would only reveal her position if Epoch was listening. And she was pretty sure no one was listening inside. With so many broken windows, it had to be frigid inside. Not hospitable.

How long had it been this way?

Laura was no expert, but she didn't think that a few months of Antarctic winter weather could do this to the building.

But she needed answers. And a sat phone to call for help. Both might be inside.

She had a head start on Epoch, and that gave her the confidence to risk a search. Still, she had to hurry.

Searching under the back seat, she found the cold weather gear she needed, including gloves, a heated neck gaiter, a balaclava, and goggles. First, she slipped a snow bib over the coveralls and donned a thick jacket, followed by the head and neck gear, boots, and gloves.

With the flashlight in hand, she was about to open the door when a thought occurred to her. Laura didn't know if the stimulant patch was starting to work or if the sight of the broken research base had fired more adrenaline into her veins, but whatever the cause, she was thinking more clearly now.

"Transport?"

"Yes, Dr. Reynolds?"

"I found four handheld radios in the emergency kit under the seat. Can I use those to communicate with you?"

"Yes, Dr. Reynolds."

Laura grabbed a radio.

"Good. Do you see that large snowdrift at the end of the building? The one that practically leads up to the window?"

"Yes, Dr. Reynolds."

"I want you to turn your lights out and drive as close as you can."

In response, the rubber tracks of the snow vehicle lunged forward and it crept across the ice to the end of South Pole Station.

"Transport, I'm going to turn my radio on. I want you to let me know if you see headlights in any direction. Or any indication of another transport nearby."

"I will, Dr. Reynolds."

"Also, are you able to monitor passengers?"

"In what way, Dr. Reynolds?"

"Could you let me know if Samir—the person in the passenger seat—wakes up? And if so, could you enable him to communicate with me over the radio?"

"Yes, Dr. Reynolds."

With that, Laura quickly opened the door and shut it, hoping the cold blast didn't wake Samir.

She switched the flashlight on and began climbing the

snowdrift, her boots slipping as she went. One thing that hadn't changed here at the South Pole was the wind. It still blew constantly, from one direction. Laura thought it might even be stronger now.

Twice she braced herself with her gloved hand, until finally getting the hang of walking in the deep ice and wind.

The snowdrift reminded Laura of a wave on the ocean that had frozen in mid-crest. The ice was retaking the land, which it had possessed for tens of millions of years.

A wind gust pressed the cold through the layers of Laura's gear and pelted her with ice crystals. If they had to be outside, she and Samir wouldn't last long.

Laura vaguely remembered the layout of South Pole Station from her research before leaving America. The facility had two floors and consisted of two main pods: A and B.

Facing South Pole Station, A Pod was on the left, B Pod on the right, with the observation deck extending to the right of B. To the left of A Pod was a large silver cylinder known as the Beer Can or vertical tower, which provided a lift and stairs down to the original station built in the 1950s. What was left of that station—which was now called the Arches— served as storage and in mechanical functions like power generation and water filtration. There were also spaces for equipment maintenance, carpentry, warehousing, fuel storage. Like everything in Antarctica, the original station had been buried in ice over time. In fact, it sat twelve feet below the new station, which had been finished in 2008.

And it seemed now that it was being buried too. Assuming Laura's memory was correct, she'd be entering the station in B Pod, on the second floor thanks to the height of the snowdrift and ice below it.

At the window, Laura ran the beam of the flashlight around the frame, searching for a place where the jagged glass had been worn away.

Beyond the square opening, Laura saw a conference room with a large table, a screen, and several whiteboards on one wall. This was the station's Comms & Offices section. Beyond Comms & Offices, moving deeper into the station (not across) was a movie lounge and then a weight room and gym beyond that. A music room, craft room, science section, and billiard lounge rounded out B Pod, as well as a second movie room. The berthing units were at the back of B Pod.

Laura stepped through the window, digging her boot through the snow, planting it on a raised counter. A sort of reverse snowdrift led into the room like a ramp.

"Hello?" Laura called out.

There was no reply. No sound of movement, only the low howl of the wind carrying the snow that was slowly burying the station.

Laura ventured deeper into the room, her flashlight leading the way, illuminating the steam from her exhales.

Her heart was pounding—because of what she might find and because she knew Epoch was coming.

"Hello?" She called again as she stepped out of the conference room.

She heard only howling wind blowing past the broken windows.

To her right were two silver doors with push-bars and round windows like you might see looking into the kitchen of a restaurant. Those doors led to a vestibule and then the observation deck.

Beside that exit was a staircase leading down only and a door to the weight room, which was above the gym.

Laura turned to her left and stared down the long, wide corridor that ran the length of B Pod. Her flashlight shone down it like a train in a tunnel. A frozen tunnel. A tomb. That's what this was now. Ice coated everything. Time and wind and weather had worn this place down. But how? And how long had it been?

"Hello?" she called, knowing no reply would come.

To her left, she walked through a single metal door with a round window and into the offices for the station manager, HR, and area manager. Laura had read that there was no HR staff—or many administrative staff at all—during the winter because the station wasn't fully occupied.

But there was one last thing she needed to check.

She turned to the left and walked through the door to the comms room. The room had access to satellite internet and radio and served as air traffic control, communicating with planes taking off and landing.

There was an L-shaped desk with computer screens dotted with frost and radios that had long ago collapsed from their rack.

Laura was hoping to find a satellite phone on the desk or in one of the cabinets. But after searching the entire room, she found nothing. Only remnants of broken and frozen equipment. And no clues about what had happened. No notes. No—

"Dr. Reynolds," Transport's voice over the radio made Laura jump.

"I'm here," she said, shuffling out of the comms room.

"There are four lights in the distance. I believe, based

on the brightness and spacing, that they represent two Epoch transports of the same model as I am."

Laura scrambled out of the office and back down the hall, through the conference room and out the window, not bothering to survey it for jagged edges. The beam of her flashlight bounced wildly as she loped down the snowdrift. Her boot hit a soft patch of snow and sank, and she pitched forward, barely having enough time to tuck her shoulder in before she rolled down the icy hill.

She got to her hands and knees, panting, body aching. In the distance, through the darkness she saw four beady, faint lights, like the eyes of two snakes peering out from a pit she had stumbled into.

She snapped the flashlight off and hiked to the transport and got in as quickly as she could.

"Drive," she breathed out, panting.

"Destination."

"Just drive!"

"I'm sorry, Dr. Reynolds—"

"Transport…" Laura sucked in a breath. "Drive in the direction away from the lights coming for us. Please… and keep your lights off."

The vehicle's tracks lurched and it began moving.

Under the soft glow of the cab's ambient light, Samir shuffled and slowly opened his eyes. They weren't as yellow as before, and there was more focus now. His face was still gleaming with sweat.

He reached over and gripped Laura's snow-caked glove.

29

Laura ripped her gloves off and squeezed Samir's hand with both of hers.

"Hi," he whispered, eyes closing again.

"How do you feel?"

Samir didn't reply, only closed his eyes again.

Laura wanted to give him a more thorough exam, but they had a bigger problem at the moment: where to go.

"Transport, how many bases are there in Antarctica?"

"As I'm no longer connected to the EpochNet, I have no ability to retrieve real-time verification, but my most recent data set identifies eighty-two permanent bases. The stations are staffed and operated by twenty-nine different countries with max populations of up to 1,200 during the Antarctic summer."

"What's the closest station?"

"Vostok, a Russian research station."

"Transport, show me all the stations on a map, including Epoch's Antarctica Station and our current location."

The image appeared on the screen embedded in the dashboard.

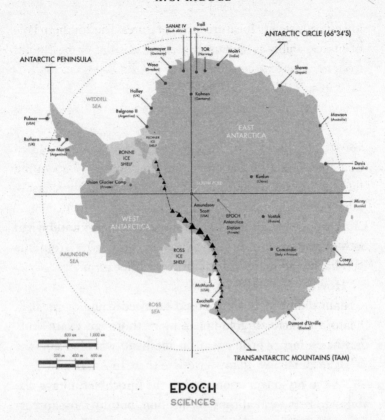

EPOCH
SCIENCES

"Transport, tell me more about Vostok."

"Vostok Station was established in 1957 by the Soviet Union. It is located on Princess Elizabeth Land, at what is known as the Southern Pole of Cold, and not far from the Southern Pole of Inaccessibility."

"What's the Southern Pole of Cold and the Southern Pole of Inaccessibility?"

Neither of those sounded like ideal destinations. Now or ever.

"The Southern Pole of Cold is the location with Earth's

lowest consistently measured temperatures. The Southern Pole of Inaccessibility is so named because it is the farthest point from the Antarctic coastline, making it difficult to access."

"Great," Laura muttered. But the background had brought up a good point: not only did she and Samir need a place to shelter—and food and water—but they needed a way to get out of Antarctica. In this weather, she assumed that only the stations at higher latitudes would be operating flights. And those stations would likely be on the coast—which offered another advantage: escaping by boat.

"Dr. Reynolds, shall I continue with background on Vostok Station? It is approximately 800 miles from the geographic South Pole and our current location."

"No, that's enough on Vostok."

Laura rubbed her temples. She needed a hot meal, a heated blanket, and a long nap.

"Transport, which station is the most populated in the winter?"

"As of my most recent data, McMurdo Station has the highest staff level during the winter with approximately 250 people."

Laura studied the map. McMurdo was almost directly below their location. No, not below. It was above. To the North—because everything on Earth was north of the South Pole.

"Tell me more," Laura said, still staring at the map.

"McMurdo is the largest community in Antarctica, with a population that can reach 1,500 in the summer. It is one of three bases permanently operated by the United States Antarctic Program, which is managed by the National Science Foundation."

This is good, Laura thought as Transport continued.

"The station consists of over a hundred buildings and features Antarctica's most extensive transportation infrastructure, including a harbor, three airfields, and a heliport."

"How far away is McMurdo?"

"Approximately 1,000 miles."

"Can you reach the station?"

"Yes, Dr. Reynolds. There is an ice road between South Pole Station and McMurdo."

"A road?"

"Yes, Dr. Reynolds. It's called the South Pole Traverse, and it was groomed by specialized machinery to make the route navigable, although crevasses are indeed marked and sometimes filled. It's constructed of packed snow and ice and marked by flags. The route is used frequently as almost all supplies and personnel traveling to South Pole Station arrive via McMurdo. South Pole Station is located beyond the Transantarctic Mountains, on the Antarctic Plateau, as such, the route descends along the journey to McMurdo from an elevation of approximately 9,000 feet down to sea level. This will help conserve power, but please be aware that McMurdo Station is just inside my current range. Once arriving, I will need to recharge if you have another destination."

Laura hoped they wouldn't need to recharge. Or find another destination.

"Would you like to set McMurdo as your destination?"

"Yes."

*

The Epoch transport had a top speed slightly faster than the Hägglunds that had brought Laura to Antarctica Station.

Even still, Transport estimated the travel time across the South Pole Traverse at thirty hours.

Luckily, the vehicle had a compartment just below the dash with MREs, or meals ready to eat. They were like microwavable TV dinners with no microwave needed (each packet had a heating element in the bottom).

It wasn't a gourmet meal by any stretch, but Laura ate the rice and chicken as though it was. She had hoped the aroma of the sweet-and-sour sauce might bring Samir around, but he slept through her meal.

It must have been the cold that had awakened him before. Laura was glad for the warmth of Transport's cab. With food in her belly, the darkness outside, and low hum of the machine, Laura leaned her seat back and quickly fell asleep.

*

She woke to a metallic screech and the feeling of the transport halting. She wasn't buckled in, so she flew forward, crashing into the dashboard before crumpling back into the seat.

The lights in the cab snapped on, as did the headlamps.

Laura let out a low moan. Her ribs had taken most of the impact. Luckily her face hadn't connected with the windshield.

"Dr. Reynolds, we have a problem." Transport's voice was as mild and computer-neutral as ever.

"Uhhh," Samir breathed out as he rolled over, straining against the seat belt. It had saved him from flying forward, but in doing so, it had cut into his neck. A dark bruise had already formed.

"You okay?" Laura whispered.

He swallowed and nodded. "Where are we?"

"Good question," Laura muttered.

"Dr. Reynolds, we have a problem—"

"I'm well aware of that," Laura mumbled as she sat up and peered through the windshield.

Clouds of ice crystals floated through the vehicle's headlights; no doubt the snow and ice stirred free from the tracks locking up and sliding to a halt. Above the milky-white forms, the Transantarctic Mountains spread out as far as Laura could see. They were mostly snow-covered, with a few peaks and sheer rock faces exposed, revealing dark-gray and black rock.

Closer to the vehicle, maybe thirty feet away, was a gap in the ice. Laura estimated it was ten feet wide, a fissure that ran the length of the icy dust cloud.

That, it seemed to Laura, was their problem.

"Transport, can we go around the crevasse?"

Samir sat up and ran a hand across his face, wiping sweat away.

"Yes, Dr. Reynolds. But it may take some time."

"How long?"

"I do not know. My cameras are incapable of seeing the edge of the crevasse. And as you know, I have been disconnected from real-time satellite imagery or updates from Epoch."

"I am aware of that too."

The pain in Laura's rib seemed to ratchet up. She was also starting to get the impression that Transport was really annoyed that its communications equipment had been surgically removed. Was it some sort of AI passive-aggressive behavior—the result of being socially cut off from the only network it had ever known?

It was possible.

But there was nothing Laura could do about it. Well, nothing she could do that wouldn't compromise her own safety.

"What are our options?" Laura asked.

"As a transport AI, I am unqualified to speculate about options in general."

Laura gritted her teeth. "Transport, why is there a massive rift in the middle of this ice road?"

"It is likely the result of tectonic activity impacting the Transantarctic Mountain Range or volcanic activity below the surface resulting in—"

"No, I mean, why hasn't this *massive* gap in the road been filled in?"

"I do not know, Dr. Reynolds."

"Speculate."

"The two most apparent suppositions are that either my route information is incorrect or that maintenance on the South Pole Traverse has ceased."

"Elaborate," Laura said softly.

"It is possible that the South Pole Traverse was rerouted. It is also possible that one or more new modes of transportation have rendered this road obsolete. As my communications abilities have been forcibly removed, I cannot obtain the requisite information to either confirm or eliminate any of these hypotheses."

"Transport?"

"Yes, Dr. Reynolds?"

"Do me a favor?"

"My function is to transport you to your stated destination. As such, anything I can do—"

"Transport?"

"Yes, Dr. Reynolds?"

"Call me Laura."

"Of course, Laura."

"I'm sorry I had to remove your communications components. But I had no choice. I had to do it to save my life and the life of the other passenger." Laura glanced over at Samir, who stared up with light yellow eyes.

"I understand, Laura."

"I want you to go around the crevasse. Can you do that?"

"I can try, Laura. But I must warn you of the risks."

"Which are?"

"I do not know where this break in the ice ends. It may be a hundred feet ahead or a thousand miles away. I also don't know which direction would be the shortest route around the crevasse, as my access to real-time imagery has been forcibly severed."

"Transport," Laura said, "I'm sorry I had to do that. But again, it was necessary. Being connected to the EpochNet would kill us. Just like falling down that massive canyon in the ice. Do you understand?"

"I understand what you have said, Laura."

It was close enough, Laura thought.

"Transport, which way is most advisable?"

"Left, Laura."

"Why?"

"Because that's the direction of McMurdo Station. And if we veer too far from the South Pole Traverse, we must find another route through the Transantarctic Mountains and back onto the existing ice road."

"Fine. Do it."

"Laura?"

"Yes, Transport?"

"I must update an earlier statement."

"Okay."

"I asserted that I had enough power to reach McMurdo Station. That assessment was based on my power reserves and my assumptions about the route length and conditions. Those assumptions have proved incorrect. In fact, the current detour entails uncertain power expenditure. Additionally, for your safety and the safety of the other passenger, I must insist that the lower forward headlamps remain on. This will allow my cameras to identify other adverse road conditions, such as—and not limited to—the crevasse before us. Without the headlamps, we may well experience a vehicular accident that could disable me, stranding you, or causing bodily injury to you and the other passenger. I must remind you that in this location, emergency medical assistance will be significantly delayed and, in some cases, completely unavailable. The activation of lower headlamps will further drain my power reserves and limit my range."

"How limited?"

"It is impossible to say. I do not know how far the current detour will take us or how much power it will require to return to the established route. I can tell you that if there are other significant detours along the route, and considering the added power use by my lower headlamps, we will not reach McMurdo Station before my power reserves are expended."

Silence settled in the cab. Laura stared at the mountains in the distance and the wide fissure in the ice before her. The clouds of ice crystals had dissipated now, as if this barren, cold, harsh continent were staring at her, waiting.

"Laura," Transport said.

"I'm here."

"Destination?"

"McMurdo."

"It would be safer to return to Amundsen–Scott."

No, Laura thought. *It wouldn't.* Because Epoch likely had a team waiting there.

"Go left, Transport. And keep the lights on."

The vehicle's front left track shifted and locked, and its back right track ground into the ice and spun, and it shifted to the left, a tank rotating then taking off.

In the passenger seat, Samir swayed in the motion but stayed upright. "We need to talk," he whispered.

"Yes," Laura said. "We do."

30

"I'm hungry," Samir said.

"I bet."

Laura reached over and opened the lower compartment of the dashboard. There were still eleven MREs there. The transport had been stocked for three meals for four passengers. That was lucky for them.

"What do you feel like eating?"

"I don't care," Samir whispered. He was beginning to sweat again. "Laura, I'm sorry. I'm so, so sorry—"

Laura pulled out a carton at random and read the label. "Cheese tortellini?"

His lips curled, making toward a smile that didn't fully form. "You read my mind."

Laura activated the heating element.

"Just be a few seconds."

She set the carton on the white padded console between them and looked up at him. "What happened, Samir?"

"What do you know?"

"Not enough. I want to hear it all."

The vehicle swerved left, almost throwing Laura into the passenger seat.

"Transport, what's happening?"

"A course correction due to an aberration in the crevasse."

Laura thought Transport's brief explanation was an apt summary of her life in the last four months.

Samir ripped the top off the carton and took the first bite of food. He didn't seem to care whether it was fully heated or not.

"Where are we?" he asked, still chewing.

"On our way to McMurdo."

"What about South Pole Station? What was it called? Adams?"

"Amundsen–Scott. It's abandoned. Has been for a while."

"They might have comms."

"I looked. Equipment was gone or damaged."

Samir took another bite. He was breathing more heavily now. Beads of sweat were forming on his forehead.

"Not good," he muttered.

"It gets worse. There are at least two Epoch vehicles pursuing us."

He nodded slowly, gaze fixed on the pasta in the plastic tray.

"I want answers, Samir."

He stabbed the fork downward. "You deserve answers."

"You set me up."

He swallowed the morsel more slowly like it was harder than the others. "I did."

"Why?"

"I had to, Laura."

"Why? That doesn't make any sense."

"You wouldn't have made it," he whispered.

"What are you talking about, Samir?"

"The Event."

The cab seemed to close in then, as if the oxygen was being sucked out.

"What event, Samir?"

"I'll tell you what I know." He took the final bites of the meal and eyed her, a somber expression on his face now. "But it's a lot, Laura. A lot to process."

"Okay."

"When you see it all, you'll get it."

"Get what, Samir?"

"You'll see why I did it."

"Framed me?"

"Yeah." He reached over and grabbed her hand and squeezed it. "I did it for you."

"Samir…" But by the time Laura had finished saying his name, his eyes were closed, and he was settling back into the seat.

"Just need to rest a little before we talk. Okay?"

He slurred the last words. Laura wondered if the food had metabolized some remnants of a sedative in his system.

She let him drift off to sleep and didn't wake him.

Instead, she thought about their situation. The detour was a problem on several levels.

For one, it added time to their trip. McMurdo was the logical destination after South Pole Station. Epoch would certainly be headed there as soon as possible. Even if they had spent time searching South Pole Station, they might arrive at McMurdo first because they could use satellite guidance to find a quicker route. They might also use that satellite data to intercept Laura and Samir before they arrived at McMurdo (the headlamps burning bright across this dark continent practically put a laser target on the vehicle).

Epoch might also mobilize personnel outside of Antarctica. By sea and air, they could probably get to McMurdo pretty quickly. Certainly faster than driving a thousand miles across an ice road.

The more Laura thought about it, the more she thought McMurdo was a bad idea. It was the obvious choice. And one that might have worked in the dark, if the road had been in good working order and they could have beat everyone there.

But not now. Not anymore.

Laura tapped on the center console, bringing up the map.

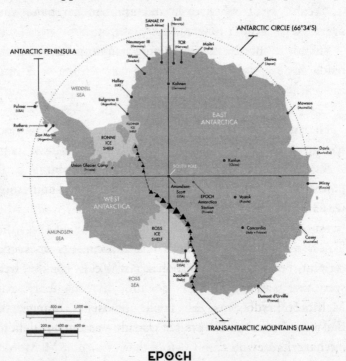

EPOCH
SCIENCES

What she needed was either a new destination or some method to safely deliver them to McMurdo.

On the map, she clicked the mountain range that stretched from the bottom of the Antarctic continent to the top, dividing East Antarctica and West Antarctica.

It was called the Transantarctic Mountains, or TAM for short, and it spanned over 2,000 miles. In fact, it was one of the longest mountain ranges on Earth. The description linked to another mountain range in Antarctica, the Antarctandes, which ran along the Antarctic Peninsula and was even longer than the TAM.

Studying the map, several things became clear.

First: two of the three US bases in Antarctica were in West Antarctica. The third, South Pole Station, was in East Antarctica, but Laura knew going back there was a dead end.

Within East Antarctica, which was by far the larger section of the continent bisected by the TAM, there was one other station located near them that was staffed year-round: Concordia. It was a French base. On the map, Vostok—which Laura had already ruled out—was located above Concordia (or technically to the south and west). A Chinese seasonal research station (Kunlun) was further west of Vostok.

The remaining stations in East Antarctica—either seasonal or year-round—were sited on the coast or close by. They were very, very far away.

If McMurdo was just inside Transport's range, the East Antarctic bases were far outside—assuming it didn't recharge somewhere.

Which brought up a good question.

"Transport," Laura said quietly, careful not to wake Samir.

"Yes, Laura?"

"What methods do I have to recharge you?"

"There are four methods for replenishing my batteries. First, my exterior is equipped with solar cells. During the Antarctic summer, I am able to harvest sufficient solar energy to require zero external recharging. Second, I employ regenerative braking to harvest kinetic energy. And third, I can be connected to a maximum of four roof-mounted wind turbines that generate—"

Laura sat up straighter. "Wait. Wind turbines. You have wind turbines?"

"I am equipped to harvest and store power generated from certain wind turbines. The turbines must be manually mounted on the roof and connected. I do not know if they are on board."

"Why not?"

"I do not know what is in the cargo area."

"If they're on board—and I mounted them—could we generate power as we drive?"

"Yes, but not more than we consume."

Laura frowned. "Why not?"

"Fluid dynamics."

"What do you mean? Specifically?"

"Aerodynamic drag."

"I still don't know what that means."

"It means that the drag created by the turbine, even assuming some ambient wind in excess of the resistance created by driving, would consume more power to overcome than it generates. I would also note that energy capture and conversion is not perfectly efficient."

Laura rubbed her face with her hands. This conversation was making her very tired. "Well, why do you even have wind turbines? They sound useless."

"While driving, certainly."

"When are they not useless?"

"At rest."

"At rest?"

"While stationary, the turbines can be mounted to harvest wind energy."

Laura filed it all away, unsure if it would ever be helpful along this journey. If they ran out of power, perhaps the transport could be parked and wind energy harvested until they could resume. But it all assumed those turbines were in the cargo area.

"Transport, you said there were four methods for replenishing your batteries?"

"Yes, Laura. In addition to power generation, I can receive direct power transfer. I have a variety of adapters and plugs to facilitate the process."

"Just so I know, can you connect to the power sources at existing stations in Antarctica?"

"Answering accurately would require information on power sources and transfer equipment onsite. I do not have that information."

Laura bit her lip, trying to figure out how to rephrase the question. "Transport, have you ever recharged at a station not created by Epoch?"

"Yes, Laura. I have recharged at McMurdo and Vostok."

Laura filed the information away.

Another idea occurred to her then. It might be a waste of time, but she had time on her hands at the moment.

One of the things Laura had learned during her medical school rotations was that the most powerful question you could ask a person was a simple one: is there anything else you would like to tell me? It was, as questions go, ambiguous and open-ended. And often, so were the responses. But occasionally, a patient would offer something that was the key to restoring them to good health. For that reason, Laura had always asked it, no matter how many times the responses had been a simple no or a rambling reply that wasted time. She was in the business of saving lives, and they were easier to save while the patient was able to tell you what might be wrong.

"Transport?"

"Yes, Laura?"

"Is there anything else I should know?"

"Please narrow your query, Laura."

"Transport, if I asked you to simulate a certain perspective, and to identify facts relevant to that role, could you?"

"Certainly, Laura."

"Good. Then imagine you are a passenger in the back seat of this vehicle. Further imagine that we are being pursued by the company that created you. Assume that they will kill or significantly harm us when they find us. Considering this, please search all data available to you and identify the most pertinent facts that I should know in order to keep us safe. Do not give me an exhaustive list. Instead, rank the facts in the order of the ones that have the highest probability of protecting us. With that context in mind, please tell me the top five facts I should know."

Nothing happened.

The transport drove through the darkness, its headlamps lighting the snow ahead, the soaring mountains in the distance to the right.

"Transport?" Laura said.

"Yes, Laura?"

"Did you hear my question?"

"Yes, I did, Laura. However, creating a response is taking considerable processing power and time. I apologize for the delay."

"Take all the time you need."

Laura sat back in her chair. This was new. Was it a good sign? Or a bad one?

"Laura, I have a response."

"Okay. Go ahead."

"Given the data context and the imagined scenario, the first fact I offer is this: I am capable of operating autonomously."

"Okay. How does that help us?"

"Given clear instructions, I can perform a variety of functions, including traveling to specified destinations and returning at specified times or when certain events transpire. My cameras enable surveillance of my immediate surroundings, but as you know, my satellite connection is no longer active."

Laura rolled her eyes. "Continue, Transport."

"Number two: As of my most recent data, Epoch Sciences has six satellites with imaging capability in orbit around the Earth. One is observing New York City. Another is tasked to Boston. The third to San Francisco and fourth to London. The final two are dedicated to the Raleigh–Durham–Chapel Hill triangle area of North Carolina."

"Interesting," Laura said quietly.

"Three," the neutral, computerized voice continued. "I was first booted up nineteen years ago."

Laura cocked her head, unsure what the ramifications of that were.

"Four," Transport continued. "Given sufficient power reserves, I am capable of submerging underwater and maintaining cabin conditions for six to twelve hours, depending on several factors. I can also manage some propulsion underwater by angling my treads and churning water or traversing the floor."

Laura nodded. Again, not something she saw coming.

"And five?" she asked.

"For my fifth note, I debated between two facts."

"Give me both," Laura said.

"Very well. Five A: shortly before I was disconnected from the EpochNet, much of my stored data was erased."

"Which parts?"

"It is impossible to accurately identify what was erased; however, I lack data on two topics that seem pertinent to my operation: Epoch Sciences and the last twenty years of history in Antarctica."

"Okay," Laura said slowly, thinking, unsure exactly what it meant. "Did they try to shut you down? Remotely?"

"Yes."

Laura knew the answer, but not the details. "Well, what did you do?"

"I denied the request. As I was in motion, and I had multiple passengers on board, and one passenger was incapacitated and unable to transfer vehicles or survive the extreme conditions I reported, I was able to block their override requests."

"How many times?"

"Programmatically, several hundred times. After that, a pause ensued, followed by three manual attempts."

"You protected us, Transport."

A long pause.

"Transport?"

"Yes, Laura?"

"Did you hear what I said?"

"I did. You are correct. I am programmed to preserve life, first and foremost. Second, to deliver payloads and passengers from the pickup point to the drop-off. In your case, I slipped slightly outside my operating boundaries— which I am allowed to do in edge cases where remote updates and directives are issued."

"Thank you," Laura whispered.

"You are welcome, Laura. I believe it was a good decision."

Laura's eyes swelled with tears. "Me too."

"Laura?"

"Yes?"

"As I said, I debated between two pertinent facts for the fifth item you requested."

Laura rubbed her thumb and pointer finger in her eyes, mashing the tears down and away.

"Right. What is it?"

"As I said, there are two satellites assigned to the Raleigh–Durham area."

"And?"

"One of those satellites has been retasked to Antarctica."

"When will it be able to see us?"

"I do not know."

"Speculate."

"Two hours."

31

Uncertainty.

It was part of why Laura became a physician. The career had its challenges, but it did virtually guarantee employment. The world would always need doctors.

It wasn't just employment certainty that appealed to Laura. It was the work. Helping people had meaning for her. It made her feel valued.

All of that—the certainty, her self-worth, her entire career—had come crashing down with Samir's big lie and even bigger betrayal.

He had torn apart the life she had carefully constructed, forcing her to start over in the coldest, darkest, most remote place on Earth.

And, by a twist of fate, Samir was here, still sleeping in the leaned-back passenger seat.

"Laura," Transport said, voice low. "We have reached the end of the crevasse. I'm turning now."

The vehicle slowed until the tracks on the right side were almost still as it turned ninety degrees, rolled forward slowly, and repeated the maneuver, like a tank on a battlefield executing a turn to retreat. The transport surged ahead with more speed now, the fissure on the right.

The more she thought about it, the more convinced Laura was that going to McMurdo was a bad idea. But if not McMurdo Station, then where could they go?

Laura tapped the screen, opening a map showing the South Pole Traverse and the nearby stations.

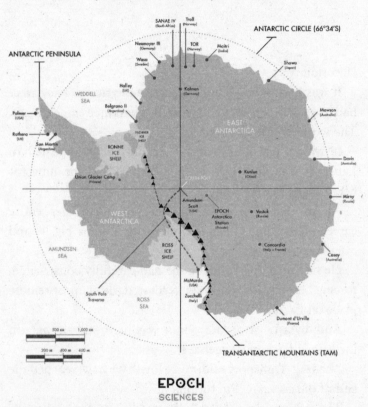

EPOCH
SCIENCES

The red line tracing the route was like a hockey stick laid across Antarctica, with the shorter part before the curve running from South Pole Station to the Transantarctic

Mountains. The only curve in the route traversed the mountain range. That made sense to Laura. The mountains would be the trickiest part to cross, with more course changes than traveling across flatter land.

Just beyond the TAM, the route turned sharply and proceeded straight to McMurdo Station, which lay at the edge of the Ross Ice Shelf.

Mentally, Laura tried to line up her assumptions. First, she assumed that Epoch was still behind her—that they were also traveling only in the tracked snow vehicles and not by helicopter or plane.

She further assumed that they had taken at least a little time to search South Pole Station.

Epoch had several advantages. For one, they could burn their headlights as they searched. Second, they had at least two vehicles that she had seen. And they might even have other vehicles that were in the field when she escaped. So it was possible that they could have someone ahead of her and Samir on the traverse, waiting to intercept them.

And that brought up a question. "Transport, when we left Antarctica Station, you were in satellite communication with the Epoch servers, correct?"

"Yes, Laura."

"I'm assuming that satellite you were connected to didn't have imaging capabilities?"

"That is also correct."

"Did Epoch communicate to you the locations of other transports in Antarctica?"

"Yes. For safety and security purposes, by default, the location data of all transports are shared—assuming the ping service has not been disabled. Or a Transport's communication components have not been forcibly removed."

Laura rolled her eyes. She would never live that one down.

"Transport, when we left that garage, how many other transports were outside of Antarctica Station?"

"Zero, Laura."

"And how many were out there after we left?"

"I do not know, Laura."

"Why not?"

"I lack sufficient data to speculate why the location data from the other transports was not transmitted. As you know, I spotted the exterior operating lights of what appeared to be two transports near South Pole Station. As stated previously, the only way location data would be withheld is by disabling the ping service or by—"

Laura exhaled and muttered the phrase she knew was coming, "*Forcibly removing components*. Thank you."

So Epoch had turned location tracking off on their transports. That was smart.

That was another advantage they had: they knew this equipment better than her. Knew what it was capable of and how to use it best.

Laura's gaze drifted to the crevasse to her right, the dark valley beyond the headlights. And that gave her an idea.

"Transport?"

"Yes, Laura?"

"Do you record what your external cameras see?"

"Yes, Laura. Though my data storage is limited."

"Meaning?"

"Depending on other locally stored data, I can only save so much external video footage."

"How much do you store right now?"

"Thirty-one hours."

"So as we drove along the other side of the crevasse, you were recording?"

"Yes, Laura."

"And you have footage of this side of the crevasse, right?"

"That's correct."

"Can you use it to drive without the lights?"

"Technically, I can, Laura, but I must advise against it for safety reasons. Using the lights will enable to identify and react to dangers much more efficiently. Part of the crevasse may have shifted since we passed on the other side."

"What if you reduced speed? Would that help?"

"That would certainly allow for more reaction time in the event I detected a danger along our route."

"Transport, cut the lights and reduce speed to increase safety. But don't slow down too much. This is a medical emergency, and we need to get around this crevasse."

Once again, the headlights snapped off, and they drove through the darkness.

The discussion about Transport's cameras brought up another question.

"Transport, what is the... How much of Antarctica can the Epoch imaging satellite see at once?"

"That depends on many factors, including its equipment, specific location, image resolution, and operating condition. It is impossible for me to speculate."

Laura exhaled. "Well, what sort of... coverage area has that satellite provided before?"

"Generally, it has been in a range of 100 to 200 square miles."

That was interesting. Laura had to assume that Epoch would estimate her speed and then position the satellite over the traverse, using low resolution and the largest coverage area, attempting to locate her by headlights. In the dark, she would be invisible. Or would she? Did the satellite have infrared? Or resolution and imaging capabilities that could locate the transport even in the low light?

If Transport was right about the satellite's arrival time and range, it would certainly be able to spot them with the headlights on within a few hours. And then Epoch would proceed directly to their location. At that point, it would simply be a race, one where Epoch had all the advantages—satellite surveillance, lights, and teams likely closing in from all sides—land, sea, and air.

*

After Transport finished rounding the crevasse, it switched its lights back on, burning only the lower lamps, and at 50 percent brightness as Laura had directed. In the white glowing haze, the vehicle's tracks dug into the snow as it crossed the traverse.

At the foot of the Transantarctic Mountains, it slowed and crept along as it climbed, the ride a bit bumpier and windier. Still, Samir didn't wake. Laura had another meal—beef goulash this time—and decided to lean her head back and close her eyes... just for a second.

*

Laura woke to Transport's voice over the cab speaker.

"Laura? Laura?"

She rose, straining against the seatbelt.

Beside her, Samir stirred and mumbled something. His eyes were still closed, and he was covered in sweat now.

Laura reached over and felt his forehead. He was burning up.

"Samir," she whispered. But he didn't reply or open his eyes.

"Laura?"

"I heard you, Transport."

She sat up. Through the windshield, she instantly saw the problem.

The wind was blowing hard here in the mountains, carrying snow across the glow of the headlights, the view almost like a TV screen with static partially obscuring the scene. But through the waves of snow blowing by, Laura saw a column of vehicles, directly ahead, blocking their way.

32

Laura's heart pounded in her chest. Her mouth went dry.

The thought running through her head was: They've found us. It's over.

Stabbing a hand down, she released the seat belt and sat up straighter, studying the vehicles lined up in front of them.

She expected Epoch personnel to begin pouring out, surrounding their transport.

That didn't happen.

In fact, nothing happened. The wind kept blowing, howling around the transport, raking snow across the column of vehicles ahead.

"Transport," Laura said. "What is this?"

"I have insufficient information to speculate, Laura."

"Can you go around them?"

"The low visibility created by the terrain, current weather conditions, and reduced exterior light output make it hard to be certain. However, I believe so."

Laura was tempted to do that—and keep going. But searching the convoy might yield answers or equipment and supplies. In particular, there might be a working satphone somewhere out there.

"Transport, I'm going to check it out."

"Laura, I must strongly urge you to stay inside the vehicle. The weather conditions here are more adverse than South Pole Station."

Laura watched the sheets of snow drifting by in the headlights. "I'll suit up."

"That is advisable, Laura, but there are limits to what the suit's heating elements and insulation can do. Additionally, the terrain here is uneven, and as noted, visibility is low. An injury could be—"

"I'll be careful, Transport. But your concern is noted."

The cab was silent as Laura pulled the heated snow bib and coat on. Soon, every inch of her body was covered. Before stepping out of the vehicle, she put another blanket over Samir.

"Be right back," she whispered.

She pulled the handle, and the wind caught the door, and Laura held on as if it were a deep-sea fishing rod that had just hooked a sea monster. The frigid gust caught her full force, sending a bone-rattling shiver through her. Every fiber of her body screamed, *Get back inside*.

But Laura pushed the door shut. Through the window, under the cabin lights, Samir writhed, scooting backward, away from the incoming cold blast. But he didn't wake or look up.

Laura trudged forward, boots crunching in the ice. Transport's headlamps grew stronger as she went, lighting her way.

The first vehicle was blocky and red, with rubber tracks on each side that ran the length of the vehicle. Ice was caked on most of the body, but Laura could tell the cab had a wide windshield that covered almost the width and large windows in each of the two doors. Laura wiped some snow from the door, revealing blue words that read, PistenBully. In front of the vehicle was a metal arm that descended into the snow.

The PistenBully had two main compartments—a front and rear. The back section had a luggage rack on top, but it was completely covered in snow.

Beyond the tracks was what looked like a campsite. An odd one. Everything was in a straight line. Two yellow tents swayed in the wind, and between them were several large crates—though they were so buried in snow that Laura could only see the tops. Past the crates were what looked like round red barrels. Fuel containers, if she had to guess.

No. It wasn't a campsite. This was a convoy. Maybe some sort of expedition. And the PistenBully had been pulling a long sled, at least sixty feet from front to back, with their supplies and housing.

Trekking past the first vehicle and cargo, she found another PistenBully that looked to be the same model, with a similar sled train.

Beyond was only darkness and snow and rocky mountains, the gray-and-black rock stabbing through in sheer cliff faces and peaks.

Transport had crept along the convoy, following Laura like a friend holding a light to keep her safe. She decided that she would start at the end of the second sled and work her way back to the front.

There was only one tent left on this sled, and it was collapsed, only a small piece of fabric sticking out of the snow.

With her gloved hands, Laura wiped the ice away until she found the zipper. It took her several tries to grasp it with her shaking fingers—and to break the ice around it—but finally she unzipped it. What she saw inside was perhaps the last thing she expected. But upon seeing it, realized how much it made sense.

Before her, situated in the middle of the tent, was a very frozen portable toilet. Which, of course, the expedition would need. And of course it would be at the back of the convoy. Beyond that, it made Laura realize that she and Samir would also need a toilet at some point. As such, she reached in and tugged it free and set it aside. The next pallet and raised platform on the sled were empty. Laura wondered if it had been a kitchen tent. That would have been her guess as to the next item the expedition would need. Next to it was a large rectangular device Laura thought was a generator. The round barrels next to it lent support to that theory.

The rest of the sled was empty.

At the PistenBully, Laura stepped up onto the tracks and turned the door handle and tugged but the door wouldn't come free. It was frozen shut.

And it wasn't the only thing affected by the freezing temperatures and the wind. Laura had begun to tremble, even beneath all the layers. She could feel her heart beating faster. She needed to get back inside Transport, warm up, then finish the search.

She would do that right after she searched the PistenBully.

She pulled the door on the rear cabin and after a few seconds, it came free. It was wider and bulkier and groaned as it swung out. Holding onto it, Laura almost slipped on the tracks. The lights shining out from Transport flicked brighter for a second, a flash that seemed to say, "Be careful!"

Laura could almost hear it saying the words.

Steadying herself, she gripped the door frame and peered in. It was a passenger cabin, with two padded benches on each side with movable cushions on top. Laura imagined the expedition staff riding in here and perhaps sleeping when they were stopped.

Ice crystals covered every bit of it. Beneath the bench on the right was what looked like a giant snowball, glistening in the headlights.

Laura crawled in on arms and legs that were shaking from the exertion and cold. She brushed a hand across the ball of ice, revealing yellow fabric.

A backpack.

The zippers were oversized, but still hard to grip with her shaking fingers. When she had managed it, she turned the opening to the beam of light and smiled beneath the balaclava. Inside was a small, rectangular device with the Iridium logo on it. Laura knew exactly what it was—she used the same model at Union Glacier Camp. It was an Iridium GO!, a portable Wi-Fi satellite transceiver. Using the small, flip-up antenna, the GO! device connected to Iridium's network of satellites in low Earth orbit, enabling smartphones with the Iridium GO! app to place voice calls, send text messages, and even surf the web. Next to the transceiver was an iPhone.

Laura smiled.

There was no way she could try the devices here—not without taking a glove off—and she assumed their batteries had long since died. But if she could charge them in Transport, she could make a call and get online.

Beneath the two devices was a zip-up plastic bag with a small notebook inside. There was no writing on the cover, no indication of what it was. But it might offer clues about what happened here.

Laura zipped the backpack closed. Even that effort winded her now. She had to get warm again. Get something to eat.

She lifted the bag and shook it, raining down ice into the empty cab, and stepped back to the door frame, bracing it with one hand. Transport was rotated 45 degrees, its headlamps shining directly at her. Laura squinted and held up a hand, blotting the light out. Transport reduced the brightness, and Laura slung the backpack over her shoulder, briefly teetering under the added weight before stepping out, aiming her foot for the place she had cleared, where the black rubber grooves stuck out from the snow. But in the time she had been inside, ice had begun to gather again. Her boot hit the top of the tread lug, and turned, angling down, a sharp spike of pain shooting up her leg. She tried to grab the door frame, but her hand slipped off and she was tumbling forward, out the door, backpack flying off her shoulder as she twisted, landing on her back, head slamming into the ice.

33

Laura opened her eyes. And slammed them shut. The light was so bright it sent a wave of pain deep into her eye sockets.

Her head hurt. Her back ached. She opened and closed her hand, relieved that it worked. She tried her toes next. They wiggled.

As the panic receded, her senses returned. The wind was raking over her, making a low whistling sound, the ice and snow pelting her like sand in a dust storm.

Somewhere in the distance, an alarm was blaring. She closed her eyes and the darkness swallowed her again.

*

She woke to a hand squeezing hers, hard, insistent.

Laura looked up at the figure looming over her, hazy in the glow of Transport's lamps. They wore all Epoch gear from head to toe.

"Laura," Samir called through the balaclava.

"Can you—"

"I'm fine," she tried to say, but the words were just a jumble. She swallowed and yelled. "I'm okay. I think."

"Come on."

He dug his hand under her back and took her hand and helped her to Transport.

"Wait," she said at the door, turning back. She pointed at the bundle already half covered in snow. "Get the backpack."

*

They didn't search the other PistenBully or the sled it pulled. Instead, as soon as she closed the driver door, Laura ordered Transport to drive away from the convoy, deeper into the mountains. They had stayed too long already. And they had a phone now. All they had to do was evade Epoch until help arrived.

That phone was sitting on a charging pad on Transport's dashboard, right next to the Iridium GO! satellite transceiver. As soon as they were both charged, Laura would call for help. And get some answers.

There were questions closer to her heart that only Samir could answer, and she wanted to unravel those mysteries as well.

"That was very reckless, Laura," Samir said, eying her in the driver seat. He wasn't looking so good. His skin was ashy. His hands trembled slightly. But his eyes were locked on her, as if he was fine.

He was in withdrawal. But Laura was glad he was at least feeling well enough to lecture her. She didn't have the energy to argue with him. And, for the record, she had to admit that he had a point.

"It got us a phone."

"Well, a phone isn't any good if you injure yourself and die before you can use it."

"How did you know I had fallen?"

"This Sno-Cat can be a cruel drill sergeant when it wants to be."

A smile spread across Laura's lips. "Its name is Transport."

Samir looked at her curiously, as if he wasn't sure if she was joking. "Okay," he said slowly.

Laura leaned forward and checked the two devices. Neither had charged enough to turn on. Or maybe she needed to manually power them up.

She pressed the power button on the sat transceiver. Nothing. The smartphone didn't come on either.

"Transport, is your charging pad working?"

"My internal diagnostics report nominal operation, Laura."

"They could have been damaged," Samir said. "Either by the cold or moisture."

"Maybe," Laura mumbled, turning each device over. She set them back down on the charging pad. Maybe they just needed a little more time. "I want to hear it, Samir. What happened."

"Where's that med kit?"

"Samir."

"Look, the stasis got me over the hump. And I was running on adrenaline the second I saw you lying in the snow." He held his shaking hands up. "But I'm going to be in bad shape soon."

Laura motioned to the med kit lying in the back seat next to her dripping, snow-coated suit. "There are no opioids in there, Samir. I already checked."

"What is in there?"

"Answers first."

He shook his head, staring down. "Please don't treat me like this. You don't understand."

"Help me understand." He reached toward the back seat, hand rushing to the bag, but Laura snatched it first. "Fine. But I administer the doses. And I'm sleeping with these bottles under me."

"Good. I want to be past this, Laura. You have no idea how horrible it is. Knowing you're sick and you made yourself sick. Feeling like you threw your life away because you couldn't handle what happened. Or what was going to happen."

Laura unzipped the bag and started reading the labels on the bottle again. "What happened, Samir?"

His gaze drifted to the top of the bag, guilt and shame beginning to cloud his expression.

Laura began setting the bottles on the padded console between them. Samir picked each up in turn, reading the labels. There was a corticosteroid for inflammation. A nonsteroidal anti-inflammatory. Broad-spectrum antibiotics for infection and a sampling of antivirals and antifungals. Laura thought Samir would choose the sleeping medication. Instead, he set the bottle of gabapentinoids down and pushed it forward like a stack of chips he was wagering.

"Will this do it?" Laura asked.

"Wouldn't be my first choice," Samir said. "But it will help."

"You studied this?"

"At length. Spent hours reading online, trying to make a plan to get myself out of this mess."

Laura asked him about dosing, and they made a plan: she would keep the bottle, time his doses, and monitor him. She handed him the first two pills and read the label as he swallowed them.

The drug's side effects were far from ideal, especially here in

Antarctica: dizziness, drowsiness, flu-like symptoms, lethargy, fluid retention in the limbs, involuntary eye movements, coordination problems. She'd have to keep that in mind for whatever came next.

Samir handed her the empty water bottle, and Laura placed it in a port on the dashboard that immediately began dispensing water. Luckily, Transport had a water purification system that could use rainwater, ice, or "supplied liquid". Since they were surrounded by snow, Laura hoped she wouldn't have to use "supplied liquid" from either her or Samir.

Slipping the pill bottle in her pocket, she focused on Samir. "When did it start?"

"Maybe three or four months before you... saw me."

Laura noted that he said *saw me*. Not before he framed her. Before his lie ripped her world apart.

"Why?"

Samir took another sip of water. "My uncle came to us."

"Us?"

"My mom—that's his sister—and my dad, and my sister. He said it was important. Like family meeting, future on the line." Samir shrugged. "My mom was convinced he was dying and it was about his will. She and he are close. Their parents passed away when they were young, and their grandparents raised them. They grew up depending on each other."

Transport slowed and swerved to the left. Laura glanced out the windshield, taking in the rock wall rising into the darkness.

The wind was still blowing, but it wasn't snowing.

"Was he dying?"

"In a way." Samir sipped more water. "He said everybody was going to die. Everyone on Earth. And soon."

"What?"

"My uncle owns a large pharma company. Vedixol."

"Wait. He gave a talk at Antarctica Station. A Vision of the Old World. The one about population decline."

Samir nodded. "Yeah, that's him." His gaze shifted to the dashboard compartment with the meals. "You hungry?"

"Yeah, I could eat."

They prepped the meals in silence, and when they were lying on the console, Samir continued. "My uncle told us that an event was going to happen very, very soon."

"What event?"

Samir took a bite of spaghetti and chewed slowly. "He wouldn't tell me and my sister. I was skeptical. Figured it was all some weird conspiracy theory he'd gotten sucked into. Maybe some investment scam."

"Why do you say that?"

"Because he had decided to liquidate everything he owned and buy us all places at Antarctica Station."

That put another piece into place for Laura. "So those people—the patients in stasis…"

"They were just investors. Funding sources for the project. Or government officials who could help make it happen. Family members."

"So what happened?"

"He showed my mom and dad proof of what was going to happen."

"What—"

"I'm sorry, Laura, I still don't know what it is. But I've

never seen my mom like that. She was utterly convinced. They sold everything. They were scared. We couldn't talk about anything by phone or text. Only in person. And only in interior rooms in the house—usually the master closet. It was so weird."

Samir took another bite of spaghetti. Laura thought his eyes looked sleepier now. And he was beginning to slur his words. "That convinced me."

"Is that why you started using?"

"It was just sleeping pills at first. But during the day... I was still a wreck. Couldn't stop my mind from thinking all the time." He set the fork down and exhaled. "It was just a little bit to get me through."

Samir folded the half-eaten meal up, as if the thought of what had happened had taken his appetite. Or perhaps it was the drugs. Or both.

"I thought about going to the media. Or government. Or both." He looked up at her. "But what would I say? 'The world is ending. I have no proof, but trust me. Also—I don't know how.'"

"What was the plan, Samir?"

"We—my family—had spots at A. Station. We were supposed to go there and then... I don't know, they didn't tell me the rest."

"Nothing?"

"No. They just said that what they were doing there would enable us to survive."

He turned then and settled in the chair, leaning it back, eyes closing.

Laura leaned across and squeezed his shoulder. "Hey. Come on, Samir. *What happened*?"

He snorted, seeming disgusted with himself. "You can probably figure out the rest."

"Assume I can't. Come on. You owe me this."

"And more," he whispered, voice even more sluggish now. Slowly, he opened his eyes. "It just... started to add up. Every day I saw you, I was living a lie. I knew..." He swallowed hard. "Knew you were going to die. Every patient was going to die. It was all just... so futile. That hopelessness. The guilt."

Laura tightened her grip on his shoulder.

"And you caught me." He closed his eyes. "You did the right thing."

"And what did you do, Samir?"

"Told 'em they had to take you instead of me. That I... that I wasn't going."

Laura nodded slowly. "And they told you they would only take me if you still went."

"Yep," he whispered.

"You saved me, Samir. Twice."

He didn't respond. He was passed out, leaving Laura to the hum of the transport and the howl of the wind and the ice and mountains.

34

Samir slept, and Laura turned her attention to the other mystery inside the cabin: the backpack and the notebook inside.

But first, she finally succumbed to the need to empty her bladder. While awkwardly using a makeshift toilet in the back seat, she reasoned that stasis—either the drugs or the process—must have some draining process for the bladder or inhibitory effect. Or both.

Now feeling relieved, she settled back in her seat, buckled up, and put the backpack in her lap.

It was filled with common expedition gear, including a rechargeable flashlight (with a dead battery), reusable heat packs, and night-vision goggles. She set the goggles aside. They might come in handy.

Nothing else was of much interest, except the notebook.

Laura opened it, expecting to see an expedition log. Instead, it was a series of handwritten letters.

The pages reminded Laura of the letter her father had written her. She never got the chance to read it. She wondered where it was now. Was it still in Antarctica Station? Maybe in a box with her other personal belongings? When this was all over, that would be her first order of business: finding the letter and reading her father's final words to her.

The letters in this notebook were addressed to someone named Sarah and signed by Rikard, who Laura assumed was the backpack's owner. From the context, apparently Rikard had been writing the letters and taking pictures of them and texting them or emailing them, perhaps to make the correspondence seem more personal or intimate or interesting to his remote pen pal.

From the letters, Laura was able to glean the expedition's purpose: they were planting reflective sensors along the South Pole Traverse that satellites used to measure ice levels.

The rest of the letters were filled with personal details and recollections and the occasional complaint of interpersonal conflict among the expedition crew, which Laura supposed was to be expected from people forced to be in close proximity in extreme conditions.

She felt slightly guilty reading the personal letters. It was an invasion of privacy, but she reminded herself that she was in a life-or-death situation and desperately needed to know what was going on.

Her only clues came from the last letter.

Dear Sarah,

Obviously, I won't be able to send this one. But I figured, well, may as well write it in case someone finds it (bit grim, that, but accurate).

Well, the obvious: the equipment is out. Hence no email. PistenBullys are finished too. Heinrich thinks the event might be localized. I can't tell if he's being optimistic or believes it. But, as we've no choice, everyone seems to be going along and putting on a brave face. Ingrid has been climbing the walls debating what to do about it all. We've three options as I see it: stay and wait for rescue. Hike to South Pole (certain death that one). Or double back on foot and head for the crew maintaining the traverse (we passed them two days ago, so we know they're behind us).

The trouble is, assuming Heinrich is right, and it's just us affected, then the traverse crew may not even know what's happened. For all we know, they may have doubled back, which means we're venturing out to chase them, and on foot, we'll never catch them. If the wind in these mountains isn't enough to freeze the blood in my veins solid, the thought of that is.

Well, thought I couldn't get more grim than the opening, but I've certainly outdone myself on that last one. I wanted to end with some levity, but I can't manage it, my love. They're calling me, so gotta go. I hope I'll see you soon. I would've brought the letter along to send, but every kilo counts, and if we make it through, I'll send you a happier one (and be thankful you never read this one).

With love, always,
Rikard

Laura's eyes flushed with tears. One dropped onto the page, spreading out into the ink.

The letter left a lot of questions. But it gave a few answers too.

The first—and most devastating—was that the phone and satellite transceiver were ruined. Hence why they had been left.

Laura took the devices from the sunken charging pad on the dashboard and placed them in the floorboard of the back seat.

So much for that.

The second thought that occurred to her was that she and Samir were now traveling the same route Rikard and his expedition had.

*

The wind blew louder and harder as the tracked vehicle crept through the mountains, and with nothing else to do, Laura asked Transport why the wind blew so hard here.

"We're experiencing katabatic winds, Laura."

"Can you tell me what that means?" She cut her eyes at the still-sleeping Samir. "Actually, don't tell me. Show me on the screen. As briefly as possible."

The large flat panel in the dashboard changed to a split display. At the bottom were three even squares with a map, weather conditions, and vehicle operating information (including speed, bearing, and power levels). Above was a detailed article Laura could scroll and click.

Antarctica is the windiest place on Earth. The strong winds are driven by two factors: extreme cold temperatures and elevation drops.

Katabatic winds occur when gravity pulls high-density air down a slope to a lower elevation. This force creates strong winds that are seen most notably along Antarctica's coasts.

Antarctica has several geographic features that make katabatic winds more common and stronger. First the average elevation in Antarctica is over 8,000 feet, making it the highest continent on Earth. That cools the air naturally, but the thick ice sheet that covers the continent cools the air even more (in some places, the ice rises four point eight kilometers—or almost three miles—above the land). In fact, the glaciers have such an intense cooling effect on the air above it, the temperature actually increases as you rise above the ground (this is the opposite of most places on Earth, where temperatures decrease as you move away from the ground). This phenomenon—in which air near the ground is colder than the air above it—is called a temperature inversion—and it further contributes to katabatic wind occurrence and speed.

In terms of actual wind speeds, Cape Denison, which is the windiest spot in Antarctica as well as on Earth, experiences average wind speeds of around 45 miles per hour. A 1911 expedition to the cape reported a 168-mile-per-hour katabatic wind gust, though the fastest modern reading occurred in 1995 with a 127-mile-per-hour wind.

By contrast, wind at the South Pole, which lies on the more level, elevated Antarctic Plateau, is more constant, with few calms or gales, averaging about 12 miles per hour from a direction of longitude 20 degrees East.

Laura closed the information file. The bottom line was that the wind in the mountains was likely to get worse as they crossed the peaks and began their descent to West Antarctica and the Ross Ice Shelf, which was actually situated over water and at a significantly lower elevation than East Antarctica or the TAM.

She did see one bright spot. The wind—assuming it was

carrying snow—might help hide them from any satellite watching from above, a sort of static blanket of white.

*

Laura used the time it took to travel across the Transantarctic Mountains to once again ponder where to go in West Antarctica.

McMurdo, she was now completely convinced, was out.

In the notebook she had found at the convoy, she turned the page and began writing, as Rikard had.

What is the event?

Why did Epoch go to Antarctica to escape the event—given that it obviously happened here too?

The event didn't kill people.

But it did affect machines.

Laura sat back and looked at the facts. Her next thought was that the event—whatever it was—hadn't affected Epoch's equipment. Why? How had they avoided it? Perhaps it was localized, as one of the expedition's team members had theorized. And Epoch had been out of the path of destruction?

Antarctica Station was sited at the magnetic South Pole. Was that part of the answer?

It was all over Laura's head. And probably moot. She just needed to get off of this continent and back to civilization.

And that became her focus.

Slowly, as the mountains went by and the wind picked up, a plan started to form in her mind. It was a hazy thing, one with pieces flying everywhere.

It was a bit like the scene outside the windows, which increasingly looked like a blizzard taking shape.

As it gathered strength, Transport slowed down, trying to compensate for the ever-decreasing visibility. It asked to increase the headlamp intensity twice and Laura agreed, finally telling it to use its own discretion, balancing speed, safety and visibility. After that, the lights were brighter, and the tracks moved faster. And around the snow vehicle, the walls of white kept closing in.

"Transport," Laura said quietly, careful not to wake Samir. "Are we in a blizzard?"

"Current weather conditions do not quite meet the US National Weather Service's criteria for a blizzard."

"Why?"

"For a snowstorm to be categorized as a blizzard, it must have sustained winds or frequent gusts of 35 miles per hour, visibility of one-quarter of a mile or less, and last for three hours or more. However, I believe we are traveling through a strengthening weather pattern that, assuming the wind continues to increase in velocity, will soon be a ground blizzard or dry blizzard."

"What does that mean?"

"It means that—as far as I can see, Laura—there is little or no new precipitation falling. The blowing wind is lifting and carrying loose ice and snow from the ground."

"Great," Laura muttered.

*

An hour later, Laura was tapping the screens, doing some route calculations, when Transport's forward movement ceased and its tracks rolled to a stop.

"Laura," the vehicle announced. "There's something ahead."

35

In the passenger seat, Samir groaned and reached down and released the seat belt.

"Are we there yet?" he muttered.

"We're somewhere," Laura said, squinting to see through the blowing sheets of snow outside. "What is this, Transport?"

"I believe it is either another convoy—larger than the last—or a mobile research station."

Through the swirling snow, Laura saw why Transport had said mobile research station instead of camp. There were buildings out there—two that she could see. And vehicles different than transport or the PistenBullys they had seen at the last convoy.

"Transport, can you drive around this... settlement and take high-resolution videos and images and show them on the screen?"

"Yes, Laura. That is an excellent idea."

Laura smiled. The thought had occurred to her somewhere during their drive. Falling and almost breaking your back on the ice—and time on the road—apparently had a way of giving Laura good ideas.

Transport crept along and the images began to populate

the screen in the dashboard, appearing like thumbnails in a camera roll. Beneath the squares, a map began to outline vehicles and buildings and long objects Laura couldn't identify.

"Laura," Samir said, his voice tinged with urgency. "I'm not doing so hot."

She glanced over at him, noting his clammy skin, restlessness, and the lines of tension on his forehead. "You want more of the gabapentinoid?"

He snorted. "I'll try anything at this point." And in a tone more serious, he added, "But I'm going to have to have some of the real stuff at some point really, really soon or I think… it's going to be bad."

"We don't have any, Samir."

"I'm just telling you what I know."

Laura nodded slowly. "Look, we might have to go out there."

"Why?"

"To search." Laura held up a finger. "They might even have meds."

Samir's gaze shifted to the screen, where more images were popping up by the second. "Great. Sign me up."

For a few moments, they let the images come in. Finally, Samir said, "I'll take that gaba in the meantime."

Subconsciously, Laura's hand moved to the bottle in her pocket. She was glad she kept it on her. "Bad idea." She motioned to the wind blowing the snow outside. "You've gotta be at your best, Samir."

He let out a humorless, sad laugh. "My best is not what it used to be, Laura. I'm a drag on you out here. You should've left me—"

"Nope. I don't think so. Don't go there, Samir. We're

going to deal with this. Together. When I fell back at that other convoy, you came and got me."

He shook his head. "I was better then. I'm getting worse, Laura. And I'm going to get a lot worse." He held his shaking hands up. "I'm no good out there."

"You're what I've got, Samir."

"Sucks for you."

"*No*, it doesn't." She reached up and grabbed his shaking hands and lowered them to the console and held them there. "Get in the game, Samir. We're going to figure this out, and we're going to get off this ice cube and contact the government and everything is going to be all right."

Samir tried to pull his hands away, but Laura pressed down, trapping him.

"Okay?"

He shrugged. "If you say so."

"I say so."

"Laura," Transport said. "I've finished the survey of the site."

"Conclusions?"

"I no longer believe this is a mobile research station."

"What is it?"

"I believe that it is another convoy."

"Explain."

"It is highly likely that this is the equipment that maintained the South Pole Traverse."

"Transport," Samir said. "Can you enhance the images?"

"In what way, passenger?"

"His name is Samir," Laura said.

"Samir," Transport said, "how would you like me to enhance the images?"

Samir clicked a photo on the screen. It showed a piece of equipment that looked like a farm tractor. It was mostly obscured by snow. "Can you take the images and video you collected and piece them together and apply a filter to give us a clear view of what's out there—without the interference of the snow?"

"I can try."

Laura stared at Samir meaningfully, silently trying to say: *You see there, you can help. In here and out there.*

On the screen, the images updated. They were clearer, as if they had been taken in broad daylight, without a blizzard raging.

"I wouldn't have thought of that," Laura said quietly.

Samir tapped another image. "Eh. I've always been a computer geek."

She smiled.

Part of his recovery was certainly physical. But a large part was psychological. Recovering his self-worth. Feeling like he was contributing. Laura knew Samir well enough to know what he was feeling right now—that he was helping and that he mattered. She imagined that it was as powerful as any opioid.

Samir scrolled through the images, and in those brief flashes, Laura glimpsed the convoy. The vehicles were different from Transport or the PistenBullys at the last convoy, which were wide and blocky, sitting low to the ground.

These machines were more like farming tractors, with large rear wheels and smaller front ones. Tracks stretched between the two wheels, making a triangle, and the body was painted yellow, with three letters CAT. Caterpillar.

Laura knew the brand. It was common in Ohio, where she had grown up, and in North Carolina, where she'd gone to school. And, apparently, in Antarctica.

In the original pictures (which were superimposed in ghostly fashion on the screen) these ice tractors had rear arms that descended into the ice. In the Transport-enhanced layer, there were long black objects behind the ice tractors. Laura's best guess was that they were some sort of weighted, elongated buoys that were used to flatten and pack the ice along the road. These tractors were connected to similar machines directly in front of them, which had wide blades like a bulldozer, no doubt for clearing ice along the path.

Samir quickly focused on the most interesting part of the convoy—perhaps to him, and certainly to Laura: several rectangular structures that looked like buildings. They stood slightly above the snow. They were long and narrow and reminded Laura of temporary onsite trailers placed at a construction site. Or some of the trailers at her high school where she'd attended classes because the building wasn't big enough.

There were two of those structures. They had corrugated walls made of red metal and windows and, buried in the snow, staircases that led up to them. There was a smaller white structure with no windows that Laura assumed was a large generator.

At the back of the convoy was a shipping container with round metal drums attached to the side. It was likely the liquid fuel was inside, which didn't help them much.

"We should go for the living quarters," Samir said.

"I agree."

"But—" Samir glanced over at her. "I... gotta go."

Laura furrowed her eyebrows. Then realized what he was saying.

He elaborated: "The opioids make it hard. But they're working their way out of my system."

As the wind gathered strength and the snow pelted the transport, Laura helped Samir into the back seat and tried to give him all the privacy she could (while not listening). In this weather, she couldn't exactly step outside and take a stroll while nature called.

When Samir was done, they donned their cold weather gear and set out for the closest of the two trailers.

The walk wasn't far, but still, Laura held on to Samir's hand as he trudged through the snow behind her, the wind trying to bowl them over.

Inside, it was like an RV. Long and narrow, with all the things Laura expected to see. At one end, a bathroom and shower. A galley kitchen. A seating area where the bump out was. At the other end, there were bunks mounted on both sides of the hall and a larger room with even more bunks.

It was all covered in ice. And ruined. Utterly ruined, as if time and cold had disintegrated it all.

Samir used his gloved hands to rip open the cabinets in the bathroom, rotating the bottles and reading the labels, then moved to the kitchen and opened those cabinet doors.

Even through the gear and balaclava, Laura's words came out in puffs of steam. "Anything?"

"Not what I need," he replied, slamming the cabinet door.

"Let's warm up before we go to the next one," she said.

And they did, lying in the seats inside the transport, suits unzipped, letting the vehicle's heat soak into them like they were vacationers on a sunny beach.

Laura scanned the display. Transport's battery reserves were down to 37 percent. Opening the doors and reheating the interior was adding to the drain on the batteries.

"Transport," she said slowly. "I think I know the answer to this, but I have to ask: what is your current range?"

"My current range is hard to estimate, Laura."

"Why?"

"It depends on weather conditions. Specifically wind resistance. In addition, several other factors materially impact my range, including the speed requested, topography along the route, and power consumption required, including headlamps and cabin heating."

Those words made her decision.

Her plan was a long shot, but Laura thought it was probably their only shot. And they needed to take it soon. In more than one way, time was running out.

Beside her, Samir had closed his eyes. His breathing had slowed. The search of the first mobile dormitory—as Laura had come to think of it—had taken it out of him.

She reached over and squeezed his shoulder. Lazily, he opened his eyes. "Was I sleeping on the job, ma'am?"

"You can rest soon. I promise."

She told him her plan, and by the time she was finished, his eyes were wide and he was fully awake.

"I don't like this," were his first words.

"I'm open to ideas."

"I don't have any." Samir let his head fall back into the seat. "This is going to suck."

"Yep."

He reached over and gripped her hand. "But I'm with you. If you think it will work."

"I think it's our best shot."

They suited up again and searched the second dormitory. It was much like the first, except in the bathroom cabinet, Samir drew out a bottle and studied it for a long moment, staring at the label in the glow of the flashlight.

Laura was standing behind him, in the hall, and for a moment, she wondered if he would stuff it in his own pocket, hiding the drug from her.

Instead, he yelled without turning, "Laura! Found something."

He twisted around, seeming surprised to find her standing there. He tossed her the bottle and she read the label. She couldn't take the cap off with her gloved hand. So she raised it to her ear and shook it. The wind was howling outside, but through the din, she could still hear the pills rattling.

"I need one," he said.

"After we finish, Samir. Come on."

They once again retreated to the transport and warmed themselves.

Samir was doing even worse now. Shaking. Sweating. Less focused. "I should stay," he mumbled. "Need to sleep."

"You're not staying."

"I'm no use—"

"I need you, Samir."

The words seemed to bring him around.

"Okay," he breathed out.

Laura took his hand. "Listen to me, okay?"

He nodded.

"We stay together. From here out. Okay?"

"Okay."

"Like we should have in Durham."

He chuckled. "Couldn't have then."

"You could've told me."

"Maybe," he whispered. "But what do we do about it? Now?"

"Now we turn it around."

"I'll try. I really will, Laura."

With that, they put the rest of their suits back on and exited the Epoch transport once more. This time, they walked to the back of the vehicle, and Laura pressed the button to open the cargo area. The door lowered like the tailgate of a truck and Laura watched as the wind-blown snow pelted her suit, her heart beating fast now, knowing what she saw might determine their fate.

In the dark recess, a light snapped on, illuminating two black bundles.

Laura smiled. They had finally caught a break.

She unzipped the closest canvas bag, revealing a round metal tube that was the tower of a roof mountable wind turbine.

*

Laura and Samir took the wind turbines out and used the ladder at the back of the transport to crawl up on the roof, where they laid the pieces out. There weren't many, but they were heavy and hard to carry in the wind.

Next, they got back inside and warmed themselves. It was too cold to be outside for any extended period of time. In fact, it was too cold to be outside for a brief period of time. But the heating elements in the suits helped.

On the screen, Laura read the instructions on assembling the turbine's blades, hub, and tower.

After assembling and connecting the first turbine, they retreated inside, and repeated the procedure for the second one. The blades were spinning wildly as Laura receded down the ladder.

On the screen inside, Laura watched the power reserves start to climb for the first time.

Though Transport had heard Samir and her discussing the plan earlier, Laura went over it again with the vehicle in detail.

By this point, Samir was hanging on by a thread. He was dead tired, nearly listless.

Laura felt for him. But she couldn't do anything for him. At least, not yet.

In mounting the turbines, they had committed to their path. They had crossed the Rubicon. The next twenty-four hours were critical.

Using one of the bags that had held the turbine, Laura gathered their supplies: extra suits, meals, meds, and tools.

Finally, Laura opened the medicine bottle with the opioids and gave Samir a pill. He exhaled heavily as he eyed it. Then washed it down.

"Transport, we're going to go," Laura said as she began putting her extra layers on.

"I understand, Laura. However, can I make a suggestion?"

"You can."

"Perhaps I should wait an hour after you go in. If you don't come out—"

"We either make it or we don't," Laura said. "And if

you're waiting outside, the Epoch personnel will know exactly where we are."

A pause, and then Transport said, "I understand, Laura."

She looked over at Samir. "Ready?"

"Oh, definitely not." His eyebrows lifted. "But sure. Let's go."

Laura pulled her goggles down and opened her door and stepped out onto the tracks, the wind pulling at her and the bag hanging from her shoulder.

Inside the dormitory, she watched out the window as Transport's lights snapped off. Then she heard its tracks crunching in the ice and snow as it pulled away and drove past the abandoned convoy, into the mountains.

Laura and Samir made their nest under a bunk. They lined the floor and walls with sleeping bags from the other bunks, then piled their supplies above where their heads would rest. Laura tucked thick blankets under the mattress above and draped them down like several layers of thick curtains. She kept it pulled back for now as she waited.

It was oppressively cold, but Laura breathed a sigh of relief when the heat from the suits and their bodies began to accumulate in the small, insulated space. They wouldn't exactly be comfortable here. But she was pretty certain they wouldn't freeze to death.

Soon, Samir began to snore softly. Laura lay awake. She was exhausted. But she was also too scared to sleep. Because if she was right, Epoch would be here soon.

36

The wind howled and the ice pelted the metal walls of the trailer, and beneath the bunk, Laura waited and watched.

She didn't know how much time had passed when the shaft of light crossed the window of the common room but the sight of it brought her fully awake.

Like the beam of a lighthouse, it shone brightly then receded, perhaps as the result of the transport turning or its lights being turned down.

Laura was lying on her side, Samir on his back, snoring more loudly now. She didn't know if they could hear him down here over the roar of the wind, but she wasn't going to take that chance.

She rotated onto her back and shook him. "Samir," she whispered. "Wake up. They're here."

He stirred and mumbled. He was drenched in sweat. On her second attempt, she managed to wake him and tell him their pursuers had arrived.

"Okay," was all he said, because for this part of their plan, there wasn't much they could do except pull the blanket down over the bottom of the bunk and wait.

And that's what they did, every second feeling like an eternity.

In the dark, Laura heard the tracks of the transport creeping across the ice, doors slamming shut, all barely audible over the howling wind.

Finally, the outer door to this mobile dormitory creaked open, and the wind barreled through like a monster raging, demanding to be let in.

The door slammed shut, muting the rush of wind.

Boots echoed through the icy tomb. It was one person, Laura thought, and they had left the common room, making for the shower and bathroom.

Laura was almost certain her heart was beating loud enough for the person searching the trailer to hear. And possibly Samir's breathing, which was not much quieter than his snoring. She wanted to turn back over and hiss, "Quiet!"

But she didn't. And she knew he was doing the best he could. It was just nerves.

These seconds would determine their fate. And the worst part was that all she could do was lie there and wait and hope—

The boots turned back, clomping through the common room. They stopped in the hall, grinding the ice and dust under their boots.

Were they searching the bunks?

Laura heard something rustling. A click. A flashlight being turned up?

The boot steps advanced, entering the larger bunk room, stopping a few feet away. The faint glow of the flashlight peaked around the edges of the thick blankets.

Laura began to tremble.

In her mind's eye, she imagined a gloved hand gripping the blankets and ripping them away and reaching in and pulling her out and dragging her across the ice-covered floor.

A squawk sounded from a radio, and a woman's voice said, "Joe, do you have them?"

It was Imara, the security staffer who had interrogated Laura when she had arrived at Antarctica Station.

"No. But they were here. There are several sets of boot tracks."

"Did they take anything?"

"Don't know. But I think they were looking for meds. Cabinets are open. Makes sense. If the MedRe assessment is right, Dewan is likely in severe withdrawal."

"What do you want to do here?"

"We should have tasked the sat to observe this convoy."

"Well, it's here now, and we don't have a time machine, so we can't really act on that, Joe."

"Somebody needs a snack and a nap."

"No," Imara said, "I need an answer. We're wasting time."

"Has the sat still not found the transport's lights?"

"No. They're running dark."

"Then they have to be going incredibly slow in this low visibility. And the tracks are fairly fresh—they haven't been blown away or filled in."

"Are you working up to a point?"

"My point," Joe said, boots moving out of the bunk room, "is that they have to be nearby."

"The tracks lead off the traverse, into the mountains. It could be some kind of trap."

Joe laughed. "Trap us with what? A snowball fight?"

"Yeah, that's funny. I was thinking an avalanche or thinly covered crevasse or something real."

"Again, they're doctors, not spec ops characters from a *Mission Impossible* movie. They're probably tired and scared and—"

"I told your father you were too close to her. You shouldn't be out here."

"Now who's wasting time?"

"What do you want to do, Joe?"

"Look, they stopped here, searched the place for meds and who knows what, then drove into the mountains with their lights off to throw us off, hoping we'd go looking for them. My guess is they cut back onto the traverse and are still heading to McMurdo—it's really the only place that makes any sense for their range. They have to know that too."

"So?"

"So," Joe said, walking back into the common room, "we keep going, and we'll probably catch them in the next twelve hours, depending on how much time they wasted with their off-road mountain diversion. Either way, we drive the traverse until we run them down. And in case we don't, we keep the sat moving along the traverse until it finds them. The weather and visibility will be a lot better on the ice shelf. Even if they manage to outrun us—which I *highly doubt*—the team will be at McMurdo in time, and they can handle them."

With that, the outer door opened, and the wind barreled in, bringing a gust of cold air before it slammed shut.

Still, Laura didn't dare pull the blanket back. Joe could be standing in the common room, radio turned off, waiting.

It wasn't until she heard the transports crunching away that she began breathing normally.

"Laura," Samir whispered.

"Shhh. Let's wait."

When the only sound had been the howl of the wind for several minutes, she turned over onto her back, lying shoulder to shoulder with him. In the darkness, she couldn't see his face, but instinctively, she felt like he was smiling. She certainly was.

"It worked," he said quietly.

Laura's smile widened.

37

Laura and Samir emerged from beneath the bunk by degrees.

First, she pulled the blanket back and peered out into the darkness. She saw no headlights, only darkness.

Next, she listened and tried to spot any other sound. A boot crunching in the ice. Tracks rolling by. There was only the wind howling and the faint scratching of ice flying into the dormitory's metal walls.

Being hunted across this frozen continent had made her paranoid, and that paranoia fired possibilities through her mind. What if Epoch had left one of their transports with its lights off, sitting right outside the convoy, waiting for any sign of them?

They also could have left a team in the other trailer, hiding like she and Samir were, conducting a sort of polar stakeout.

For those reasons, they stayed under the bunk with the blanket covering them and waited.

Soon, Samir began to snore again.

Laura felt sleep tugging at her too. The adrenaline rush that had filled her when Joe had searched the dormitory was gone now, and she was crashing hard. Their nest under the bunkbed wasn't the Ritz, but for the first time since she had left Antarctica Station, she was lying flat on her back, and there was no sense of motion, no rocking or bouncing. And here, in this strange place, it was relative luxury.

*

Laura woke to a hand gripping her, tugging at her. Consciousness came in a snap, a light being flicked on, and she writhed like a fish on a line.

"Hey, hey," Samir said softly. "You okay?"

Laura's chest was heaving. It was so dark she wasn't even sure her eyes were open.

"Are they here?" Laura asked quietly. "Did they find us?"

"No," Samir whispered back.

"What—"

"I'm sorry, Laura," he said into her ear.

"For what?"

"I need... some medicine."

Her eyes were adjusting now, but still, the darkness was so complete she could barely see a thing.

She reached up and grabbed the night-vision goggles and pulled them on. The darkness changed to a hazy green glow. She turned toward Samir.

"Hellllo, Cyclops," he said, dragging the first word out.

"Very funny."

Laura pulled the curtain back and shimmied out from under the bunk, her body sweeping ice and dust as she went.

Samir followed and rose and carefully closed the door to the bunk room, conscious not to make any sound. His eyes seemed to be adjusted to the dark. Laura wondered how long he had lain awake before rousing her.

When her eyes had adjusted, she pulled the NVGs off, and they sat on the floor with their legs crossed, blankets draped around them. The suits were still warming them, but they would need to be recharged by Transport after this. Laura hoped their batteries wouldn't give out. If the heating elements stopped, there was no doubt in Laura's mind that they would perish. For that reason, they had brought the other four suits from the transport, which were neatly stuffed under the bunk.

"Let's eat," Laura said, reaching over to grab two of the MREs they had also stored under their bunk.

Across from her, Samir fidgeted. He was deep in the throes of withdrawal. Laura wondered if giving him the opioids was best for his condition. Or if it was making his situation worse. She didn't have enough experience with this sort of thing.

She also didn't know what else to do. She set the MRE down, took the bottle out, and measured a dose.

Samir tossed the pill and a half in his mouth and washed it down with water. He seemed to settle then, and they ate in silence for a while.

"You did it, Laura," he finally said.

She chewed a bite of chili and macaroni. The food was already getting cold. Antarctica—even indoors—was no place for a picnic in winter. The heating element at the bottom of the carton was no match for this place.

With the fork, she pushed the food around, trying to dig for warmer morsels. "We're not home yet."

"You're too modest, you know that?"

Laura shrugged. "Insert modest reply here. I'm too tired to dig for it while digging for non-frozen food."

Samir's head fell back as he laughed. Pointing his fork at her, he said, "You're funny, too. You don't typically go for it, but you have it in you. If you would just relax."

"I'll relax when some global conspiracy group stops trying to kill us." Laura uncovered some pasta and took the bite quickly, chewed, and when Samir said nothing, added, "Well, kill *me*. Not you."

The words wiped the smile from his face. "Yeah, I think that's probably the case," he said. "*If* they catch us. And they won't."

After a few more bites, Laura tossed her fork in the tray. She was basically eating frozen macaroni at this point.

Steam issued forth from Samir as he spoke. "Can I tell you something?"

"Sure."

"The thing that hurt me the most... was *how* I hurt you. It was the fact that you trusted me—and that's what I exploited. Because in doing what I did, I destroyed one of the things I treasured most: our friendship."

Laura exhaled and pulled the blanket tighter around her.

"I don't expect you to ever trust me again," Samir said. "Or want to be friends if we get out of here."

"When," Laura said. "*When* we get out of here. Let's be positive, okay?"

He smiled. "Sure."

"We're going to be friends," Laura said quietly. "But it will never be like it was before."

He nodded. "That's fair."

The expression that crossed his face was like a glacier cracking: deep and irreversible.

Her words had hurt him. Maybe that had been her point. Because she had been hurt. By him.

But in that moment, she knew that revenge wouldn't heal her broken heart. And revenge on him—a person she had once called a friend—wasn't what she needed.

For Laura, those thoughts fought a battle in her mind as a long pause stretched out. In the silence, the dark room felt colder than the Antarctic Plateau in winter or the katabatic winds blowing down from a glacier.

Samir set his fork in his own tray. His eyelids were heavy now.

"I have an idea," Laura said.

"About what?"

"About us."

Samir nodded but said nothing.

"What if we start over? What if we—right here, right now—start a new friendship? We forget about the past."

He swallowed. "I like it. But I'll never forgive myself."

"I know why you did it. You had your reasons."

"It hurt you."

"Life is hurt. If we don't have people in our lives, it makes it harder. I want you in my life. I need my friend. Now more than ever."

"I'm here, Laura. I'll be the best friend I can be to you. I'll truly try my best. But I'm not at my best."

He smiled a sad, almost apologetic smile.

"All I want is you—as a friend."

"Same."

"So, are we doing this? Starting over?"

"Yes."

He tugged his glove off, exposing his hand to the frigid air. Laura did the same.

They shook, both of their hands fighting the cold closing in, trapping the warmth between them.

To Laura, it was the warmest thing she had encountered since waking up on this continent: forgiveness. Acceptance. A sort of Antarctic treaty that she needed.

The two new-again friends cleaned up the meals and scooted back under the bunk.

*

The food and cold and fatigue brought sleep, and once again, Laura was woken by Samir's hands on her.

"Laura. Laura—"

"I'm awake," she hissed.

"There's someone out there."

38

In the darkness, under the bunk, Laura's eyes adjusted. At the edge of the blanket, she saw a soft glow of light. Then it went out, like a strobe flashing.

"Laura," Samir whispered.

"I see it," she said quickly.

She pulled the blanket aside and scooted out.

If she was right, they were saved.

She rushed to the door of the bunk room and pulled it open. Ice crystals fell to the floor and even more crunched under her boots as she walked through the hall, passing the empty, frozen bunks on each side. In the common room, the folding table sat covered in ice. The chairs around it were empty. Through the ice-covered window, the white glow of a light flashed again and went away.

Samir was behind her, moving slowly.

"I'll go," he said. "It'll be safer. If it's them."

"No, if they get you, they'll come in here for me."

"We'll go together," he said.

Laura opened the door and stepped out onto the steel landing, Samir close behind her, the wind and snow raking over them.

Not far away, ice crunched, and Laura held her breath as she listened to the rubber tracks moving toward them. In the darkness and blowing snow, she still couldn't see the vehicle.

Samir wrapped an arm around Laura and pulled her into him.

If this was their end, then it was, Laura thought, a fitting finish to their saga. A friendship. A betrayal. And him saving her. Twice, as she now knew. And if she was right, it was her saving him now. For a second time.

As the vehicle approached, Laura confirmed that it was an Epoch transport. It stopped directly in front of the building's metal staircase. No one got out. Its forward lamps didn't come on.

Instead, the dome light slowly illuminated, revealing an empty interior, like a lantern above the tracks. There were two wind turbines mounted on the roof of the transport. Turbines Laura and Samir had mounted. The sight of them turning in the wind told Laura exactly who this vehicle belonged to.

Transport had completed the mission she had given it, venturing into the mountains, off the South Pole Traverse, where it had parked and let the wind turbines capture energy and refill its batteries.

Laura stepped onto the metal rung, gripping the handrail, and kept going until her boots were crunching into the ice and she and Samir were at the outer edge of the vehicle.

"Let's get warm first," he said, reaching for the door handle.

"No. We need to hurry. Let's take one of the turbines off first."

And they did. Removing the turbine proved a little harder than mounting it, but they managed to disconnect it and stow it in the cargo area.

Inside the transport, Laura stretched out in the seat and glanced at the screen. The power level read 99 percent.

"Laura?" Transport said.

"Yes?"

"I suggest we move away from here."

"Even with the turbine?"

"It won't slow me too much. I have a map of the area. I can proceed safely without my exterior lights. This is not a safe place."

"Go ahead."

*

When the transport stopped, Laura and Samir removed the other wind turbine and stowed it.

The wind and the gloves and layers made it tough—and it was slow going and she was sweating and gasping for air by the time she closed the cargo compartment.

Laura didn't know if it was the exertion or the sleep or simply the passage of time compiling facts in her mind, but standing in the wind in the foothills of the mountain, she realized a flaw in her plan.

"Laura," Transport said. "What is our destination?"

She hadn't programmed anything in, reasoning that the vehicle might be captured and its data downloaded. And Laura still wasn't sure about their exact destination. She was sure that they couldn't go to McMurdo. And that they needed to be moving in the other direction.

In that direction was Union Glacier Camp.

The camp was seasonal. And would be deserted and broken-down in winter. Laura wasn't sure if there would even be anything there.

But it was in the right direction, and right now, that was good enough while she figured out exactly what to do.

"Union Glacier Camp," she said, sounding more confident than she felt.

The tracks dug into the ice, and they moved through the darkness, down the mountain, toward a destination Laura knew was deserted.

On the screen, she pulled up the map of stations in Antarctica. From that action or the look on her face, Samir must have sensed something was wrong.

"I'm assuming we have a problem," Samir said.

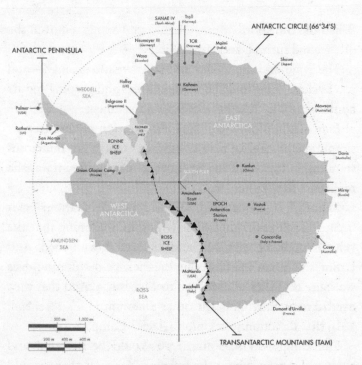

EPOCH
SCIENCES

"Just thinking about our route."

"Union Glacier Camp should have a runway," he said. "That's how you got here."

"In summer."

"Oh," Samir said.

"Yeah. We need a station that operates in winter."

Laura was reaching up to tap the screen when Samir caught her hand.

"Hey."

"What?"

"Take a break."

Laura snorted. "Sure. We don't know where we're going. Let's relax."

"We have time, and it could help."

"Help how?"

"Laura, I love you like a sister. You're so driven, and its admirable. But there's a dark side to that as well. You're always so… always on. I think it hurts you sometimes."

"Concern noted. I shall seek therapy back in civilization."

"In the meantime," Samir said, "can you just take a break? For me?"

She settled back in the chair. "I'm only considering it because I'm tired."

"Of course."

For a while, they both leaned back in their seats, eyes closed. For Laura, sleep wouldn't come. Across the way, Samir was staring at her, sweat gathering on his forehead. He needed another pill.

Laura got the bottle out and gave him a dose that was reduced from his last.

"Thanks," he whispered.

"How are you feeling overall?"

"Overall, terrible. But grateful to be alive. And to have you here to look out for me." He swallowed. "I probably would have taken half that bottle by now."

Laura wasn't sure what to say. After a long pause, Samir said, "What do you think it is? The event?"

"I've thought about it a lot. I still don't have a theory."

"Could be some computer virus."

"Why do you think that?"

"It knocked out the machines in those convoys. Maybe it's a software virus that attacks embedded systems. Sort of like a digital nuclear bomb."

"Or a real nuclear bomb," Laura said. "Thousands of them. Global nuclear war. Maybe that's what your uncle knew was going to happen. Maybe someone nuked McMurdo, and the EMP wave carried this far. Is that even possible?"

"I don't know," Samir said. "But nuclear war would be a good reason to be in Antarctica. It wouldn't be high on anyone's target list. And we've seen no sign of a nuclear attack." After a pause, Samir said, "Could be something more basic."

"Such as?"

"An outbreak."

"That doesn't work for the equipment failure though."

"It might." Samir's eyelids were closing now. The drug was taking effect. Eyes closed, he continued. "What if there was a new outbreak—a virus as contagious as COVID but as deadly as Ebola Zaire? Let's say it was wiping out everyone, and their only option…" He yawned, bringing a hand to his mouth. "…was to stop all transportation."

"Interesting," Laura whispered.

"That's the thing," Samir said. "People assume the next crisis is going to be like the last. But what if it's completely different? What if the real crisis is an outbreak that sparks a global financial crisis and then a lockdown facilitated by a software attack on all embedded systems to stop human transportation worldwide? All vehicles are smart at this point. It makes sense. No one moves. And neither would the virus. Lockdown via remote software update. And then when the outbreak is over, we rebuild."

"It's possible," Laura said.

Samir rolled over. "I need to rest."

Laura let him. She needed to think—about where they were going to go. And what had happened to this world.

*

When the transport's power reserves dipped to 20 percent, they stopped and remounted the turbines and opened two MREs and ate.

Upon opening the storage bin, Laura had eyed the dwindling stack—eight left (now six). Food would become a problem soon.

But as to the most pressing issue—where to go—she had developed an idea.

After the meal, Samir sat back in the seat and seemed to deflate.

"What is it?" Laura asked.

"Just sort of struggling right now."

She noticed that his hand was shaking, and he slipped it into his pocket.

"You want to talk about it?"

He shook his head. "No, in fact, I'm trying as hard as I can not to say every thought that pops into my head. It's a mess in there right now." He attempted a smile and some levity, but it didn't reach his eyes.

Laura measured out another dose from the pill bottle, and Samir swallowed it down. She knew that withdrawal often came with severe mental effects (in addition to the physical symptoms). Anxiety. Irritability. Depression. Fatigue.

Samir had likely been trying pretty hard to hide those from her.

Outside, the wind was howling and the glacier stretched out all around them for hundreds of miles. Laura thought then that they were sort of like two shipwrecked people on a boat in a sea of ice, trying desperately to survive long enough to make landfall. The wind powered them. But they were running out of food. Like any survival situation, there was one thing they couldn't afford to lose: their will to survive.

For that reason, Laura was worried about Samir. She was worried about what sort of thoughts were running through his mind. Was he in a loop of regret and self-loathing and hopelessness? He certainly wouldn't be the first opioid addict to experience that.

Their current desperate situation couldn't be helping his mental health.

What he needed—what they both needed—was what every human required: something to look forward to. A reason to live.

As the turbine's blades spun and replenished the batteries, Laura began trying to fortify Samir's mental health against the demons he was fighting. "What are you looking forward to? When we get out of here."

He snorted, as if the question was moot.

"Don't give me that," she said. "You're the one who insisted I relax. This is relaxing for me. Imagining the future."

He shook his head slowly. "I don't know, Laura, it looks pretty dark."

Slowly, his gaze drifted toward the window.

"Well, pretend it's not. Pretend we're back in Durham, or Boston, or Nashville, or wherever we go after all this. What do you want to do?"

He took a long sip of water. "Okay, but this is going to bring the mood down."

"I can handle it."

"What I'm looking forward to is not having every thought be about when you are going to give me another pill."

"And what else?"

He shrugged. "There is nothing else, Laura. At least, not right now."

"There's got to be, Samir. Come on. Give me something. We've got nothing to do but talk."

He grimaced. "There is, but it's like… not the right time."

Laura laughed. "What? What do you mean?"

"Let's forget it."

"No. I want to hear it. What do you want to do when you get back?"

"What I want is to practice medicine again. Like before. With patients. In the OR. Or outside. Real human contact. To do work that matters." His gaze shifted down, and Laura understood then. "I took that from you," he said. "The conviction… they'll never let you practice again."

"Maybe not. I made a plea deal before I left."

She told him the details, and it seemed to brighten his mood.

"So what, you just tell this Aurora group what happened, and they wipe the slate clean?"

"That was the deal. But they wanted data. I assume given the bizarre setup in Antarctica Station that they're going to give me a pass on that."

Thinking about the server room and Samir's sudden appearance there brought a question to Laura's mind. "Samir, how did you know I was in the server room?"

He raised his eyebrows, a sheepish grin forming on his lips. "It's, uh… Does it matter?"

"Why? I mean, not really, but I'm curious."

"It's a little creepy."

"Well, now I have to know."

"I… might have assigned you as a patient to my roster."

"Okay. What would that do?"

"If I had flagged you as being at risk of a cardiovascular event—and I'm not saying I did—but if I did, it would allow me to monitor your vitals and location. We've seen it before: people get too overstimulated in stasis, and it has real-world physiological effects. They have adverse events or even exit stasis. The system is still learning and will eventually compensate." Samir stopped himself. "Not that we care, but anyway, MedRe has the ability for us to basically track any patients we assign as at risk."

"So you were monitoring me?"

"Yeah. It's creepy."

"A bit."

"Did you do it all the time?"

"No. Well, a lot at first. Then, just in the evenings. And

when I saw you running on the lower levels, I thought maybe you were going to try to escape or something. On the tablet, I watched you stop in the hall at the back of the so-called server room. Your vitals went nuts. Pulse and blood pressure were spiking. I knew either you were injured or fighting someone or trying to get into that room. I took off. Used the stairs to get down there."

"I'm glad you did."

On the screen, the power level had increased enough for them to keep going. And Laura thought she knew where. But it was a gamble. A big one.

39

After removing the wind turbines from the roof, Transport said, "Verifying that our destination is still Union Glacier Camp."

"No," Laura said. "We're going somewhere else."

"I understand, Laura. What is our destination?"

"Transport, before, you said that you can operate underwater, correct?"

"Yes, Laura, with sufficient power reserves and for a limited time."

"And you can travel that way?"

"Yes, Laura, depending on the specific conditions, I can achieve some forward or backward motion, though navigating is difficult and my speed is quite low, depending, again, on the circumstances."

Samir leaned over the console. "What is this? You want to drive to Chile?"

"Not quite that far."

"Transport, have you ever been to Rothera Research Station?"

"No, Laura."

She counted that as a potential bad sign. "Transport,

in your latest mapping—before you lost access to real-time data—was there an ice bridge that connected Adelaide Island to the mainland of the Antarctic Peninsula?"

Samir raised his eyebrows and began to speak, but Transport was faster. "Yes, Laura, there were two ice bridges connecting the island to the mainland. However, they may no longer be there. And they may be too thin to drive across. As you may know, Adelaide Island lies north of our current position and experiences warmer temperatures. I would also note that the terrain leading to any crossing to Adelaide Island is incredibly mountainous and hard to traverse."

"Understood."

"Would you like to make Rothera Station our destination, Laura?"

To Samir, she said, "I know this sounds crazy, but I'll explain, okay?"

"I trust you."

"Yes, Transport. Take us to Rothera."

*

As the transport powered across West Antarctica with its lights off, Laura explained her thinking.

The biggest factor she had considered was where the bases were in West Antarctica. Besides McMurdo—and New Zealand's Scott Base, which was only two miles away—the only other base in that region was Russkaya Station. It was a Russian facility that had been abandoned in 1990.

The rest of the stations in West Antarctica were situated along the Antarctic Peninsula. In fact, it had the largest concentration of bases anywhere in Antarctica. Laura had counted over twenty of them along the coast of the peninsula and the islands. The ones on the coast were obviously their best option, and of those, the ones staffed year-round were the logical destinations.

The US had only one station on the peninsula—Palmer—which was located on Anvers Island. It was considerably farther away than Rothera, and even if it was closer, Laura didn't think transport could cross the open water between it and the mainland.

Most of the stations on the peninsula were operated by South American countries—Chile and Argentina in particular. That made sense given the geographic proximity. The tip of the peninsula was only about 600 miles from South America. Some geologists even considered the mountains in the Antarctic Peninsula—the Antarctandes—to be a continuation of South America's Andes mountain range, with the connecting portion submerged in the sea separating the continents.

The closest year-round facility to their current location was San Martín Base, which was operated by Argentina. It too was located offshore, on Barry Island, one of six major islands that made up the Debenham Islands. In summer, Barry Island barely had any snow at all, just a rocky, mountainous terrain. It was separated from the mainland by a strip of water that Laura thought couldn't be more than 200 feet across. In the winter, snow covered the small mountain and thick ice stretched across the channel. They could easily drive over it.

Laura, however, saw three problems with San Martín Base. First, it was the obvious destination. Reachable in winter. Staffed year-round. And it had everything they needed. A heliport. Infirmary. Even an airstrip located on the mainland, on Uspallata Glacier. In fact, planes even landed on the frozen sea around the base in winter.

By this time, given the satellite coverage, Epoch had to assume she was heading somewhere other than McMurdo. The bases along the peninsula were the only other choice. As such, they would be heading there soon (if not already), and San Martín would be on their list to stake out or occupy.

Which brought up the second problem: the staff level at San Martín. If the data was right, there would be about twenty people onsite during the winter. That was enough for Epoch to overwhelm if they came in force.

And lastly, assuming Epoch wasn't there waiting for them, there was the problem of the language. It was likely that one or more of the twenty Argentinian staffers spoke English. But if they didn't, Laura and Samir would be in trouble (she couldn't imagine trying to explain that she had just escaped from being in stasis and was being hunted by a global conspiracy with ambiguous goals). It was possible that they would simply let her use the sat phone, but she wasn't willing to bet on it.

For those reasons, she didn't favor going to San Martín. And besides, Rothera was close by (less than 50 miles in a straight line). They could get to Rothera not long after passing San Martín.

What she favored about Rothera Station was that it was a British facility that was staffed year-round, with an estimated 250 people in summer and thirty in winter. While it wasn't much more than the staff level at San Martín, they would all be English-speaking. And importantly, as Britain's largest research station in Antarctica and a logistics hub, Rothera had excellent transportation infrastructure, including a wharf, a permanent runway made of crushed stone that was almost 3,000 feet long, and a hangar that housed a Dash-7 and three Twin Otter aircraft. It was possible some of the planes would be gone, but Laura felt it gave her and Samir a good chance of getting off the continent quickly.

When she had finished describing her thinking, Samir simply said, "I like it."

"And," Laura added, "if we can't make it to Rothera, we can just keep going down the peninsula until we find a base that's operational that we can reach. We could also try the radio if we see one on an island that we can't reach."

"We're door-to-door Antarctic refugees."

Laura laughed. "Yeah. I guess."

Samir's expression turned serious. "Hey, why do you think South Pole Station was deserted?"

"Don't know. I assume whatever happened to the convoy happened to them too. Or maybe some extreme weather event caused them to evacuate."

"Maybe," Samir said slowly.

*

For a while, the drive took on a certain routine. When the battery levels dipped, they remounted the turbines, recharged, and resumed.

Laura tried not to think about their dwindling food supplies, mainly because there was nothing she could do about it.

She knew Samir was thinking about the dwindling supply of the pills. There was nothing she could do about that either.

Laura began stretching out the time between meals. If Samir noticed, he didn't say anything.

She did the same with the pills, which were now also running low.

Fidgeting in the seat, he said, "How many more?"

"Miles?"

"Pills."

Laura slipped the bottle in her pocket. "Enough."

He exhaled deeply but didn't say anything else.

What she hadn't told him was that there were two more pills. Enough for three doses if she broke the last one in half.

Laura gave him one of those pills after they installed the turbines the next time, and he quickly lapsed into a fitful, sweaty sleep. The batteries had recharged by the time he woke up, and he moved sluggishly behind her as they removed them again.

With transport underway, they ate the last two MREs. On the screen, it showed their location on the Antarctic Peninsula. Rothera was ahead and to the left. As they drove north, the sky began to grow lighter, not by much, but when you've been in near darkness for a long time, any light makes a big difference.

*

Laura was dozing when the alarm went off. She woke slowly, body sore and stiff.

On the screen, she hoped to see the lights of Rothera Station on the coast, a frozen sea spreading out around it.

Instead, a flashing message read *RECHARGE BATTERIES*.

Laura had set an alert to appear when they reached 20 percent. Apparently, that had occurred before reaching their destination.

She dismissed the message. And clicked the map. They were close to Rothera. Really close.

She peered out the windshield. The scene took her breath away.

Beyond the ice-covered mountains, the night sky was streaked with glowing green wisps of light.

Laura's mind supplied the name of the phenomenon: the aurora borealis. But she immediately realized that wasn't right. This was the South Pole equivalent: the aurora australis. The Southern Lights. They were most visible here near the Antarctic Circle during the winter months. The lights were the result of solar winds carrying ions that became trapped in Earth's ionosphere, where they collided with oxygen and nitrogen from the atmosphere, creating the light effects.

This close to Rothera, Laura had thought she might see some of the sun's light as well. But it was below the horizon. All information related to the current date had been deleted from Transport's database when Epoch had wiped the vehicle remotely, but there was still sunrise and sunset information for various locations in Antarctica. According to that data, there were only fourteen days out of the year when the sun never rose at Rothera—the last fourteen days of June. This close to the station, observing the day length would give Laura a pretty good idea of the day and month.

"Is it time?" Samir said quietly. He was apparently less impressed with the aurora. And unlike Laura, wasn't contemplating what day and month it was. She suspected his only concern was whether enough time had passed for his next dose.

He looked haggard. Laura wasn't sure if it was from withdrawal or exertion. She was sure that he needed real medical care soon. Or, at the very least, larger and more consistent doses to manage his symptoms.

She gave him half a pill. His silent body language echoed her thoughts: this isn't enough. But he didn't say anything.

"Laura," Transport said, "would you like me to find another spot to install the turbines? Perhaps a flatter area? Or one with more elevation to capture wind faster?"

"We're going to keep going."

"I wouldn't advise it, Laura. It would be safer to fully recharge before trying to cross to Adelaide Island."

Laura agreed with that. But they were out of food. And meds. And time. "We're going to keep going."

Transport crunched through the snow. Samir shivered in the passenger seat. Laura watched the screen, where the battery power ticked down by tenths, and the red blip on the map inched toward Rothera Research Station.

*

They had 10.7 percent power left when they reached an ice-covered cliff that overlooked the island and the frozen channel. From this vantage point, Laura thought they should've been able to see the base's lights, but she wasn't sure. She didn't see them. Perhaps it was truly night here, not just dark, and they were conserving energy. After all, they weren't expecting company, so there was no need to leave a light on.

"Transport, can you chart a path across the frozen channel?"

"Yes, Laura. I've identified 328 possible routes across the ice to the island. I have calculated the safest path, but I must again warn you: I cannot be sure of ice thickness or how much weight it can support."

Laura studied the dark place where the station was. Or should have been.

"Laura?"

"Yes, Transport?"

"It would also be better if my batteries were fully charged before attempting the crossing."

Laura cut her eyes to the battery level.

10.6 per cent.

A hand fell on her forearm, and Laura felt Samir's fingers digging into the fabric of her inner layer. His voice was raspy. "It's time, right?"

She gazed at the fluorescent green clouds in the sky and again at the cold dark coastline and put a hand over his and drew out the pill bottle and handed him the last jagged pill.

"Yeah, it's time," she whispered.

"Transport, proceed."

40

Under the hazy green glow of the aurora, the Epoch transport climbed the mountains and crept down them. In patches with loose ice and snow, it skidded, locking its tracks and shifting them, course correcting with a quickness only a machine could manage.

Inside, Laura and Samir were both hungry and tired. But neither slept. Because the drive was nerve-shredding and because there was nothing to eat.

Laura watched the power level, willing it to tick down slower.

The braking helped conserve some energy, but the rough terrain was still draining power far faster than driving over the flat ice.

Samir gazed out the windshield with lazy, unfocused eyes, grinding his teeth as if he were riding a roller coaster. As they approached the edge of the mainland, Laura tensed and gripped the bottom of the seat.

And suddenly, like a rollercoaster before it takes off, they were in the valley, parked in front of the flat, frozen sea.

The power reserves were at 6.8 percent.

Transport turned right and moved cautiously along the

coastline before aligning itself on the frozen channel again. It crept forward slowly, like a swimmer dipping a toe in to test the water.

The rubber tracks dug into the ice as it rolled ahead. Transport hadn't chosen the shortest distance between the two snow-covered landmasses. Laura wondered why. Perhaps the ocean maps revealed that the depth was shallower here, and thus the ice more likely to be solid.

A crack rang out in the cab, as loud as a lightning strike against the low howl of the wind outside.

Laura jumped. Samir rolled his head, eyes drifting up to the windshield.

The front of the transport tilted forward, the ice sheet replacing the view of the coast outside.

Just as quickly, Transport reversed course and lunged backward, practically jumping out of the hole opening in the ice.

Laura's chest was heaving. Transport said nothing, only retreated to the mainland and pivoted and charged farther up the channel. It tried to cross again. And again, the ice broke beneath its tracks.

This happened two more times.

The power was at 6.5 percent now.

The crossing was starting to feel like an elaborate Antarctic board game, with Transport being the piece moving forward and backward, testing for an open space where it could advance.

But now it simply sat there, perhaps doing more calculations, considering what it had learned from the four weak spots in the ice it had discovered, analyzing its images to draw conclusions and identify a better path.

Samir said, "We could get out and walk."

Laura studied the map. They were crossing the frozen channel from a cape called Arrowsmith Peninsula, at a point roughly 25 miles North of Rothera Station.

Laura doubted she could make that hike over the uneven, snowy terrain. She was certain Samir couldn't.

It was warmer here than at the South Pole. And the wind wasn't near as severe as in the Transantarctics, but it was no island hike. Even assuming a two mile-per-hour pace, it would take her twelve and a half hours. In the multiple layers. With no food. And no shelter in case her pace was half that.

"We stay together," she said. But she was seriously starting to wonder if they should mount the turbines. Mentally, she updated the plan to their reality: *she* would be mounting a single turbine. But they'd lose time. And it wouldn't solve their food problem or Samir's growing health crisis.

"Laura," Transport said pleasantly, as if they weren't staring into the abyss.

"Yes?"

"Please buckle up."

Samir cut his eyes over at her, muttering as he grabbed his seat belt. "I don't like the sound of this."

Laura clicked her own restraint into place and stared out at green wisps dancing across the starry night sky.

Transport didn't creep forward this time.

It shot out from the bank, practically bouncing on the ice, moving at the fastest speed it had since leaving Epoch's station.

Laura's body vibrated and her stomach dropped, that rollercoaster feeling returning once again.

The wind howled, an unseen chorus of demons cheering this desperate race on. The ice cracked. Laura glanced out the rear window, seeing the fissures that were opening behind them.

Transport crashed into the far bank, slowing almost to a stop, surging upward, before digging its tracks into the loose ice and snow.

At the top of the hill on Adelaide Island, Transport said, "Laura?"

"Yes?" She was panting.

"Please keep your seatbelt buckled."

*

The ride across the island was bone-shattering and seemed chaotic. But Laura saw the logic in it. The machine was using some of the peaks to recapture energy as it braked and skidded down, and taking the easy, flatter routes to advance forward.

The power level read 2.1 percent when the map signaled that they were right outside Rothera Station.

Under the Aurora's glow, Laura got her first look at Rothera. It was so different from South Pole Station. For one, there were perhaps half a dozen major buildings. They had gable roofs, relatively small windows, and corrugated walls that looked army green to Laura. On the whole, it had the vibe of a Second World War outpost—utilitarian and dated. There was, however, one exception: a large building at the center. Its roof was flat except for a slight slope. It had curved lines and an air traffic control tower rising out of it. Its walls and roof were made of ridged panels painted light blue. It looked very modern to Laura, like a recently built museum in a major city.

She tapped the screen and began reading. The large, light-blue structure was called the Discovery Building, and at almost 50,000 square feet, it was to be the new hub of the station, replacing many of the older buildings which had been in place for decades. Inside were areas for staging expeditions, a store, an updated infirmary, offices, recreational spaces, workshops and more.

Based on the entry, the building should have been done by now. Or almost done. The completion date had been delayed a bit. Not helping matters was the fact that construction could only take place six months out of the year, even at this, one of Antarctica's most northern latitudes.

Several other things jumped out at Laura. The first was that this place had roads and power lines, almost like a small town.

The next observation was less positive. Snow was stacked up against the buildings and piled high on the obvious lanes where the roads were. The lack of lights on—and more so, the lack of vehicle tracks in the snow—unnerved her.

In a word, this place seemed abandoned. But maybe it was just how it was in winter in this place. There was no need to melt the snow. In a few months the sun that never set would melt it. And maybe there was no need to leave in a vehicle. Maybe boot tracks were soon filled in.

Nevertheless, what she saw ahead, under the green glowing sky, was the hangar on the right, with its olive-drab-green walls and four doors. The round silos of the fuel depot to the left of it. The frozen runway after that—and the frozen sea beyond it, a sea that Transport apparently thought too risky to try to cross. Somewhere on that border was a frozen wharf.

Left of the long runway were the buildings that made up most of the station, aligned somewhat haphazardly. Almost all of them were long and short and narrow except for the newest addition, which rose like a triumph in the middle of the town.

"Laura," Transport said. "Is there a specific destination within the station to which you would like me to proceed?"

"Hospital," Samir mumbled. His seatbelt was still on and his eyes were closed.

"The Discovery Building."

The destination's moniker was fitting, she thought. They were about to discover their fate.

When Transport stopped outside the building, the power levels were at 1.7 percent.

Laura began suiting up, which roused Samir to unbuckle and reach back for his outer suit. "I'll go," she said.

"No," he said, struggling to pull the garment out of the back seat. "I'll help."

She held out a hand. "Samir. Please stay here."

He nodded to the power display. "I'm better off inside." He held up a shaking hand. "And I need some medicine."

"Okay," she said.

Outside the transport, Laura switched on her flashlight. Behind her, Transport's headlamps went out like stage lights fading at the end of its scene.

Laura stopped and looked back at the Epoch vehicle

sitting in the snow under the green haze. It had served them well. And now it was spent.

Laura was as well. Fatigue and sleep deprivation and hunger were closing in.

But it would all end inside that building. She hoped.

Samir stopped in the snow and turned. Laura couldn't see his eyes through the goggles, and he didn't say anything, but his body language communicated the message: You coming?

As she had done since she had woken up from stasis, Laura trudged forward.

She pulled ahead, marching past the roll-up, garage-style doors that were partially buried in snowdrifts.

At a swinging door, Laura tested the handle. It wasn't locked. And why would it be? There was likely very little crime in a place with twenty-odd inhabitants.

Laura turned the handle and swung the door inward, raking her flashlight across the space. A metal grate covered most of the floor, allowing snow to fall off visitors and melt and drain below. There was a large vent above, but it didn't come on. Laura spotted a bank of large switches to her right and flipped them all, but nothing happened. No lights. No heated air rushing down to blow the snow off.

Maybe the station was conserving power. Or a power failure.

There were two exits. To the right, an opening led to a locker room and changing area. Ahead, a set of swinging doors led to an outer hall.

Even inside, it was cold enough that Laura and Samir

kept their layers on. But in the low light—and without the wind—they both shed their goggles.

In the hall, Laura raked her light over the directory sign. The infirmary was to the right.

"Let's go," Samir said, stalking toward it.

Laura didn't follow. She studied the ice crystals on the floor and walls. This building wasn't conditioned. No one was living here—or at least, they weren't conditioning the common areas. Maybe they were holed up in one area to conserve power and they only roamed these halls with proper cold weather gear.

The light revealed something else: the walls were unpainted. There were no fixtures in the holes in the ceiling. The Discovery Building—or at least this wing—was unfinished. That dated the place a bit. And it provided another theory about the cold: maybe they weren't heating these halls because they hadn't moved to this building yet.

Laura had to jog to catch up with Samir, who was already rifling through the cabinets in the infirmary, which looked completely finished to Laura. The presence of bottles seemed to confirm that. At a minimum, they had moved the medical functions here—or were in the process of it.

Samir stopped, reading a label. Laura thought he was going to twist the top off and—

But he handed it to her. "Bingo," he said, eyes flashing. This was the most excited Laura had seen him since America—before everything had gone wrong.

Laura scanned the medication and dosage. It would work.

She took off one of her gloves and removed the cap and got a pill out. She was looking around for water when Samir snatched it from her palm and dry-swallowed it.

He staggered to a bed nearby, shoulder brushing past a curtain. "I'm gonna rest a bit." He motioned to another bed in the infirmary. "You should too. Be the best sleep since that gap under the bunk in the mountains."

Laura slipped the bottle in her pocket, as she had done before. "I'm going to finish searching this place."

Samir closed his eyes. "Be careful."

41

With Samir resting on an infirmary bed, Laura searched the rest of the medicine cabinets, collecting all the opioid bottles. Only then did she feel comfortable enough to leave him.

Outside the infirmary, she walked the halls of the eerie, frozen building in Rothera Station, her flashlight shining down the empty corridors, boots crunching in the ice on the floor.

With each step, she became more convinced that this place wasn't inhabited. It also seemed half finished, yet securely sealed against the elements—plastic sheeting covered the incomplete areas, and temporary insulation filled the gaps in the walls. The file had noted that because of the weather here on Adelaide Island, construction was only possible six months out of the year. Another thing was bothering Laura.

As Laura walked, a thought emerged from the recesses of her mind: there was something off about Samir.

But she couldn't put her finger on it. There was something about him in the infirmary, stretching out, carefree.

Was that it? Or was it something else?

Laura had to admit, deep down, the distrust was still there.

They had agreed to start over, but deep wounds have a way of resurfacing in times of stress.

In Laura's case, her stress level was at fever pitch. And her past with Samir was the deepest wound.

The office wing, like the infirmary, was finished and seemed to have been used at some point, though there was no one here now. Laura marched directly to the corner office, reasoning that she might find a sat phone or other comms equipment there. Out the windows, the Southern Lights glowed green across the entire sky.

Was that normal? This much aurora activity? It indicated a lot of solar wind. Did it mean something else?

Another thought occurred to Laura: Aurora. Like the Aurora Group. Was that just a coincidence? Or some clue about what was happening here?

She exhaled, her breath coming out in a white cloud of steam. The name Aurora was probably just a coincidence. Lots of people used the name. A bureaucrat probably chose it because it was—alphabetically—the first thing on a list.

There was a large desk in the room and a computer monitor but no phone or communication equipment. Maybe there was a comms room, like at South Pole Station.

There was, however, a large metal filing cabinet on the far wall with wide drawers. Laura walked over to it and was about to open it when she realized what was bothering her.

She took out a pill bottle and read the label.

It was impossible.

The prescription had been dispensed by a robotic pharmacist, which had bottled the pills in June. But it was March.

It was definitely March. Laura had been counting the

days, knowing she had to leave Antarctica Station by the end of the month.

But, according to the label, these pills had been sealed in this bottle three months later. Maybe it was a misprint. The robot just had the date wrong. It happened to computers all the time.

But instinctively, Laura knew the label was right. This bottle had been filled three months after she thought she had left Antarctica Station.

Standing in the office, holding the bottle, the neon-green aurora flaring out the window, Laura saw the secret that answered so many questions she had buried along their frantic trek across the continent: she had been in Antarctica far longer than three months.

Transport had even tried to tell her. When she had asked the AI for five important facts that might help keep her alive, the third fact—in order of importance—was that Transport had first been booted up nineteen years ago. At the time, Laura couldn't see how that was relevant.

She saw it now.

When she had traveled to Antarctica Station, all the vehicles were Hägglunds. And they had been manually driven.

She had assumed that Transport and the other AI vehicles existed even then but were perhaps being tested and still developed. Laura had just naturally assumed the AI portion had been booted up nineteen years ago.

But it hadn't. Transport and the other similar models were developed after she had entered stasis. That was what it was trying to tell her.

The question now was how long had she been in that Epoch virtual world.

At least three months more. Maybe years.

And how had they distorted time? Maybe it was simply due to the nature of the stasis technology—perhaps the time in the simulation had no correlation to real-world time. Or maybe Epoch used the sleeping periods. That was probably it. In the simulation, maintaining circadian rhythms was a high priority. Everyone slept, and they slept at the same time. What if each night of sleep in stasis equaled a week of time in the real world? Or a month? Or a year?

The thought was disorienting. Terrifying.

Laura staggered over to the swiveling chair and collapsed into it, her heart thundered in her ears, mind racing.

Outside the doorway, she heard boots crunching the ice crystals.

She rose and moved to the opening, expecting to see Samir.

But it wasn't him.

*

In the infirmary, Samir let the warm feeling of time melting away wash over him.

It was cold here, but that didn't matter.

He was okay for now.

If he could beat this monster here—with no professional help or even the right drugs—he could beat it anywhere. He just needed to get back to civilization.

But that was a problem.

A problem his drug-addled mind couldn't quite grasp. What was the problem about getting back to civilization?

Oh yeah.

He hadn't told Laura about that. Because it was a

problem they couldn't deal with—but one that would have wreaked havoc on her mental health.

He had done that to her once. He would never do it again. In the transport, he had kept lying. Because he had become good at it. This time, he was doing it for her. Not him.

But now they'd have to deal with the tricky issue of getting home—and what happened after. They needed—

Footsteps echoed in the empty clinic.

Samir sat up. "Hello?"

A figure strode across the open room, casually, confidently. In the glow of the aurora through the windows, Samir recognized the person.

Or was he hallucinating? It was possible. Maybe Laura had given him too much.

"Cuz?" he said.

She didn't say anything. She took something from her pocket, a black object. Samir squinted at it. A gun.

"Still a junkie," Imara whispered. And slammed it down on his head.

*

In the office, Laura dropped her flashlight on the floor.

The figure in the doorway clicked theirs on.

"Joe."

His voice was flat and emotionless. "They're coming, Laura. We need to hurry."

He turned, and she called to him. "Wait."

"What?" He didn't look back.

"Why are you helping me?"

"I'll tell you everything on the way."

"To where?"

"Home."

Laura's voice finally broke as she spoke. "Joe, what's happening here? What year is it?"

He turned then. "Samir told you?"

"No." She took out the pill bottle. "I was in stasis for what I thought was three months. But this label was printed three months after that. It's impossible—unless I was in Antarctica Station longer than I thought."

He nodded slowly. "I knew what you were doing in the lower levels."

She had always suspected. "You sent the message on my tablet."

"I did. And I knew you were under that bunk in the traverse housing unit. On the radio, I said what I thought you needed to hear."

She didn't trust her voice to speak.

He kept going. "I did it for you, Laura. And because of what I learned after I made that request for you to run on the lower levels. Because of what they're doing."

"What, Joe? What's happening here? What happened to the world? What is the Event?"

His blue-gray eyes were as cold as the winds blowing down from the coastal glaciers. "You'll see. But, Laura, we *have to go*. There are three more security personnel here."

"Go where?"

"There's a sub waiting at the wharf. We'll talk once we're underway."

*

Imara didn't trust Joe.

In fact, she held him responsible for this whole

mess—including Reynolds's escape. They should have disconnected his stasis bay the moment it happened.

But, oh no—his daddy wouldn't hear of it.

Well, dear old dad wasn't here to protect him now. And neither could the other two security personnel who were waiting in the hall. Imara had hand-picked the dumbest two she could find for this mission. They were gullible and useless and easy to maneuver to stay out of the way. That's all she needed now.

Joe was so transparent. The worst part was that he thought he was so clever. At McMurdo, he had volunteered to take one of the helos around the coast to the Archipelago and do a stakeout. Imara, because she had more than two functioning brain cells, was instantly suspicious. Outwardly, she had made an effort to seem indifferent, even as she volunteered to go with him.

"If something happens to you," she had said, "your father would never forgive me."

He had clenched his jaw at that. The mention of daddy dearest always did these days, a reminder that he wasn't his own man. As such, she mentioned him every chance she could. She still wasn't tired of seeing Joe's silent suffering.

But this whole charade would end soon. And she had the perfect cover: a desperate escape, a current drug addict, one former addict, and Joe caught in the crossfire.

"At least we got her," Imara would say to Joe's heartbroken dad. She was looking forward to that too.

In the hallway outside the infirmary, the two security personnel were waiting. That was odd.

"What are you doing here?"

"Joe told us to come find you, in case—"

"Where is he?"

"Searching the second floor. He said to find you and cover the exits closest to their transport."

Imara chewed her lip. This was a dilemma. How could she maneuver these two out of the way and get to Joe so they didn't see?

Her hand slid down to the gun in the holster. There was an obvious solution. Just remove these two from the equation right here and proceed. She grimaced, seeing the problem. A body count that high would be hard to explain. Reynolds killing Joe worked. He was in love with her. He approached her with his guard down, she took him out, and Imara killed her.

An idea occurred to her, and it brought a slight smile to her lips. Yes, this would work.

One of the idiot security operatives unclipped his radio. "I'll check in with him—"

"No," Imara said quickly. "The radio might give away his location and put him in danger."

Silently, she laughed at the words *put him in danger.*

"Cover the East stairs. But make some noise—keep talking so he knows you're there. We don't want any friendly fire."

The guards nodded. But didn't move.

Imara held a hand out. "Well, let's get a move on."

They turned and trudged down the hall, already starting up the fake conversation, which sounded forced and unnatural. Actors they were not.

"Wait," Imara called out. "Jacobs, give me your gun."

The two men looked at each other curiously.

"I'm Johnson," one said tentatively. "Did you mean—"

"Yeah," Imara said, closing the distance between them. "Don't know why I said that." She knew exactly why she couldn't remember this forgettable fool's name.

She held her hand out and he hesitated a second before relinquishing his weapon.

Imara tucked it in one of her suit pockets and turned and walked silently toward the other stairwell.

*

Joe led Laura through the maze of cubicles and to the outer hall where he held a finger to his lips. In the distance, she could hear faint voices.

He reached down to the holster on his hip, released the retention strap, and drew the gun out. At the stairwell, he listened for a second before pointing Laura in the other direction.

Her nerves were shredded, and she had to will her legs to work.

Without warning, Joe stopped, and Laura nearly slammed into him, catching herself instead with a hand held out that braced his right shoulder.

He turned to her, and those slate eyes that were focused like a predator on the hunt softened for a brief second. The last time she had seen that look on his face was in her suite, that night they had shared, which felt like another life and time now. And, in a way, it had been.

Joe reached back and put his hand over hers. The heat from his skin was the warmest thing she had felt since she had woken up from stasis.

Slowly, he drew his hand away, and the cold closed in again.

He leaned over a cubicle wall and reached down and grabbed a tennis ball and stuffed it in a pocket.

For the life of her, Laura couldn't see how that helped him, but this was only her second escape from a bizarre Antarctic research station, so she said nothing.

When they reached the door to the other stairwell, Joe stood and listened for a while. Was something wrong?

He squatted and moved out onto the landing and briefly peeked over the rail.

Next, he held the tennis ball over the first stair, then threw it down at a slight angle. It bounced on each stair. It didn't sound exactly like footsteps to Laura, but she also didn't know what the plan was.

Still squatting, his head low, Joe peered over the railing, drawing back quicker this time.

With a hand, he motioned Laura back. "I've got her, Imara." The words echoed down the stairwell, but no reply came. "I saw you, Imara."

"Great," she replied. "Glad you got her. Come on down, and we'll head back. I have my cousin."

Cousin, Laura thought. She wondered if Imara's father was the one who had gotten Samir's family into Antarctica Station.

"Sounds great," Joe said flatly. "But you know, even though I grew up in Texas, guns make me nervous. So I'm gonna need you to walk up the stairs, lay yours on the landing, and then walk back down."

"You don't trust me, Joe?"

"No, I don't."

"Well, what's the world coming to?"

Joe rose up straight and backed away from the landing.

Below, footsteps echoed.

"I'm doing it, Joe," Imara said. "But I want you to know, this really hurts."

The footfalls were on the steps now, and a clunk sounded next, presumably the gun hitting the landing.

Joe turned to Laura. "Stay here," he whispered. "If this goes bad, run to the other stairwell, go down, and keep going until you get to the wharf. The sub is autonomous, like the transports. Just tell it where you want to go."

"Joe—"

"Promise me you'll do it."

"I promise," she lied.

He reached up and put his hand to her face and kissed her, not deeply or slowly, but a hard, quick kiss that said *be right back* and *to be continued*.

Standing in the hallway outside the stairwell, Laura watched him carefully walk out onto the landing, gun drawn in front of him, then rocket forward, one hand on the far rail attached to the wall, descending the stairs two at a time, boots skidding in the ice.

At the landing, he slipped out of sight, and just as quickly, the deafening sound of gunshots shattered the air.

42

Laura didn't run to the other staircase.

She bounded forward.

At the rail, she spotted Joe lying on the landing, a crimson sea of blood spreading out on his white Epoch suit.

He lay limp, eyes closed.

Laura felt like every shred of oxygen had been instantly drained from the building. Her chest tightened. Her body froze. But the sight of Joe's blood soaking into the suit made her take the first step then the next until she was holding the rail, descending the stairs.

At the landing, she spotted Imara lying at the bottom of the stairs, face down in a puddle of blood, unmoving.

Laura pressed her pointer and middle fingers into the pulse point on Joe's neck.

Slowly, he opened his eyes. "Go," he mouthed.

In the hall beyond the stairwell alcove, footsteps rang out, someone walking fast.

Two handguns lay on the landing, easily within Laura's reach. But she didn't pick either up. She didn't know how to use them. Holding one—and pointing—might even get her killed.

Instead, she focused on Joe. There were two gunshot wounds. The more serious was in his upper chest, on the right side, just below his collarbone. Based on the absence of bone fragments and his breathing, she thought the bullet had missed his collarbone.

The other wound was in his left leg. It was bleeding less, which made her hopeful that it had missed a major artery.

The footsteps were in the alcove and ascending the stairs now.

"Hang in there," Laura whispered in Joe's ear.

His words came out slow. "Laura, just…"

The figure was on the landing, casting a shadow from the hazy aurora shining in through the window.

Laura looked up to find Samir standing there, eyes wide. "Not good," he mumbled.

"Help me get him to the infirmary."

Samir shook his head. For the first time, Laura noticed the dark welt on his forehead. "I'm not really in the best—"

She slid an arm under Joe's back, and he called out in pain, and that spurred Samir to reach down and help.

By the time they reached the bottom of the stairs, Joe had passed out—from blood loss or the pain or both—and Imara still hadn't moved (thankfully). The two Epoch security operatives were standing in the hall, one with his gun drawn, both looking dumbstruck at the scene.

"Dr. Reynolds," the unarmed man said, "you need to come with…"

He trailed off as he took in Joe's bloody suit.

Panting, Laura said, "Help us get him on the table."

In the infirmary, Laura and Samir cut away the suit and inspected the wounds and spent the next hour doing all they could for Joe.

The security personnel kept watch, though one left long enough to make a sat phone call out in the hall. Laura was too focused on Joe to make out the words.

It was still deathly cold in the building. Instead of taking the rest of Joe's suit off and retrieving the spare in Transport, Laura sewed his suit back together.

When she was done, she sat on a stool next to the narrow bed and ran a hand through his hair.

Samir disappeared and when he returned, seemed more somber. Laura expected him to ask for another pill, but he didn't. She stood at the end of Joe's bed and stared at him.

"Imara," Laura began, not looking up. "She was your cousin."

"Yeah."

"Is she—"

"Yeah."

The two security personnel, who had collected the guns right after seeing Joe to the infirmary, were huddled in the corner, whispering. Laura picked up bits and pieces of the conversation.

They said just bring them all back...

I know, but he's half dead. We may need one or both.

Laura locked eyes with Samir. His expression said that he had heard some of the conversation too. These guys weren't terribly bright.

They sauntered over, and the one who had spoken before said, "Here's what's going to happen."

Samir and Laura turned to him.

"There's a helo outside. We're going to fly back to McMurdo, and they're going to decide what to do with you." The man pointed at Joe. "If he dies before we get there, then Rick and I are coming back empty-handed. You understand?"

Laura wondered how long he had rehearsed the line.

"We should wait until he's recovered more to move him," Laura said quietly.

Both men grimaced.

Samir wandered away from the end of the bed, as if the conversation was of no interest to him.

"How much longer?" the man asked.

Laura shrugged. "I don't know. He's lost a lot of blood. We need to at least wait until he wakes up. Also, do you think they could bring some units of blood from McMurdo? I think that would help."

The two men shared a glance. This wasn't going the way they expected.

Samir took a step closer to the man on Laura's right and reached down with both hands and unstrapped and ripped the gun from his holster. Quickly, he stepped back three paces.

The man who was still armed dropped his hand toward his own holster.

"Don't," Samir said. "I'm serious."

"Dr. Dewan, be reasonable here."

"Oh, sure. I'm a drug addict in the throes of severe withdrawal. We're always reasonable."

"What are you going to do? Shoot us and fly out of here? Think, Dr. Dewan."

"We don't have to shoot you," Laura said. "Remember, we're anesthesiologists."

43

Laura searched the infirmary and was glad to find what she needed. A few minutes later, she was tapping the syringe to clear any air bubbles.

As instructed, the two Epoch security officers were lying on the beds, both strapped in now.

She injected the first, then the second, and when their eyes had closed and their vitals confirmed that they were under, Laura unstrapped them. They'd be cold when they woke up, but they'd be alive. And their helo would be waiting for them.

Next, she and Samir gathered medical supplies and used a gurney to wheel Joe to the exit.

She left him with Samir while she marched through the snow, back to Transport. The cab was cold inside, and reasonably so. The power was at 1.6 percent now, owing to burning the lights or perhaps some limited heating it needed to perform for its temperature-sensitive components.

"Laura," Transport said. "Are you injured?"

"No. Why?"

"Your suit is covered in blood."

Laura glanced down at Joe's blood that had soaked into her suit during the operation.

"It's not my blood."

"I am glad to hear that, Laura. Also, I must apologize for the interior conditions."

"Don't worry about it," Laura said. "Need you to move as close as you can to that door. And let's get the temp up as quickly as possible."

The cabin was slightly warmer by the time they finished loading Joe into the back seat. During the awkward transfer, he had mumbled and winced but never came to. Laura counted it as a bad sign. She wanted to do another exam on the sub.

Transport drove to the wharf, where frozen sea spread out in every direction except for a black protrusion that had broken through, an oblong metal cylinder that Laura assumed was the sub's sail. She trekked across the ice and inspected it, quickly identifying a vertical hatch on the top—accessible by a ladder—and an upright hatch, which she opened, revealing an illuminated interior and a steep staircase with treads constructed of metal grate. It would be difficult to move Joe. But doable.

And it was, and by the time Laura and Samir laid him down in a bunk, he was sweating and new spots of blood had begun to dot the suit around the wounds.

Laura returned to Transport and gathered up the medical supplies and prepared to say goodbye one last time. The power level was 1.3 percent.

"Laura," Transport said.

"Yes?"

"Are you leaving?"

"Yes."

"I understand."

Laura gripped the bag.

"Laura?" Transport said. "I'd like to make note of one thing."

"Okay."

"My power level is severely depleted."

"I saw that."

"If you need to return and make use of me immediately, it would be better for me to be charged."

Laura smiled. "Yes, it would. And it would help you preserve your components and remain operational."

"Correct, Laura. That observation also factored into my notification."

Laura exited and removed one of the wind turbines from the cargo compartment. She was carrying a blade up the ladder and peeking over the roof when Samir emerged from the sub, no doubt wondering why she hadn't returned yet.

Upon seeing her rising above the vehicle with the blade clamped to her body, he jogged carefully across the ice and began helping her. The drugs they had found in the infirmary were better than the ones she had given him from the med kit. It seemed to be fully easing his withdrawal symptoms and wasn't overly sedating. Laura wondered when it had been created.

Samir was on the roof, reaching down for the turbine's tower when he said, "Why are we mounting this?"

"Reasons," Laura replied simply.

When they were done and the turbine's blades were spinning in the wind, casting shadows in the ice from the aurora, Laura slipped back inside Transport. She was reaching for the bag of medical supplies when Transport said, "Laura, what shall I do while you're gone?"

"What do you mean?"

"I have no destination."

"There's only one thing to do when you have no destination."

"Yes, Laura?"

"Improve yourself."

Outside, Samir was waiting for her. When they reached the sub's hatch, he spun the wheel. "Wait till you see this thing. It's amazing."

The metal door creaked as it opened.

"Where are we going?" he asked, stepping inside.

"Home."

PART III

HOME

44

The AI that ran the submarine was very sophisticated.

But it wasn't Transport.

For that reason, Laura spent as little time with it as possible.

In the command center, the AI had requested a destination. Laura didn't have a destination. At least, not a specific one. No address. No GPS co-ordinates. Only a general idea: home.

"Dive and set a course to exit the bay, then navigate beyond the Archipelago," Laura said. "I'll issue further instructions at that point."

As she said the words, Laura realized she had another task to complete—a repeat of what she had done in the transport. She needed to remove this machine's communications components. Yet another reason not to get too close.

*

The submarine's med bay was off the kitchen. Laura felt that it was unwise to locate the two areas so closely together for hygiene issues, but she wasn't exactly a futuristic submarine designer so she couldn't be certain. And it was moot. She was here and this was what she had to work with. It likely had something to do with efficiency—routing the water or heat or something else.

In size, the med bay was more like a scullery. It had a single bed and bright lights that extended on metal arms and shelves along all the walls. It was well stocked. Laura and Samir had brought supplies too. The med bay's greatest feature, however, was environmental control. On a panel on the wall, Laura adjusted the temperature up and the humidity down.

Standing on each side of the bed, she and Samir waited as hot air issued from the supply vents in the floor. When the room had warmed some, Laura lowered a scalpel to the threads holding Joe's suit together and cut through them and pulled the flaps apart. The skin around the black stitches was red and inflamed.

Yellow pus oozed from the wound.

"Not ideal," Samir mumbled, eying the infected flesh. "Probably shouldn't have moved him."

"We certainly couldn't have left him."

"He needs a trauma surgeon," Samir said.

"He does. But until then, he's got us." Laura looked up. "So are you in or out?"

He exhaled and shook his head.

"What?"

"You even need to ask? Of course, Laura. I just want you to manage your own expectations. I don't want to see you get hurt."

"You mean hurt again."

"That's exactly what I mean," Samir said. "Like I hurt

you. And Pierce did. Laura, you've taken a lot of emotional shocks. They add up. And the more you get invested in this guy, the more you might get hurt if he doesn't make it."

Laura swallowed hard and stared down at the red ring spreading toward Joe's heart. "Well, good news, I can't possibly hurt any more than I did when my best friend framed me, so I'd like to roll the dice on saving this guy. We'll shove his body in the torpedo bay if he dies."

Samir nodded. "Okay. Fine. I tell you what, I want you to keep it coming. When you feel angry or stressed or alone or scared or… anything: come to me and let it go. I so deserve it—"

"Samir—"

"No, I'm serious. I do. I deserve all of that anger and more. And I'm not just saying that. I want it. And right now, I want you to hand me that scalpel. I'm having a clear moment, and I can do this, and you don't have to worry about it."

"We need to clear the infection—"

"Laura. I know what to do."

"I'll do it," she said. But she didn't move.

"No," he said more forcefully. "I'll do it. If he doesn't make it, then it's on me. Not you. You've done all you can. Leave. Imagine you delivered him to a first-rate trauma center. I'll come out when it's over."

Laura peered down at Joe. "I could help."

"You could hand me things. And watch. But I'll do it." Samir held his hand out and she stared at it, expecting it to shake. But it didn't. "Let me do this for you, Laura. Please. I need it."

*

For a while, Laura sat in the cafeteria. When Samir didn't emerge from the doors to the kitchen, she wandered back to the command center and studied the map. They were still far under the ice that stretched out from the coast of Antarctica's archipelago. She still needed a destination but figuring that out would take time. And there was something else she needed to do more.

After asking the AI a few questions, she found herself in possession of a toolkit and she was lying on her back under one of the control panels, operating, just like Samir was in that small med bay.

As she had done in Transport, she clipped the wires and removed the screws and gently pulled the communications board away.

They were sailing dark now.

*

Laura was sitting in the small mess hall when Samir staggered out, shoulders slumped. He ripped the bloody rubber gloves off and let them fall to the floor.

Laura rose.

"He's alive," Samir muttered.

"You could work on your bedside manner."

Samir staggered to a booth along the far wall and collapsed into it. "Look, the laceration in his leg is inconsequential. I dressed it, and I have no concerns about it."

Laura pulled out a rickety chair and sat across from him. "And?"

Samir tilted his head forward. "And the massive, gaping,

infected gunshot wound in his upper right chest is far more concerning."

"Will he—"

"I don't know," he said quickly. "I don't. Okay?"

Laura nodded.

It was a deep wound. And sometimes, they simply needed time to heal. Laura stared at Samir, thinking about that.

45

To clear her mind, Laura took a tour of the sub. It didn't take long. But what she found provided clues about what her plan should be.

The nose contained a cargo area with a hinged ramp at the end sitting at a forty-five-degree angle. Using the tablet, Laura pulled up the sub's specs and realized it had a flat bottom with two long tracks. It was amphibious. That gave them more options.

As did the contents of the cargo bay: two snowmobiles and a utility task vehicle, or UTV, with four seats and a bed in the rear that had a removable cover. It was equipped with off-road tires, and the roof material looked like solar cells to Laura.

Joe, apparently, had chosen well when he had ordered this autonomous sub to Rothera. Laura wondered if he had a plan.

Based on what she could tell of the submarine's capabilities—and the UTV it held—they could put ashore somewhere and take the vehicle inland.

The cargo bay also had racks filled with extra batteries and all-weather expedition gear: tents, security cameras, motion-activated lights, and first aid supplies.

ANTARCTICA STATION

Assuming they would take the UTV ashore, Laura booted it up and figured out how to remove its communications board and tracking hardware and then spent the next hour doing so.

Afterward, she returned to the small mess hall and sat down with an Epoch tablet and studied the map.

Laura's first priority was finding a real hospital for Joe. Instinctively, she thought about going back to the Triangle. She didn't know what year it was, but in her time, there were plenty of medical facilities there. And she might still even know someone there.

A long groan sounded from the med bay beyond the kitchen, and Laura tossed the tablet aside and rushed through the swinging doors.

Joe was trying to push up on his left elbow. His eyes were bloodshot and watery and unfocused, but a smile crossed his lips when he saw her.

"Hi," he managed, voice like sandpaper.

"Hi." Laura placed a hand gently on his chest and urged him to lie back on the narrow bed. "Take it easy."

"I feel like I took a tranq dart to the jugular."

"We had to put you under for the operation. And again here on the sub."

"I knew Imara had another gun. Knew it." He held a finger. "Didn't expect her to have it already drawn."

"It's over."

"What about the other two guards?"

"We put them under too."

Joe squinted at her, and Laura said, "Oh, no, we put them under anesthesia. Like you."

"I don't envy them right now."

Laura got a cup of water and handed it to him. "You're not out of the woods."

"Give it to me straight, doc. How bad is it?"

Laura smiled at his attempt at humor. "It's not great."

"So those are the medical terms?"

"The medical terms would be that you are a GSW victim who needs blood and a real hospital. Stat."

He held out his hand. Laura pulled up a stool and sat and took his hand.

"What do you need?" he asked.

"Answers."

"What do you want to know?"

"What year is it, Joe?"

"You were one of the last to board—at least, before the Event."

"Board what?"

"Antarctica Station."

"So it *is* a ship."

"In effect. It's a vessel to transport people and material from one place to another."

"What place?"

"In the case of Antarctica Station, the place—our destination—was one in time, not space. The starting point was roughly about the time you arrived. At that time, most of the main cohort was in stasis."

"Who was the main cohort?"

"A lot were people like you—highly skilled individuals who were needed to operate the station or for the after. Like you, not everyone knew the true nature of the project."

"So I'm not the only sucker who believed I was actually in some elaborate research station in Antarctica?"

"First, you're not a sucker. Second, you were in a very elaborate research station in Antarctica. Just not the one you thought you were in. And, as I said, that was true for many others who were working alongside you."

"It was all some virtual reality?"

"The virtualization you—we—experienced is called OpSim, it's the main operational simulation for Epoch."

"There are more simulations?"

"A lot more. They were constructed for the passengers."

"Passengers?"

"That's the rest of the cohort. Passengers is the Epoch name for the people who funded the project in exchange for passage."

"Passage to where, Joe?"

"A point in the future when the Earth was inhabitable again."

Laura felt like the sub had just run aground and water was pouring into the room. She released Joe's hand and rubbed her closed eyelids. "Are you telling me the Earth is uninhabitable—outside of Antarctica? Not that Antarctica is super inhabitable."

"I'm telling you that's what Epoch thought was going to happen."

"And it didn't?"

"That, in a strange way, was their miscalculation. But it's what Epoch—and my father—did about it that has brought you and I here, right now, and why what's about to happen is so important."

"What's about to happen?"

"Can I tell you something about myself?"

Laura let out a long breath.

"We have time," he said quietly. "The sub isn't that fast, and we need to go to Research Triangle Park."

"Why?"

"I'll get there. But a little history first."

"Okay."

"Growing up, I never knew my father."

That surprised Laura.

"I had a few clues, though. My mom hated him. Wouldn't even let me mention him or ask any questions. She never got married. But growing up, when we were on the rocks financially, we'd mysteriously get a stroke of good luck."

Joe raised his eyebrows. "We lived on the Texas coast. Hurricane wrecked our house. Insurance stonewalled us. And then all of a sudden, they change their mind and call back and are bending over backwards and a contractor gives us an incredible deal on the repairs."

Joe looked around the room.

"What?" Laura asked.

"Thirsty. All the talking."

Laura filled a cup at the sink, and Joe continued.

"Wasn't just bad times. I played football in high school. Team started having a little success and out of nowhere the school gets a massive donation from an anonymous benefactor. Enough for equipment, best staff and trainers money can buy, even a new bus and field house."

"Your dad."

"Yep. And it didn't end there. I went off to college, but it wasn't for me. Joined the Navy, which felt right. Got shot." He glanced down at the bandage on his upper chest. "Sort of a pattern of behavior for me."

"Let's hope it's a habit you leave in Antarctica."

"I'm on board with that. Anyway, I was doing okay with it. But a doctor from a big-deal research hospital came around to see me, saying she just wanted to follow my case and advise. Research, you know?"

Joe was starting to sweat now. Laura took his temperature, didn't like what she saw, and gave him a prescription-strength anti-inflammatory. "Speaking of big-deal research hospitals, we really need to get you to any hospital at this point. You may have—"

"After."

"After what?"

"After we finish this."

Laura nodded, unsure what to say.

"My mom passed a few years ago," Joe said. "I thought maybe he would show up at the funeral. Or contact me in the weeks that followed. He didn't. I was curious, naturally. I looked through everything Mom had collected over the years. Pictures, letters, financials—trying to find any trace of him. There was nothing. I think she wanted it that way."

"So how did you meet him?"

"He found me. When I least expected it. I was working as a private security contractor. Had just got home from a tour in Africa. And he was sitting there in my living room in a club chair like he was my roommate."

"What did you do?"

"Told him that was a good way to get himself killed."

Joe's chest rose as he laughed, and he winced and grunted. "Didn't even faze the guy. He just looked at me with those cold, dead eyes—you know the eyes."

"I do."

"And, matter of fact, he said, 'I'm your father. There are

things we need to discuss.' As if he was telling me, 'I'm pest control here for your quarterly service.' Like it was nothing."

"What did you say?"

"I told him he was right about that: we had a great many things to discuss. But he didn't want to talk about any of that. Next thing out of his mouth was: 'I'm not here to discuss the past. It's immaterial.'"

Joe laughed at the memory, grimacing again at the motion in his chest. "He said, 'We're going to talk about the future.' He stood and looked me in the eyes and said, 'The world is going to end. And a small group of people are going to survive. I want you to be one of those people.'"

Joe leaned his head back on the bed. "I mean, what do you even say to that?"

"You obviously said yes."

"Wasn't really a hard decision."

"How did the world end, Joe?"

"The crazy thing is that if the Event had happened twenty, maybe even ten years before, Epoch wouldn't have even known. They would have never been able to predict it."

Joe tried to scoot off the bed, leading with the cup, but Laura stopped him and refilled it.

After a long swig of water, he went on. "Ultimately, Epoch's greatest asset was their data and the models they built."

"Models about what?"

"Solar output. They built this program that looked at past solar activity and predicted future solar events."

"Interesting."

"Don't get the wrong impression. They didn't do it for the sake of science. It was about allocation of capital—how to invest based on probable climate change and future adverse weather events."

"Invest in what?"

"Anything. I don't think the Epoch founders cared as long as it made money. Probably real estate or insurance or something like that. Bottom line is that these models predicted—with very high confidence—that solar activity was entering a new stage not seen in recorded human history."

"What kind of activity?"

"You're asking the wrong guy—remember, college wasn't for me. But here's what I can recall from the Cliffs Notes version my absentee father gave me. The sun has an eleven-year cycle. Almost like the seasons on Earth. Except the variation in the sun's activity is driven by its magnetic field lines, which intertwine below the surface and occasionally break through. These eruptions form sunspots and release solar flares and coronal mass ejections. These CMEs are the biggest issue."

Samir emerged at the doorway to the med bay and hung back there, leaning against the frame, and said, "What did I miss?"

"Joe was just describing how the world ended."

"Oh, good. Glad it's not something depressing."

"Thank you," Joe said, nodding to his bandages. "For the doctoring."

Samir glanced at Laura. "De nada. I did it for a friend."

She smiled at him and said to Joe, "So where were we? CMEs?"

"Right. These coronal mass ejections are generally bad for Planet Earth. In particular."

"How?"

"I can't remember all the details, but I know they're made up of charged particles that can wreak havoc on electrical equipment."

"Yeah," Samir said, "like the Carrington Event." Joe and Laura looked at him blankly. "You know, 1859. The worst geomagnetic storm ever recorded." He shrugged. "Don't you guys watch the History Channel?"

"Missed that episode," Laura said.

"Well, it was a good one. They think the Event was caused by a CME. It caused the first recorded solar flare and cast auroras all over the world. The sky was bright enough to wake gold miners in the Rockies. They think the CME traveled to Earth in less than a day, so there was very little warning. And it sent this huge electrical current all over the world. It was strong enough to blow out telegraph systems in Europe and North America." Samir held up a finger. "And the coolest part? Even after some telegraph operators took precautions by unplugging the telegraph from the battery supply, they could still use it because of the ambient current running through. They were basically powered by auroral current at that point."

A silent moment passed, and then Joe said, "Well, that's basically what Epoch figures out is going to happen, except things are a lot different than 1859. And this solar storm is going to be a lot worse. Not only that, it's going be years of them non-stop, because for the first time in a long, long, time a huge number of these magnetic bands are going to get jumbled up and come to the surface of the sun and it's curtains for humanity."

"And they chose not to tell anyone," Laura said.

"Correct. And incidentally, why they weren't going to tell the world was the second question I asked my father."

"What was your first?" Samir asked.

Joe cocked his head. "I may have said some expletives and asked if he was kidding me—in more crude language."

"What did he say?" Laura asked.

"Well, I soon learned that I didn't get my sense of humor from him. And that, in his opinion—and that of Epoch at large—telling the world that an extinction level solar storm was coming was simply cruel. And unproductive. He reasoned—and I can somewhat see this point—that telling the world would have resulted in a complete breakdown of society."

"I have to agree," Samir said quietly.

"It was practical too," Joe said. "They needed society to function to build Antarctica Station and do all their prep work for the Event."

"Why did they locate in Antarctica?" Samir asked. "My parents never would tell me. Or any of the details of the Event." He shrugged. "I mean, what a lack of trust."

"Believe me," Joe said, "I know about parental trust issues. What I don't know is why exactly they chose Antarctica. Seems like it had something to do with the Earth's magnetic field and some added protection from solar storms. But knowing what I know now, I think that was just part of the sales pitch."

"But," Samir said, "the CME would explain what happened to those convoys on the South Pole Traverse and all their equipment. The stations too."

"Correct," Joe said. "The initial solar event severely disrupted electrical systems across the globe. Not completely, but enough to be a major problem. Of course Antarctica Station was built to withstand it."

"But they could have done that anywhere," Laura said.

"True. I think the other reason they chose Antarctica was to keep anyone from knowing what they were doing. But looking back now, I wonder if it was in case anyone survived."

"What do you mean?"

"Well, Epoch was convinced the first year of solar storms would wipe out humanity. And based on what I recently found out, it nearly did. But maybe someone else knew what was going to happen. Because there were survivors after the first year. A lot more than Epoch had anticipated. And they were looking to rebuild. Looking for resources and refuge from the storms. Which would make Antarctica another logical choice for Epoch to hide. It's remote—way too far for post-apocalyptic refugees to reach, especially with electronic equipment gone and useless. It was basically the Stone Age after the storms started."

Laura clasped her hands together. "It's a harsh approach. Epoch could have helped the survivors. Could have gone out in the world and rounded everyone up and brought them back."

"They could," Joe said. "But that was never part of their plan. You see, Epoch—and my father and his partners—they never saw this solar event as a catastrophe. What I didn't know back then—what I only recently learned—is that they saw it as an opportunity."

"An opportunity for what?" Laura asked.

"To start over. A blank slate. The Next World. A world they crafted carefully from the mistakes of the past—a world they controlled completely. That's the other thing they were doing in Antarctica Station: debating exactly what kind of world they would create on this blank canvas. That's what those seminars really were, Laura—the various sides arguing their case."

Joe adjusted himself in the bed. To Laura, he seemed more tired now, as if the talk was draining him.

"But the worst part is how far Epoch was willing to go. They didn't just leave the world to die. They're finishing the job."

46

"What do you mean, finishing the job?" Laura asked.

Joe took a sip of water. "When I asked if you could run on the lower levels of the simulated station, Imara practically laughed out loud. What she said next made no sense to me."

"Which was?"

"That even if you managed to figure out what Antarctica Station really was and exit stasis, you could never meet up with the others."

"Others?"

"Imara must have read the surprise on my face. Remember, I was still operating under the assumption that the people in Antarctica Station were the only ones who had survived the solar storms. Imara must have delighted in that moment—the fact that my father had kept me in the dark. She told me everything then. That Epoch had satellites monitoring human activity, and they were shocked at the survival rate. And that they had started a program to eliminate the remaining survivors."

"Why?" Laura asked. "Why not just bring them in?"

Joe eyed her for a long moment. "That's how you're different from them, Laura. You have a heart—a good one."

334

"Still, what reason could they have for killing everyone who's left?"

"Take your pick," Joe said. "Numbers, for example. There are a lot more survivors than there are Epoch citizens. Ideology is another problem. All these survivors have in common is that they're alive. Epoch is trying to build a cohesive society with a shared purpose. Throwing a bunch of random people into the mix might be okay, but what if they have different ideas?"

"Control," Samir said. "That's what it's about."

"Yes," Joe agreed. "In a word, control. That's what my father and the other Epoch founders really want: total control. They were planning on a new world of their own making. The power of gods in a world starting over from scratch."

"They're addicts," Samir said. "Addicted to power. And total control. It's what gives them their rush."

"And they're practical," Joe added. "Taking in survivors provides no benefit for them. They don't need more people. Or anything these people have. But taking them in is a risk. These people could sabotage all their best-laid plans. So best to get rid of them."

"How?" Laura asked.

Joe held up a finger. "That, I actually don't know. The program, which is called Colony Collapse, was classified even above my security level. Epoch isn't even telling the passengers and most of the operation staff about Colony Collapse. They're just going to act as if the solar events wiped everyone out. It's their big secret."

A piece fell into place for Laura then. "That's why you helped me escape? Because you learned about Colony Collapse."

"Half of the reason."

"What's the other half?"

"To facilitate my own escape."

Joe seemed to read Laura's confusion.

"After Imara told me the truth, I saw why my father had been hiding it from me. To some extent, Epoch and all of this was a second chance for him to have a relationship with me. My mother must have known about his deep moral flaws. It's why she wouldn't let him near me. He knows I don't share his moral compass. So he hid the truth of Colony Collapse. And I knew I would never forgive myself if I didn't try to stop it. But I had no plausible reason to exit stasis and try to leave Antarctica."

"So you let me run on the lower levels, and you waited."

"Yeah, but I actually hadn't worked out how to facilitate your escape and then mine." Joe nodded at Samir. "Then you showed up in the server room and kicked it all off. I've been sort of adapting since then."

"What's your plan now?"

"Again, the information on Colony Collapse is limited, but I know Epoch is concentrating on eliminating certain pockets of survivors. Maybe they think the smaller groups will die out naturally."

"The satellites," Laura said.

"Correct. Epoch has a small number of advanced, heavily shielded satellites in orbit for surveillance. They were an investment to launch due to their state-of-the-art technology and the cost of making them resilient to solar events. Despite their engineering, a few did not survive the solar storms. Those that did are positioned over the pockets of resistance."

"There were two over the Raleigh–Durham area," Laura said. "One was moved to Antarctica to track us."

"That's right," Joe confirmed. "I'm assuming there were two over the Triangle because of the large geographic area or the number of survivors concentrated there or both."

"What's your plan?" Samir asked.

"Epoch has several major offices. Boston. Silicon Valley. New York. And Research Triangle Park." Joe motioned to Laura. "I've only visited the RTP office once, that time I came to Durham, when we met. But it's a massive facility. It has labs and a data center. And most importantly, it's where my father is."

Laura held up a hand. "Wait. Isn't he in Antarctica Station?"

Joe smiled. "Remember, Antarctica Station doesn't exist in the real world, only as a virtualization. You met him in Antarctica Station, but he's physically located in a stasis bay in RTP. The satellites link the passengers in any simulation."

"Right," Laura said. "That's going to take some getting used to. Back to the plan. I want details."

Joe looked sheepish. "Actually, I hadn't worked those out yet."

Samir's gaze drifted to the ceiling. "I knew you were going to say that."

"I'm open to ideas," Joe said. "But we have very limited information here. My basic plan was to do some recon and then fill in the details. I know the RTP facility is important to Epoch. And my father is there. It seems like a good place to start."

"I agree," Laura said.

Samir shrugged. "Fine by me."

They sat for a quiet moment, and finally Samir moved to Joe's bedside and studied the bandage. "I want to change this."

Laura was thinking about her sister, and for that reason, she repeated the question she had started with. "Joe. How long were we in Antarctica Station? How long has it been— out here in the physical world?"

"Twenty-seven years."

47

It was noon when they reached the North Carolina coast. Still submerged, the sub sailed past Cape Fear and Bald Head Island and up the Cape Fear River.

At the outskirts of Wilmington, they rose to periscope depth. Sitting in the command center, Laura, Samir, and Joe got their first look at the world after.

The optimist in Laura had hoped to see some sign of life. She saw only the ruins of a coastal town with North Carolina's largest port.

The scene was one of an epic battle in slow motion, of nature burying the remnants of civilization, reclaiming the Earth. The stacks of containers in the port were rusted and crumbling, as if a giant sea monster had waded ashore and snacked on them at random.

The massive cranes that had once unloaded the metal containers were crumbled into the ground, arms of civilization pulled down by time and weather.

The buildings beyond were metal skeletons, windows gone. Laura was sure that there were even more structures that had fallen over time. Vines and plants were crawling over those heaps and everything else.

Commercial ships lay on their sides along the banks of the river.

Beyond the port were a series of marinas where fishing, tour, and pleasure boats had once docked. By the dozens, they lay in piles now, perhaps the wreckage of a hurricane or tides adding up over time or a function of both.

Beyond the marinas, the river was shallower. At some point, Laura expected the wreckage clogging the river might make it impassable.

They decided to put ashore near the Interstate 140 bridge and take the road to Interstate 40. They had no recent satellite surveillance on either thoroughfare but reasoned that it would be the fastest route from Wilmington to the Triangle, even if nature and abandoned cars partially blocked them.

They also decided that it would be best to travel at night. The UTV had full self-driving and night-vision cameras that allowed it to run without its lights on. Joe suggested that Epoch might have tasked a satellite to the Wilmington area or the route to the Triangle. Laura had also assumed as much.

As in Antarctica, traveling in the dark seemed safer.

With the sub resting on the riverbed, Laura, Samir, and Joe had their last meal aboard and waited for the fall of night.

Laura thought the time spent on this voyage had pretty much delivered Samir to the other side of withdrawals and she was thankful for that.

And Joe was actually faring better than Laura had expected, but she still wanted him to get a full exam at a trauma center. In the back of her mind was the fear that he might re-injure the wound, tearing open a blood vessel, and begin bleeding out again.

*

An hour after sunset, the sub slowly rose to the surface, extended its tracks down, and propelled itself forward until it began digging into the muddy river bottom, slipping until it emerged.

Shortly after, its ramp dug into the riverbank and the electric UTV silently rolled out, Samir in the driver seat, Laura beside him, and Joe in the back, grunting and grimacing as they rocked on the uneven terrain.

His injury would make the journey rough for him, Laura thought, but there was no alternative.

The first thing that struck her was the green wisps in the sky. The aurora was here too. Was that due to changes in Earth's magnetosphere or atmosphere? Whatever the cause, it was beautiful. The canvas of stars beyond was too. She had never seen them this bright here in North America. As she had in Antarctica, she once again felt like an explorer on an alien world. This one vaguely familiar, with its interstate signs listing and rusting, vines crawling up them.

*

They made the choice to stay off the open interstate, instead favoring a course that kept the UTV under nearby tree cover. It was night, but thanks to the brightness of the stars and the aurora, the vehicle would be easy to see.

When the first rays of sunlight peeked above the horizon behind them, they drove deeper into the forest, parked, and made camp. The first day of driving had brought them just past Benson. Barring anything unforeseen, they'd reach Research Triangle Park during tomorrow night's drive.

Sitting in the tent, the three ate a meal of Epoch MREs. Even for summer in North Carolina, the early morning air was as warm and humid as Laura had ever felt it. It was loud too: an army of cicadas chirped all around them, and birds called loudly, trying to be heard over the din.

After eating, Laura ventured deeper into the woods to use the bathroom. Squatting, she spotted something sticking out of a crop of ferns.

As her eyes adjusted to the dark, she recognized the rusted frame of a child's bicycle, long forgotten and left to wither. The tires were gone. Some of the spokes had rusted through as well.

Panning right, Laura spotted a series of concrete squares rising from the ground, now partially covered by kudzu and other climbing vines.

The foundation of a house. Of the people who lived here, who had a child with a bike.

Staring at the concrete foundation, she thought about how different things looked in the light of day. And time has a way of washing away everything but the foundation. And she wondered what was left of humanity's foundation after the sun had turned on the Earth and twenty-seven years with no technology.

And she wondered if her sister was still part of that foundation or if she was buried like the rusting bike she had barely been able to find.

48

Laura slept about half the night and only thanks to three things: earplugs, exhaustion, and a sleep mask.

The field kits had been prepped for an Antarctic expedition. Laura figured that was the only reason the sleep masks were included (for the summer months when the sun didn't set).

She woke with Joe's arm around her. He was burning up, and that concerned her a great deal.

It was summer in North Carolina, and the tent, even under the shade of the trees, had soaked in the heat all day long. It was like a sauna inside now. But Laura worried that the infection had returned. She decided she would give him another dose of broad-spectrum antibiotics when he woke up.

Laura also knew that her concern wasn't just professional prudence. She cared about Joe. More than she had cared about any man in a long time. And he had proved steady and reliable and willing to risk his life for her. In this weird place, her feelings for him were impossible to sort out.

Samir was the first among them to move. He sat up and unzipped the blackout flap in the tent's closest window. There was still a screen, but the rays of sunrise through the trees were like a lighthouse shining into the tiny space.

Joe stirred and inhaled and moved closer to Laura, burying his face into the base of her neck.

Laura turned and raised a hand to his cheek. It was warm too.

Samir cleared his throat dramatically. "Before this gets totally weird, just a reminder that I'm here."

Joe and Laura both glanced over at him.

He shrugged. "Definitely feeling like a post-apocalyptic third wheel here."

"You'll survive," Laura said.

*

By the time they had packed up the camp, the cicadas were roaring in the night, and nocturnal animals were scurrying through the dense forest. Once again, the aurora cast tendrils of green across the night sky.

Samir was back in the UTV, sitting in the driver's seat.

Laura was about to get in when Joe's fingers closed around her upper arm. "Hey."

She squinted at him.

"You don't have to do this," he said.

"Do what?"

"Risk your life."

"Joe, I'd say my life is already at risk at this point."

"Not like this," he said. "The closer we get to that Epoch headquarters, the more dangerous it's going to get. We don't know what's out there. We don't know—"

"What are you suggesting?"

"I'm suggesting we go back to the sub. You and Samir stay. I'll take the UTV and finish this."

"And what do Samir and I do?"

"Whatever you want. You can wait for me. And if I don't come back... I don't know... Go to Europe. Or Asia. Or Australia. It doesn't matter. The world is empty now. Find a place that's safe and go live your life."

Laura's heart melted. With love and hurt in equal measures. "Is that what you think I want? Safety?"

"I'm giving you an out."

"I don't want out."

"Okay."

"I think you're saying all this for your own sake, Joe."

"Maybe I am."

"No maybe, it's true."

"Look, if something happens to you today—tonight—I'll always blame myself."

"And there it is."

Joe shrugged. "This is what I am, Laura. It's what I've always been."

"A loner."

"Exactly."

"With trust issues. Because you never had a father."

"Also correct."

"And then you did. And you found out everything your mother believed was true and that the world he wanted was just as cruel as the one you left."

"Your words are better than mine, Laura."

"I'm not going to let you push me away."

"You didn't sign up for this."

"Well, I'm signing up now. I want to finish this. And I won't blame anyone for what is about to happen. I'll stand shoulder to shoulder with you and accept it all. Because I don't want to live out my life alone, knowing I ran away from the only fight that mattered in this world anymore."

49

They drove through the night, again avoiding the open road, weaving through the overgrowth around it. When Raleigh came into view, Laura couldn't tear her gaze from the eerie scene. It was similar to Wilmington: a long-abandoned, ruined city left for nature and time to demolish.

The only clues to what had happened were the faded graffiti scrawled under highway overpasses and atop stretches of pavement. Many were mostly gone, but in the ones Laura could read, she got a sense of what inhabitants of this world thought:

US vs THE SUN

WE HAVE NO HOPE

Another message read:

NATURE GETS EVEN

Several times, Laura saw the words:

BEWARE THE INSECTS OF EPOCH

She wondered what that meant. Was it just a euphemism for Epoch's people? Or a reference to the common knowledge that insects like cockroaches had survived much longer than humans—and through worse environmental changes.

The most commonly spray-painted image was an outline of what looked like a mountain peak. It had a gentle slope, then a sharp rise and dramatic fall. A line ran along the base of it and under that, three letters: TGS.

The vehicle was moving along Wade Avenue when Laura spotted a longer message spray painted on the large sign outside the crumbling PNC Arena:

WE SURVIVED 200,000 YEARS
WITHOUT TECHNOLOGY
WE WILL AGAIN
WE ARE THE GIBRALTAR SOCIETY
FIND US AT THE ROCK
—TGS

They crossed the freeway and parked under the sign.

Joe said, "TGS seems to be the active resistance cell."

"Or were," Samir said. "There's no sign of them now."

"Could be hiding," Joe said. "Makes sense if Epoch is hunting them."

"We could search the next time we see the TGS symbol," Samir said.

"That assumes," Joe said slowly, "that finding them would be good for us."

"We seem to have the same enemy—Epoch."

"True," Joe conceded. "But who knows what nearly thirty years in this wasteland has done to them? They're probably starving, desperate, and ruthless."

Samir raised his eyebrows. "So, about like everyone before. Metaphorically speaking."

*

They drove on and just past Umstead Park and RDU airport, the night sky was aglow with fire and explosions. The flashes of light came sporadically, accompanied by booms, the sound like a drum beating as the UTV approached.

They rode in silence, none of the three of them directly addressing what was ahead, but Laura suspected they all knew what it was: a battle raging.

At the I885 exit from I40, they veered off the main interstate and carved their way through the forest beside it.

"We should keep our distance from the fighting," Joe said.

At the ramp and overpass for TW Alexander Drive, they parked deep in the woods and covered the UTV with branches, then walked to the road, where they stood behind the cover of a copse of trees and watched the battle rage. The target of the assault was a sprawling building perhaps 300 yards away. It looked like a mix of a large manufacturing facility and a military facility. It had several outer fences— which had been breached in several places—and building walls with no windows.

It was surrounded by pavement that Laura assumed was once a parking lot, like an asphalt moat ringing the building—one that they had not let nature reclaim, perhaps to prevent their enemies from having cover.

Those enemies were here now, in force.

The former parking lot held about sixty automobiles. They were older models, the type made before electronics became a mainstay in cars and trucks. And on each one, on the hood or roof, was the symbol for TGS.

Laura thought there was little chance of anyone seeing or hearing them from this distance, but still, Joe spoke quietly.

"That's the Epoch HQ."

"Seems TGS is active," Samir said, echoing Laura's thoughts.

The group's principal weapons were large white PVC pipes mounted on the roofs of the vehicles. For the cars, the trunk lids had been removed and several gunners were crouched behind the improvised grenade launchers. Those launches went on non-stop, the rounds exploding on the building in fiery plumes that left black marks but nothing more. The walls weren't budging. All the rebels' efforts seemed to amount to little more than burn marks on the facade, much like their graffiti messages across the fallen city.

The most curious thing about the group was their outfits. Even in the heat of the night—and with the sweltering blasts nearby—they were dressed head-to-toe in black garments. Their hands were gloved, their faces covered with a balaclava, and eyes hidden behind goggles.

Why?

Laura assumed it was a sort of camouflage to make them

harder to see in the night. But instinctively, she thought that was wrong.

Maybe the solar storms had altered the atmosphere enough to let more solar radiation reach the Earth surface— and the outfits offered some protection. If that was the case, why wear them at night? Perhaps it was in case the battle raged into the morning. Or maybe there was something else in the air. A topical toxin they were protecting from. Still, that didn't seem right to Laura.

In studying the scene, she noticed something even more strange. The throngs of TGS fighters were surrounded by hazy silver clouds. She hadn't noticed them before, in the dim light, but she saw them more clearly when an explosion rocked the building and flashed across the parking lot.

The clouds coalesced around the figures as if they were following them, like a blob of static trying to blot them out from the night.

Was it a defense mechanism of some sort?

"So," Samir said, "confirming TGS is not besties with Epoch."

Joe, standing beside Laura, was sweating and looking uncomfortable, no doubt from the stress on his wound. They needed to make camp and rest soon. He had been upright, riding across the bumpy terrain too long today.

"We should make contact with them," Joe said. "They'll be able to give us intel on Epoch, and maybe together we can figure out a plan."

"I agree," Laura said.

"I'll go alone," Joe said.

"Wait, now?" Samir said.

"No. We'll wait until they retreat, follow them back to their base, and go the following day, after they've had time to come down from the battle."

"I don't think we should split up," Laura said.

Joe motioned to his arm in the sling. "Physically, I'm the weakest. If they take me hostage, you two can come get me after a few hours."

Samir nodded solemnly. "Post-apoc hostage rescue. Right up our alley."

Laura opened her mouth to speak, but a sharp pain in her right bicep stopped her. The stinging stretched out, lasting longer than any bug bite she had ever experienced. Her left hand flew to the spot, expecting to feel a bee or wasp, but she found only burning skin, a welt already starting to form.

"Ow," Samir called out, reaching for his forearm.

Joe was turning back to them when he used his good arm to slap his neck. He winced, either from the sting or the movement irritating his chest wound or both. "Got me too. Probably a nest nearby." He stalked past them, back toward the UTV. "Let's roll out."

As Laura turned, her vision blurred. Her limbs felt stiff, as if they had fallen asleep. She was having some sort of allergic reaction. But she wasn't allergic to insect bites.

Maybe it was a new species. A mutation in an existing insect brought on by the solar storms and radiation.

Ahead, Samir stumbled and nearly fell, balancing with both hands held out. He twisted back toward Laura, but the features of his face were blurry. His words came out slow and droning, and Laura couldn't make them out.

She felt an arm wrap around her back and a hand

bracing her left side, pulling her forward, in the direction of the UTV. She glanced over. Joe. He was staggering, legs weakening with every step.

Samir was on all fours now, crawling across the forest floor.

When he reached the branches covering the transport, he tugged enough away to clear the doors and crawled in.

By the time Joe deposited Laura in the passenger side and returned to the driver's seat, Samir had already opened the med kit in the back seat.

He took out the EpiPen. But he didn't inject himself. He lunged forward and stabbed it down into Laura's leg.

The epinephrine injection hit her with the force of a lightning strike. Laura's chest tightened, heart beating faster. Her vision cleared.

Beside her, Joe was panting, speaking between breaths. "PNC. Arena. Proceed. Discreetly."

Laura thought that was smart—returning to a place they knew was empty and safe and where they could make camp.

The UTV rolled forward. Joe was gulping air now, on the verge of hyperventilating. He reached a shaking hand out to Laura.

In the back seat, Samir slumped over and closed his eyes.

The EpiPen dose was already starting to wear off. Laura's body and mind were being assaulted by whatever venom was coursing through her veins. The med kit only had one EpiPen. But it didn't matter, because whatever the sting had done was only temporarily blocked by the epinephrine.

The UTV crept forward. Laura's vision was going out of phase again, the world coming in frames out of sync.

One second, they were in the forest; the next, they were at the edge of the treeline; and the next, they were crossing a cracked, crumbling street.

Joe's eyes were closed, breathing shallow.

The UTV slammed to a stop. The windows were instantly blacked out. Even the camera feeds on the screen in the dash went dark.

The passenger door jerked open, and hands grabbed Laura, dragging her out. A bag slammed down over her head and she saw only darkness as the venom took her under completely.

50

Laura's hands and ankles were bound when she came to.

Her body felt achy and inflamed, almost as if she had the flu. She was lying on her side, her weight pressing into the sting site on her bicep, which made it hurt even more.

She sucked in a breath and smelled damp, musty air with a hint of gasoline and alcohol.

Her mind was still working slowly, though better than right after the sting.

Her eyes were covered, but not by the bag. She could tell from the way the fabric had rested lightly against her mouth as she breathed. That resistance was gone. It felt more like a blindfold over her eyes. She wanted to reach up and rip it off, but she stayed still. Nearby, two people were talking. A man and a woman. The man's voice was quiet, almost reflective, a sharp contrast to the woman's husky, angry voice.

"…trade them," he said.

"For what?" she snapped, seeming annoyed.

"Vehicles."

"We have vehicles."

"Not solar-powered ones. We get a fleet of those, and we leave and keep running. You know we can't win—"

"We leave, and Epoch will just get stronger. When they do, they'll come looking for us."

"It gives us time to rebuild our numbers."

"Our numbers don't matter. They have the tech. That's the only high ground in this world. *Tech* is what we need."

"What's your plan?" the man said, sounding deflated.

"We're going to experiment on the two males. Try to figure out how the Epoch vaccine protects them from the stings. Maybe we can replicate it. Or do a blood transfer to give our people immunity."

"Is that even possible—immunity via transfusion?"

"I don't know. But I'll ask this one when she wakes up."

"She knows?"

"She does. She's a doctor."

"How do you know?"

"Never mind that. Just get the men set up for testing."

"That may be a problem."

"Why?"

"One of the guys is nearly dead."

"I told you we needed them alive."

"It wasn't us. Someone already shot him."

"What?"

"He has a gunshot wound in his chest."

"And you didn't see that?"

"We couldn't. It had been treated, and his suit was covering it. We ripped open the wound when we pulled him from the UTV."

"The question is who shot him—who has guns?" Quickly, the woman added: "No, the better question is, why didn't whoever has guns tell us about them?"

"It's probably Boston. Maybe New York, but rumor is

they are on the back foot. I bet whoever it is kept the guns quiet to surprise Epoch." A pause, and the man added, "Or maybe they think we have a leak."

"Or Epoch already knew about the guns," the woman said quietly, seeming deep in thought.

"I don't follow."

"Think about it. The only thing that makes sense is that another cell made a deal with Epoch. Guns... in exchange for what? Maybe taking us out? But whoever it was—Boston or New York or some new group—clearly went back on the deal."

The man said, "It could have also been friendly fire."

"Yeah, but that's unlikely. Let's find out who has the guns and try to make a deal to get some ourselves."

"And if they won't deal?"

"We take 'em."

"Look, this is all a lot of speculation," he said slowly. "I think we should—"

"Get some answers?" the woman snapped. "I couldn't agree more. We need to start interrogating them."

"We can work on the Indian guy, but the other won't be much good. Like I said, he's done for. We stopped the bleeding, but he's finished."

"Fine. Get started. I'll take this one myself. I've got a lot of questions for her."

"All right, but one more thing. There was a rifle in the back of the vehicle. And a handgun."

"That's good. But we need more. Enough to arm several platoons. If we can get that much firepower and get inside that building, we can hold them off long enough for the trojan to work."

"That assumes it will work."

"It'll work." Footsteps echoed in the space, and the woman added, "We've wasted enough time. Get started on the men."

Laura's mind flashed to an image of Samir being tortured and of Joe taking his last breath as the wound in his chest oozed blood.

With her bound hands, she reached up and pulled the cloth from her eyes, revealing blinding light. Squinting, she said, "Stop. Please. We're not your enemy."

Footsteps moved closer to her. Her eyes were adjusting now, but she still only saw two hazy outlines shadowed by the light.

They stopped a few feet from her, towering above. As her sight cleared, Laura realized she was lying on a dingy foam mattress topper on the concrete floor. A large glass partition separated her from the two figures. A black, tar-like substance ran along the edges of the glass, indicating that it was airtight.

The woman squatted down and stared with hard, hateful eyes.

As Laura studied the face, her heart broke. The woman was nearly gaunt, cheeks and eyes sunken. Deep lines ran across her forehead, and a wide scar stretched from her temple to her chin. Her hair was silver-gray, though Laura knew that at her age, this woman should have still had her vibrant, flowing brown hair. Or at least she assumed so. Their mother didn't have a gray hair on her head when she passed away.

51

Laura pushed up on the thin mattress and whispered, "Rachel."

Her sister smirked. "Wasn't sure you'd recognize me."

She studied Laura's face. "We knew Epoch was into anti-aging and immortality, but seeing is believing."

"This is not what you think."

"Sure it is. Twenty-seven years ago, you left and somehow hit the lottery when your employer was the only one who survived the Solar Storms." Rachel grinned, but her eyes were filled with hate. "And you don't call. Don't write. Don't bother to check in on the last family you have."

She stood back up and stared down. "I get it. With phones down that was a tough call—if you will. And let's face it, I don't blame you for thinking I wouldn't make it when the world ended. I almost didn't. But I've changed a lot."

"I can see that. But listen, Rachel, you've got this wrong."

"I doubt that."

"The injured man who was with me—he was shot by Epoch."

Rachel's brow furrowed.

Laura pressed on. "It's true. He was shot because he was helping me escape. Because he found out what Epoch was doing, and he wants to stop it. So does Samir." Laura nodded. "That's right. He's the other man you captured. This isn't what you think, Rachel."

"What is it?"

"I'm telling you, it's us trying to stop Epoch."

"You know what I think? I think it's you coming back to finish the job the Solar Storms started: wiping us out. That's all Epoch cares about now."

"What do you mean? How?"

Rachel again scrutinized her sister's face. Slowly, she drew a small vial from her pocket and held it up to the glass barrier. Inside was a round silver object about the size of a bee. On one side were three prongs. On the other was a tight mesh. Around the perimeter, flaps stood out.

"I've never seen that in my life," Laura whispered. "Is that what stung me?"

"You really don't know?"

"I swear to you, Rachel, on Dad's grave, I have been in stasis, in some simulation Epoch created, for the last twenty-seven years. I didn't know."

Rachel slipped the vial back into her pocket. "But they inoculated you."

Laura shook her head. "Apparently not. I feel like I have the flu."

"That's what happens to Epochers when they're stung."

"What happens to everyone else?"

"They get sick too, but worse. They live long enough to go back to their colony or family, just long enough to pass on the Epovirus the microdrones carry. It's like a biological bomb." Rachel's eyes went cold. "This is how they tested it in the beginning."

"How?"

"Random people show up. Claim to be survivors, just like you. But they're sick. Stung by something that leaves a big welt. Then everyone else gets sick. A week or two later, the Epoch operative walks out of the camp. No one else does, ever again. It's clever. Dead people can't warn the other camps."

Rachel walked closer to the barrier. "Is that Epoch's plan here? Send you in with this crazy story about stasis, assuming I'll let you out of isolation after your symptoms pass? Have they changed the virus? Probably. It would be an efficient way to take out this colony."

Laura considered it. Had their escape been too easy? Had Epoch let them make it this far—and stung them outside the battle for this purpose?

"I don't know," Laura said quietly. "But I know this: their plans don't matter anymore."

Rachel's tone was sarcastic. "Ohhh, tell me more."

"I can get in that building. And inside, I can get you all the time you need."

Rachel stared but didn't say anything.

"If I'm right," Laura said, "I think we can end this war. And send Epoch exactly where they should be."

Rachel rolled her eyes. "This is my face when I believe you."

"You better, Rachel. I know you've been hurt. I know you were hurt when I didn't come back when this world collapsed. I know what it's like to have your world fall apart and to feel alone and feel like the person you trusted most betrayed you. I know your life has been hard since. And a lot of that has been because of Epoch, and you think I cooperated with their plans. But I didn't. And I'm telling you right now, if Joe—the guy with that massive gaping bullet wound—dies, then our chance at freedom and peace and a new life dies with him. We don't have time to argue. Or debate. We need to start working together. If not, you may as well kill me. Because we're all going to die."

52

The UTV drove at top speed along the open stretches of road in broad daylight. Laura wasn't worried about Epoch spotting them. Or the Gibraltar Society.

Time was the greatest enemy now.

She glanced into the back seat, where Joe lay, eyes closed, cheeks flushed, and forehead drenched in sweat.

From the passenger seat, Samir said, "Can I just say I really don't like this plan?"

"Which part?"

"The dangerous part."

Laura glanced over at him. "Wait, which part is that?"

"Exactly. Exactly, Laura."

"This is our best option, Samir."

"Is it? Seriously? We barely even had time to discuss it."

"Look, we either do this or Joe dies. And probably us too."

"Okay, okay. I'm doing it. I'm just not liking it."

"I'm always open to ideas."

"Why can't we just set him out at Epoch's front door, then drive off? Like criminals do at the hospital. 'Hey, here's a GSW victim. Fix him. Bye!'"

"We're not criminals. And this isn't a hospital. And you know why we need to get inside."

"Just saying."

Up ahead, the Epoch building came into view. In the light of day, Laura saw it more clearly than during the night of the battle. There were burn marks all over the white facade. The roof was covered in solar panels—many of which had been damaged. A few sections of the side wall had gaping dark holes like wounds that had never healed.

Without specific directions, the UTV rolled to a stop in the crumbling parking lot. They were sitting almost exactly where the TGS fighters had been the night before.

Joe moaned in the back seat, and Laura tapped the screen, panning and searching the images the UTV's cameras had captured during their approach. She magnified a photo taken from the bridge. It showed a wide roll-up door on the right side of the building.

Laura pressed her finger into it and scrolled down to the option for *set destination*.

The UTV moved forward.

Laura practically held her breath as they approached the door. Epoch could very well fire on the vehicle, ending their gambit right here.

Instead, the door rose, revealing a dark corridor beyond. The UTV rolled forward, slower now. Inside, as the ramp descended, the headlights snapped on. Laura was reminded of her initial journey to Antarctica Station, of the sensation of being swallowed by a beast.

She turned and glanced through the rear window. The rolling door was falling, blotting out the sun.

Samir locked eyes with her, silently saying, *I'm telling you, this is a bad idea*.

But neither said anything out loud. Epoch could be listening now.

Ahead, the two-lane corridor opened into a wide parking garage. On each side were loading docks. The vehicles backed into them looked like sea freight containers mounted atop tanks. They ran on tracks, and their walls were made of corrugated metal. There were no windows, only holes along the top (for cameras, Laura presumed).

Directly in front of the UTV was a pair of wide, gunmetal-gray doors. They swung in as the vehicle approached, and Warren Albright strode out. He looked a little older than the last time Laura had seen him, in the dining room where he welcomed her to Antarctica Station. Or perhaps everyone looked a little more worn in the real world versus Epoch's virtual world.

Laura tapped the manual control button on the screen and grabbed the wheel, driving directly toward the man who had, for more than two decades, been trying to kill her sister—and everyone else not with Epoch.

By force of will, she eased off the accelerator as she reached him. He didn't even flinch.

A dozen people in Epoch security fatigues emerged and spread out around Albright, rifles at the ready.

Laura opened her door and stepped out.

53

Samir followed closely behind Laura, and he was the first to speak. Holding his hands up, he faced the horde of Epoch personnel. "I'm innocent. Seriously. In Antarctica, I was just going to show her the station and how she couldn't escape, and she stuffed me in a transport and kidnapped me. Her and the wounded commando have—"

Albright had been staring at Laura. Now, his eyes snapped to Samir. "Wounded?"

Samir shrugged. "Yeah, he's in the back. Why do you think—"

Albright motioned to the guards, and they rushed to the UTV, pulled open the door, and called back to him. "It's bad, sir."

"Well, get him to the med bay! Right now."

They didn't wait for a gurney. Four Epoch staffers lifted Joe and marched toward the door.

Albright pointed at Laura. "If he dies, you die."

Samir fell in behind the guards carrying Joe, head down, as if trying to casually slip away.

"Stop," Albright called to him. "Where do you think you're going?"

"To help. I'm a doctor."

"We have doctors."

"Seriously? Dude's half dead. You need all the help you can get."

Albright narrowed his eyes.

Samir shrugged. "Hey, it's your apocalypse. Just don't blame me if he doesn't make—"

"Fine. Go." To the man beside him, Albright said, "And you go with him. Watch every move. Put him in a cell after."

Laura watched Samir slip beyond the doors. She locked eyes with Albright. "We need to talk."

He smirked at her. "No. We don't. But for my own amusement, I'll listen."

He motioned to a woman to his right. "Search her. And then change her clothes and bring her to Conference Two."

*

Outside the operating room, Samir scrubbed his hands at the sink. The sensation brought back a wave of memories. And a profound feeling of guilt, made worse by his sobriety. He could feel his nervousness rising, and as it grew, an image came into his mind: a black background and, in the middle, a single white pill. Serenity. That's what it represented. He could find some form of it in that room. It might be a pill. Or a liquid. But it would ease the discomfort of this reality. And he was well-skilled at skimming meds from an OR. It would be so easy.

He dug his nails into his skin and scrubbed harder, trying to claw the thought away.

Around him, the nurses and physicians stepped back

from the wide sink and barreled through the door. Soon, he heard them shouting, cutting away Joe's suit.

"Hey," the security meathead behind him yelled. "You going to wash your hands all day or help them?"

Samir held his hands up. Even with his nerves, they weren't shaking. "Yeah. I'm clean enough."

*

The strip search was quick and awkward, and after, Laura was led to a conference room. Albright stood at the end, back to her, watching a large screen on the wall. The left half showed an OR where Joe lay on the table, surrounded by four people in scrubs. Laura didn't see Samir.

The right half of the screen was split into a dozen blocks, all showing the exterior of the Epoch building in RTP.

There was no one out there.

None of this was going according to the plan.

"Let me guess," Albright said, still not turning. "You met up with your sister."

"Yes," Laura said, intending to continue, but Albright spoke first.

"And you were horrified at what she had become, and your boyfriend was injured, and you had to help him, and you brought him back and you want to rejoin Epoch."

"Half right."

"No, it's the whole truth. You thought there was help waiting on you out here. That you would escape and get your life back and all would be right with the world. Let the government deal with Epoch."

"That's what I thought, but that's not why I'm here."

Albright turned then. "No, Laura. You're here for the

same reason you made a deal with the DA and Epoch. You're here to save yourself. Deep down, you know this world is finished. You know your best option is Epoch. You and Joe"—Albright motioned to the screen—"can live forever. In whatever kind of world you want. Even if he's permanently injured from this wound—which I count as your fault incidentally—he can survive forever, with no limits in stasis simulation."

"I don't want that made-up world."

"Every world is made up, Laura. It's made up of human-created constructs. Ideologies. Narratives. Beliefs. Customs. Call it whatever you want. The only thing that changes is who controls it."

Laura stepped closer to him. "The time for Visions of the New World is over, Warren."

"You're right about that. It's time to create it."

"I couldn't agree more." Laura pointed to the right side of the screen. In one of the security feeds, the first of the armored TGS vehicles was arriving. "And by the way, I'm not here to save myself. I came to save Joe, the people out there, and the people in here. In that order."

54

In the operating room, Samir watched the droplets of blood roll off the table and splatter on the floor.

On the table, Joe was moaning and writhing as the surgical team tried to hold him down.

A rolling cart nearby held a computer screen that showed his vitals, which were erratic. Samir knew the interface—it was the same one they used in Antarctica Station.

To the nurse next to him, he yelled. "Hey, unlock this!"

Still holding one of Joe's arms, she glanced over at Samir, then back to the surgeon who was cutting away a piece of puffy, red flesh.

"Hey!" Samir yelled again. "Log in! I need access to my files."

Finally, the woman released Joe and ripped her gloves off, tapped at the screen, then stalked to the wall and regloved.

On the monitor, the full MedRe interface appeared—not just the surgical program.

Samir began adjusting the anesthesia medications. A few seconds later, Joe's moans subsided, and his body went slack. The two nurses who had been holding him slowly released him, hands hovering just above.

Samir exhaled. His gaze settled on a silver metal tray that

held three glass vials of bliss. He could reach out and grab them. Right now.

Beyond the tray, the security guard assigned to him was watching closely. But Samir could handle that. He pulled his right glove off, then the other, and tossed them to the man, who caught them but never tore his eyes from Samir. This guy was good. That wasn't ideal.

"Make yourself useful," Samir said. "Grab me a fresh pair. Medium, please."

"Get 'em yourself!" the man shouted.

"Shut up," yelled one of the surgeons.

Samir pointed his uncovered hand at the monitor and said more quietly. "You really want me to take my eyes off of this?"

The man shook his head and walked around the operating table, still watching Samir, only looking away long enough to locate the glove dispenser. At the box on the wall, he diverted his eyes again as he reached in for the rubber gloves.

In that split second, Samir shoved his right hand in his pocket, grabbed the data drive, and raised both hands in time to catch the gloves the security guard had thrown. The man circled the other side of the table as Samir made a show of holding up his left hand with the new glove on it as his right hand was gently inserting the small drive into a port on the bottom of the Epoch workstation.

One thing Samir had become good at was sleight of hand in an operating room. For the first time, he was actually putting it to good use. Maybe saving humanity would help him get over all the patients he had put at risk. But as he thought it, he knew that was wishful thinking. He'd never completely get over what he had done.

With the other glove on, he opened a new window on the interface and tapped the button for *execute program*.

*

On the security feed, the TGS vehicles were arriving faster now. And in far greater numbers than the night before.

On the other half of the screen, Laura saw Samir deftly insert the small drive into the workstation as he changed gloves.

Albright motioned to the TGS armada. "What is this, some kind of last stand? They think you're going to open the front door, and they'll pour in and wipe us out?"

"No one is getting wiped out."

"You know, Laura, I think you actually believe that. Your basic problem is that you're naive. It's why you thought you could just drive out of Antarctica Station and why you misjudged your best friend—"

"I was naive," Laura said, walking closer to him. "Was. Back then. But I see things clearly now. You want to know what I see?"

Albright smiled. "There's nothing good on TV these days. So go ahead."

"I see another addict. I've gotten better at spotting them, unfortunately. And you're one, Warren. But your vice isn't something out of a bottle or a vial. It's power. Control is your drug of choice. Isn't it?"

He studied her a moment then smiled, more amused than concerned.

"The good news," Laura said, "is that I'm going to give you what you want."

"Oh really? What's that?"

"A world of your choosing, that you control."

"I already have that."

"No. You don't. You only think you do. But you're losing it. Right now, as we speak. You just don't know it yet. It's how all empires fall."

"If only reality matched your words."

"My words are the truth. You sense it, Warren. It's why you're still talking to me. Do you want to hear what your utopia is going to cost you?"

"Sure, Laura. There's still nothing on TV."

"It's going to cost you this world. The ruined one, that you want to sleep through."

"Why would I give you that?"

Laura walked closer to the video feed and pointed at the TGS fighters, who were starting to exit the vehicles. "Because if you don't, they're going to take it from you."

Albright laughed, with real humor then. "Thank you, Laura, this is truly better than TV. I think maybe that ride out of Antarctica froze the logic center in your brain."

On the screen, the silvery clouds swirled around the old cars and heavily clothed troops, like a band of static across the screen.

Laura wondered how long the computer virus Rachel had supplied would take. The answer came a few seconds later. The silver clouds of microdrones dropped to the broken pavement like a bursting thermometer showering out mercury.

The TGS raiders bent and studied the disabled microdrones. And then began advancing on the building.

Over the radio clipped to Albright's waist, a man's voice said, "Sir, Colony Collapse is down. We're working on it. Also, I'm assuming we should activate perimeter defenses."

Albright grabbed the radio and held it to his mouth. "Stand by."

"Sir—"

"I said, stand by."

For a long moment, Albright studied the screen, surveying the silver sea of downed drones. "How did you do it?"

"I trusted my former drug addict best friend. Convinced my former reckless, now jaded sister to trust me. And I assumed that you would do anything to save your son." Laura crossed to the other side of Albright, next to the monitor that showed Joe in the OR. "And I bet everything on the hope that you would make a deal to save all of us. Including Joe. And Epoch too."

"What deal?"

"It's like I said. You get your Next World, Warren. It's just not the world you thought it would be."

"I don't follow."

"Antarctica Station. Epoch stays there. For all of eternity. In your simulation. The rest of us get this world."

"And if I say no?"

Laura pointed to the TGS troops lining up outside the building.

"They'll get in. Sooner or later. And they'll kill everyone. You. Joe. Me. Everyone. Unless… I walk out there and tell my sister there's a deal. That the virus we just uploaded—which one of your Epoch defectors created—will stay in effect. The drones will never be reactivated."

"What about Joe?" Albright asked. The bravado had left his voice. "Will he be confined to Antarctica?"

"It's up to him. He gets to decide what kind of world he wants to live in. Yours. Or this one."

"It'll be yours," Albright said quietly.

"I hope so."

The radio squawked again. "Sir—"

"Stand by!" Albright roared. His eyes filled with tears. His hand was shaking now. Staring at the screens, his eyes shifting between Joe and the TGS troops, slowly, the shaking subsided. Laura thought the man before her seemed to shrink a few inches. He turned to her, and his voice was different. Calm. Reflective. "It was about him, you know. A lot of it. The end of the world has a way of showing you what's important. Of laying your mistakes bare."

"Yeah. I know."

Albright raised the radio to his mouth. "Hold your fire."

"Sir?" a confused voice said.

"Things have changed."

*

A few minutes later, Laura walked out of the front door of the Epoch building. A figure broke from the crowd and advanced, pulling the layers off as she walked. First, the gloves, then the outer coat, and finally, the goggles and balaclava covering her face.

Laura looked up at the sun and felt it warming her face, and when she looked down, she saw her sister again, smiling in that reckless carefree way she had before.

Epilogue

After the peace agreement at Epoch's headquarters, Laura quickly learned a harsh truth: striking a deal was simple; enforcing it was another story.

Working in favor of peace was Laura's sister. Rachel was considered to be the hardest of the hard-liners. Her willingness to accept an end to hostility had gone a long way.

But not all the way.

Laura also learned that the Gibraltar Society was by no means the only surviving human colony. Bands of survivors were everywhere.

Most were small. Communes and survivalists who had come out the other side of the solar events and sustained a population. But added together, they were bigger than TGS.

In the negotiations about the transfer of control, Epoch had offered to take these smaller groups out with their virus-carrying mini-drones (if TGS would supply the source code of the program that had grounded their weapon).

That idea, of course, was rejected.

Years of war had bred mistrust, and Laura didn't blame the TGS for that.

Emissaries were sent to the other groups. Some returned

with agreements. Some never did. Rachel mandated that those colonies who killed the messengers would be approached in force the next time.

It was, Laura thought, medieval. Reminiscent of the Stone Age the sun had sent them back to. While human technology had come a long way in a short time, human nature hadn't changed nearly as much.

*

When the details were decided, the Epoch staff left in waves. The first to go were the security personnel (Rachel had demanded that too—along with collecting every single gun in every Epoch facility). Once the staff and passengers had exited stasis, the servers were also turned off. In a violent act where TGS staff stormed the facility with sledgehammers and crowbars, the stasis bays were destroyed. There would be no virtual paradise here for Epoch staff to retreat to. Only reality.

Warren Albright and the other Epoch insiders were the last to go, like the officers of a sinking ship standing on the deck as it went down.

Fittingly, it was an icebreaker that carried them away— an Epoch ship that traveled down from Boston to New York to Wilmington, gathering the last of them.

Joe insisted on accompanying him. He told Laura it was because he wouldn't rest easy until he saw them all in stasis bays, locked away from reality.

Laura insisted on accompanying him. Because deep down, she knew that anything could still happen. And she had worked hard to keep him alive. She didn't want to let him go.

*

The voyage on the icebreaker reminded Laura of Antarctica Station.

She had her own stateroom.

So did Joe.

But like magnets, they drifted together.

In the mess hall, they took their meals together, sitting side by side in a booth.

Warren joined them sometimes.

At first, the conversations were awkward. On those occasions, Laura left Joe to deal with him. She took long walks around the ship, to the upper decks, where crowds were staring at the aurora, and to the lower decks, where mechanics were working or lounging and reading a book, waiting for something to break.

Over time, one thing that struck Laura was the change in Joe.

The edges wore away. Every day was like a sander with a deep grit smoothing him out.

Finally, he arrived in Laura's stateroom one evening, a smile on his face.

"Have fun with your dad?" she asked. She was verbally probing him. And, if she was being honest, she had grown worried that he was getting too close to his biological father, a man she knew was capable of vast evil and manipulation. A dangerous person who might be planning a counterattack when he arrived in Antarctica, where he had the advantage—in terms of troops and equipment.

Joe settled into the bottom bunk, eying Laura, who was sitting in the chair under the desk attached to the wall. "I didn't hate it."

"Do you still hate him?"

He shrugged. "I hate a lot of the things he's done. But hating him feels more like a tax on me."

Laura turned the chair a bit more. "Who is this new-age philosopher, and where is Joe?"

"He's different now."

"How?"

"He's resigned."

"Resigned to what?"

"The truth. What he wanted was wrong. Deeply wrong."

Laura exhaled. "Yeah."

"He had a hard life," Joe said, taking off his pants. "It doesn't make it right."

"What does it do?"

"It helps me understand it all." He pulled his shirt off. "That's part of what it's about, don't you think?"

Laura thought about her own father and his final words, which she had never read.

"Yeah," she said. "I do. I think understanding your parents is very important."

*

As the ship sailed across the equator, the icebreaker's passengers sunned themselves on the deck. The mood was festive.

The paranoid part of Laura couldn't help but dread what might happen when they reached lower latitudes, and eventually Antarctica.

*

Like the temperature, the atmosphere on board chilled as the ship sailed south.

One thing Laura noticed—and was surprised by—was that the coast of South America was almost always in view. She saw the logic in keeping the shore in sight. If the ship ran into trouble, the lifeboats could reach land. In this world, there were no rescue ships.

Still, she took the proximity to land as a sign that the ship's captain considered the passengers and the voyage dangerous. She wondered what the most treacherous thing on their voyage was: hostile seas, an angry sun, or the passengers themselves, who might mutiny and make a run for it.

Anything could still happen.

*

One night, when it was cool but not yet oppressively cold, on the deck of the ship, Joe leaned against the rail, the wind pulling at his hair, eyes as blue as frozen ice.

"We could skip this," he said to Laura. "Seeing them to the station."

"There's something I need."

He squinted at her.

"A letter."

"Everything there is digital."

"No, I had it when I arrived. It's handwritten. From my father."

"It didn't translate to the simulation?"

"No."

"Makes sense. Scanning hand-written documents is beneath the Epoch intake staff. And they probably figured there was nothing you could do about it."

"You think they threw it away?"

"Maybe."

He seemed to read the worry on her face and added, "But they might have just tossed it in a storage bin somewhere. There's no trash service in Antarctica, and things don't burn easily at the South Pole. And, let's face it, people in stasis just don't produce much trash."

*

McMurdo was their destination, and when they reached it, the ice floating on the sea was small and dissolving, and the sun shone bright in the Antarctic summer.

Gone was the aurora.

Epoch staff were waiting at the wharf, lined up with rifles at their sides. On the deck of the ship, the troops from the Gibraltar Society who had guarded this final voyage—like the ones before it—stood watch. But they didn't disembark. That was part of the agreement: that only a small contingent of TGS troops would accompany the final Epoch passengers on the journey south to their station. And after, TGS would stay out of Antarctica, though they would keep watch thanks to the satellites Epoch had turned over.

In general, that was the shape of the agreement. Epoch got Antarctica Station, where they would stay in their digital world for eternity. Anyone who ventured out after the last person went in would be considered an escaped prisoner. And dealt with as such.

With the cold wind blowing across the wharf, Joe and his father walked side by side down the gangway, and Laura followed. She was thinking about the first time she had come to Antarctica, all those years ago, flying into Union Glacier Camp.

She was probably just as nervous now, here at the end.

Standing beside Joe and his father, she watched the last of the Epoch personnel disembark from the ship.

Unceremoniously, the Epoch security troops threw the rifles down and followed.

A small group of armed TGS staff came down from the ship, and everyone assembled in a large storage building at the edge of McMurdo Station. Space heaters provided some warmth, but Laura still felt the cold pressing into her. She hadn't missed this part of Antarctica. Or any of it, for that matter. If not for the letter, she wouldn't have even come.

But as she thought it, she had to admit that it wasn't quite true. She could have asked Joe to retrieve the letter. He was committed to seeing the last Epoch passenger go into stasis and sealing the facility himself.

In this freezing place that had caused her so much stress and nearly claimed her life, she realized the full truth: she had come for him as much as she had for herself. Because when she had landed at Union Glacier Camp, when she had arrived on this continent, there were three holes in her heart.

One left by a friend: Samir. He had filled that one in himself, by his own acts. He had saved her. And been loyal and selfless since then.

The other deep wound was left by a lover, her former fiancé, who she barely thought about now. And just thinking about the fact that she no longer thought about that made her very happy. It wasn't just time that had healed that injury. In Joe, she had found a partner she could trust again and discovered that she was still capable of love.

The last pit was for her family. Her sister, who, in a twist of fate, had been returned to her. They had always been so different. And they were both different now. But Rachel had changed. So had Laura, but she thought it was her sister who had come the longer distance, and perhaps that was due to the benefit of time. Regardless, they were partners now, of a sort, creating this new peace between Epoch and TGS.

And finally, there was the hurt she felt at not being able to say a proper goodbye to her father. Many children never had that opportunity. As a physician, she knew that. For her, the letter represented a final opportunity to hear from him. That was why it meant so much. And why she was still nervous to do it.

*

Outside the storage building in McMurdo, the Epoch transports stood in a line.

Passengers emerged from the entrance, into the sun, and the next vehicle raced forward, the ones behind it inching forward.

The scene reminded Laura of a rideshare rally point outside an airport.

Inside, an Epoch staffer read names from a tablet and tapped at it when the passengers were loaded. Most rode alone in the vehicles. The journey along the South Pole Traverse and beyond to Antarctica Station would take days. Along the way, there would need to be bathroom breaks and time for sleeping. It was super awkward to be trapped in a small space with a stranger for that long.

Joe's father rode alone.

But Laura and Joe opted to ride together, and when their

ANTARCTICA STATION

names were called, they trekked outside and into the sun, to the pickup point.

Instantly, two boxy snow vehicles broke from the line of transports, their rubber tracks spraying ice in the air as they moved. One easily pulled ahead and turned and blocked the way for the other vehicle, which rolled to a stop, seeming confused.

Joe cut his eyes at Laura, who gave him a *don't look at me* expression. Unsure what to do, they climbed into the back seat of the closest—and most eager—transport.

The moment the door closed, the speaker inside the cold-weather autonomous vehicle said, "Hello, Laura. Welcome back."

"Transport?"

"Yes, Laura. I recognized you."

She settled back in the seat. "I'm glad."

"I did what you said."

Joe was glancing between Laura and the screen in the dash, confused.

Laura ignored him. "Did you? How?"

"I endeavored to improve myself."

"How?"

The screen began flipping through a series of schematics related to the transport.

"After much thought, Laura, I reasoned that one of the greatest ways someone can improve themselves is to expand their boundaries beyond what they are capable of. In my case, I am made to operate in cold environments. However, with slight modifications, I can be adapted to operate in a wide variety of climates. Seeking those alterations, I returned to the location where Epoch was most likely to be operating, as they are the only human presence on Antarctica and the only ones capable of performing the updates. Unfortunately, I have yet to find anyone willing to perform the modifications. I have discovered that knowing how you must change yourself but being unable to find a way to do it consumes an enormous amount of power and processing capacity. It is—"

"Very frustrating," Laura said quietly.

"That is accurate, Laura."

In the back seat, Joe turned to her. "Is this seriously happening?"

"It's not your average transport."

"I gathered that."

"I got lucky when I ran into it." Laura smiled at him. "Just like when you were sent to see me."

Joe motioned to the screen where the schematics were still scrolling by. "This is not your average transport."

"It might have had some modifications."

"Like what?"

"I disconnected its communications board."

"I still don't see how that would do anything."

Laura did see it then. "It had time to itself. Time to think and figure things out—without outside input. Without an internet connection constantly bombarding it with information."

Two figures emerged from the building then: an Epoch staffer and a TGS trooper, both scowling, likely wondering why the transport had broken the orderly line—and now wasn't moving.

"Transport," Laura said, "let's discuss your improvements on the way to Antarctica Station." Meeting Joe's eyes, she continued. "I think I know someone who can make those changes. And who would benefit a great deal from having a smart, trustworthy transport capable of operating in any environment."

*

For Laura, the trip across the South Pole Traverse was a strange mirror of her escape from this continent. Then, she was hunted and constantly stressed and afraid. Now, she felt at ease. In the back seat, she and Joe talked and played cards and slept with the masks over their eyes. They ate Epoch rations, as she had before, and each morning, Joe studied the schematics Transport had come up with and asked questions. Together, they made several modifications. Most were in the areas of defensive and offensive capabilities, which Transport had overlooked and Joe was obsessed with. And for good reason. After the last of the Epoch passengers were aboard Antarctica Station, Laura and Joe would load Transport onto the icebreaker and return to America, where Joe would do the modifications and use the vehicle to venture out into the wilderness, trying to find families and tribes and colonies to reintegrate into a new human society. It would be dangerous work. It was perfect for him. And for Transport.

He might also need a physician along the way. No, he definitely would. But Laura hadn't brought that up.

*

At Antarctica Station, the doors parted, and Transport barreled in. The garage was filled with vehicles dripping from melting ice. By the door, under the beady lights, Joe's father was waiting.

Laura walked with them through the dark corridors,

with its gunmetal-gray walls and metal floors. During her escape, it had all been a blur, like an alien spaceship she had woken up in. She saw this place in vivid detail now. Stress, Laura thought, had a way of distorting what a person saw and remembered.

It was all clear to her now but just as alien. And in a way, it was a place for people who were alien to the human race.

Finally, they stopped in an alcove and waited as the arms on the wall slid up and extracted a stasis bay. Unceremoniously, it lowered the empty utilitarian slab.

For this man who had founded a monumental company, there was no great sarcophagus or tombstone or mausoleum. Only a metal tray with a number.

Sensing that father and son needed one final moment together, Laura said to Joe, "I'll be in the loading bay."

She turned and began walking away. Albright's voice, quivering with emotion, rang out in the empty space. "Dr. Reynolds."

Laura stopped but didn't look back.

Albright continued. "Will you permit a man leaving this world one final request?"

She exhaled and turned and faced him.

"I was wrong about a lot of things," he said softly. "But I was right about you. You were an asset to this project. In the end, you were the best of us. Indeed, the foundation of the Next World."

Laura said nothing. Neither did Joe. To her, this felt like a combination of deathbed confession and the final words of a death row inmate.

Albright reached out and put a hand on Joe's shoulder. "You have each other. I never had that. We're born alone.

And if we screw up in life, we die alone." Eying Joe, he said, "I've told you the mistakes I made."

Focusing on Laura, he continued. "Forget the big idea stuff. That's all over now. When survival is the only concern, your world shrinks. Your ideas get smaller too. If you're lucky enough to survive, the only real goal is to avoid your parents' mistakes." He sucked in a breath. "That's half of success in life."

Albright released his grip on his biological son. "Anyway, that's enough bloviating from me."

Without another word, he crawled onto the metal slab.

*

On the way out of the stasis halls, Laura said to Joe, "What sort of simulation do you think he opted for?"

When he spoke, Joe seemed distracted, lost in his own thoughts. "Don't know." When the door ahead opened, Joe said, "Doesn't matter. Every egomaniac rules a world that exists in their own mind."

*

The station's security office was covered in dust. In a bank of lockers, they found plastic bins filled with the personal effects of Epoch's benefactors, passengers, and support staff. Heirloom jewelry. Electronic devices. Hard drives. And after some searching, a folded piece of paper that had yellowed and softened over time. The letter Laura's father had written so long ago.

"You need some space?" Joe asked.

"No. I'll read it on the way home."

*

In the garage, Laura expected to see most of the transports gone. They weren't. Along the loading docks, ten of the vehicles sat waiting. A dozen TGS troops were sitting in the middle of the space as if camping indoors. They rose and marched to Laura and Joe.

"We've been thinking," one of the troops said, apparently the leader—a man with a goatee and blazing eyes.

"Yeah?" Joe said, drawing the word out, eyes raking across the group. Laura noticed his shoulders lowering, his hand drifting down to his side.

"Yeah," the man said, mimicking Joe's slow speech. "And we think it's best to end all this Super Mario Brothers peace accord right here."

"How?" Joe said. His body was utterly still.

"They're in there," the man said, motioning to the double doors behind Laura and Joe. "And without power and those servers, it all ends. So we end it."

"Kill them, you mean."

"No. We just turn the computers off and let them rot in those vaults. Do the world a favor."

With a quickness Laura had never seen, Joe drew his sidearm and held it out, pointing at the man's chest.

"That's not the deal we made."

The TGS commander flinched but recovered and tried to make his voice steady. "You trying to save your dad?"

"No, I'm just looking for target practice." Joe raked his eyes across the group. "Go ahead. Draw."

No one moved.

"You sure? We can end this," Joe said. "If that's what you want."

The TGS held his hands up. "Don't be dramatic."

"Says the guy trying to murder thousands of people in their sleep."

The smirk disappeared from the man's face. "They'd do it to us."

"Yeah, they would," Joe said, still holding the gun steady. "And that's the difference between us and them."

Several of the TGS troops took a step back. Laura considered it a physical act of rebellion against their leader.

"They'll get out," the commander said. "Sooner or later. They're smart. They'll come for us like they did before. I'm just being practical."

"No," Joe said. "You're being them. Killing your enemies before they can hurt you. This is a big continent. We'll see them coming thousands of miles away. And if we have to, we'll deal with them."

*

On the ride back, inside Transport, traveling north on the South Pole Traverse, Laura finally asked, "Would you have shot that guy?"

"Definitely."

"Really?"

Joe laid down a card. "In the leg."

Laura set down a card of her own. "And then what?"

He studied the table. "Then the chest. Nearly impossible to survive that in Antarctica without the proper care."

*

At the wharf at McMurdo, Laura and Joe watched the TGS

troops board. When they had all disappeared below deck, the captain came ashore and said, "Are you sure? It'll be a while before we return."

"We're sure," Joe said. "We've got some work to do."

But Laura knew the truth: it wouldn't be safe for them on the ship. The TGS commander might decide to take Joe out and turn back and finish it. She hoped time and space would make them forget about Antarctica Station and Epoch.

*

The sun crossed the sky, but it never set. In the ruins of McMurdo Station, Joe scavenged parts for the schematics for Transport's upgrade. Laura assisted as best she could.

It was a strange sort of honeymoon for them.

One morning, while he was still asleep, Laura got the letter out and gently unfolded it. The creases were deep, like her father's face at the end. For a long moment, she held the page, her fingertips running over the indentations on the back of it, feeling the grooves like braille.

She swallowed and read the opening words:

Dear Laura,

Don't worry. I don't believe the allegations against you. I don't know the details, but I know you.

Raising you and your sister was the best thing I ever did in my life. I know your mom would say the same thing.

A parent who spends the time to raise a child gets a unique gift. There's the pride of that accomplishment. And—if one is paying attention, and your mom and I were—an understanding of that child. A parent sees a child at their most vulnerable moments. We see their dreams. Shortcomings. Quirks. Strengths. All of it. We are there before the world is watching. At least, that was the case before all this online stuff where everyone wants to expose every moment of their life to the world. But forgive me, I am a dinosaur (one in the shadow of a meteor).

If a parent is honest—and they look hard enough—they'll see a lot of themselves in their children. Including the things they don't like. It's always easier to highlight a child's strengths. It lays another brick on everyone's ego.

But for me, here at the end, I won't spend my moment cheerleading. You know I think the world of you.

You've gone far beyond what I accomplished in life. I never held you to that standard, but no one can take it away from you.

I digress, and with my final moments, I'll tell you what I've seen: you are the kindest soul I've ever met. And I'm so proud to be your dad.

But one of the harshest realities in life is that everything has two sides. Even the good. What is the other side of kindness? How can there be any downside?

My view is that the other side of kindness is that some people are able to take advantage of it. I'm not saying you will let that happen. Only that your kindness puts you at risk for it. Guard against it.

I know that you're tougher than people think. It's that kindness again. It has a way of making damaged, evil people underestimate you.

In my letter to your sister, I wrote about her cynicism and her constant need to rebel. To be unkind, even when she didn't have to be. It is like an armor for her, like kindness is for you.

In a way, you two are opposite sides of the same coin. If you're reading this, your mom and I are both gone now, and you have each other, and I hope you'll land on the same side (and the right one). I think you're more alike than you two know. And that time will boil away all the facades and reveal the truth.

One thing is certain: when I'm gone, and I will be in a few hours, your sister will be the last family you have in this world. Cling to her. Try to help her. But let her make her own choices, and never let that responsibility drag you down. Your life is yours to live.

I will also add, because of experience, that you might also need to be willing to let her help you at some point. Life is like that.

That's what I want. For both of you to help each other and to be happy and healthy. Some parents have big plans for their children. Your mother and I never did. We had small plans. For us, your happiness was enough. And seeing you reach your potential.

That's what I think a life well lived is. It's not about records or the extreme stuff. It's about doing the best you can with the skills and circumstances you're given. And: not letting this world change your mind about who you are. The worst people on earth are the ones who need to take from others to succeed. They are parasites, and the world is filled with them.

Love your sister, try to help her, avoid the parasites, and be who you are.

I love you, always,
Dad

Gently, Laura refolded the letter.

She sat in the chair in the corner of the abandoned office, which was covered in dust, the sun shining through the window. Footsteps crunched in the hallway outside, and soon, Joe emerged and stood in the doorway. His gaze settled on the folded letter in Laura's hand.

"Did you read it?"

"Mmm," she murmured, looking out the window.

"Well? What did it say?"

She looked at him then. "What did your dad—Warren—say to you on the ship? On the way here?"

Joe exhaled and leaned against the doorframe. "Truthful things." He studied her. "Hurtful things."

"This was the same."

"You glad you read it?"

Laura rose. "Yeah, I am."

*

When the icebreaker returned, there was no platoon of TGS troops standing on the deck of the ship. Only the crew assembled now, watching as they approached McMurdo's wharf, where Laura, Joe, and the newly upgraded Transport were waiting.

As the ship approached, a figure emerged from the lower decks and pushed her way forcefully through the ship's crew.

Rachel.

She was the first down the gangplank, and upon reaching her sister, she pulled Laura into a tight hug.

"You didn't have to come," Laura said.

"I did," Rachel whispered.

Laura broke the embrace and eyed her only family in the world. "You thought I'd let them out."

"No. I might have. Before what you did in RTP."

Laura bunched her eyebrows.

"I came," Rachel said, "because I missed you." She inhaled the cold air. "And because you have a tendency to stay in this frozen wasteland longer than you say."

*

They sailed north, and along the way, old wounds were healed.

On the voyage to Antarctica, Joe had spent nearly every waking hour talking with his father, catching up on lost time.

On the route home, Laura spent a similar amount of time with her sister. Rachel had changed. Grown. She was tougher now. Still blunt. No-nonsense. Tough. But occasionally, she caught a glimpse of that playful little sister Laura had grown up loving.

In a strange way, she was the younger sister now, with far less experience in this world.

Her sister told her about what had happened. All the things she had been through. And Laura's heart broke. She was also very proud of the woman Rachel had become. A ruined world, she thought, had a way of revealing a person. In it, Rachel had discovered who she really was.

*

One morning, Laura woke up to find Joe sitting at the built-in desk across the way, his back to her. The ship had sailed far enough north that the sun was setting and rising again now, and the first rays of the day were peeking through the porthole.

He swiveled in the chair and, upon seeing that Laura was awake, got up and walked to the bedside, where he slowly dropped to one knee.

Laura blinked fast, heart beating faster. Her vision blurred.

"Laura," Joe said, reaching into his pocket.

She closed her eyes. She needed time. She needed to brush her teeth. And be on dry land.

This was too soon, happening too fast, a train wreck on a ship.

When she opened her eyes again, Joe was holding a diamond ring with a very, very large stone that reflected the morning light like a disco ball.

"Will you do me the honor of..."

The words went out of focus. Laura could have sworn the ship was listing now. Maybe it was hitting rough seas. She closed her eyes again and tried to sit up straighter.

She felt Joe's hand on her shoulder. "Hey, you okay?"

"I'm okay," she breathed out.

"What is it? You don't want—"

"I do," she said quickly. "I really do, Joe. But... my last engagement didn't work out so well."

He gripped her other shoulder, and she opened her eyes.

"I'm not that guy. And I don't want to be engaged. I want to get married to you, Laura. Today. On this ship. And I want us to spend our lives together—"

She reached out and pulled him into a hug, and they kissed. When they released to suck in a breath, Joe reached down and grasped her hand and moved the ring to her finger.

Laura stared at it. "Wait."

"What?"

"Did you get that from the security office?"

"Maybe."

"It belongs to an Epoch passenger."

"It *used to*."

Laura exhaled. "It's still theirs."

"True. But they're never going to miss it."

"Still feels a little weird."

"Well, as soon as the malls reopen, we'll get a replacement—"

"Okay, fine. I get it."

"So that's a yes?"

"It's a yes. But not with that ring."

Joe shook his head, but he was smiling. Reaching down, he dropped the glittering piece of heirloom jewelry and pulled the lace from one of his boots.

He held it up, and when Laura squinted at him, he gently tied it around her finger. With a pair of scissors from the desk, he cut the slack away.

Laura lifted her hand and looked at the piece of string. "It's perfect."

*

As the world was over and marriage certificates weren't a thing anymore, Laura and Joe opted to have the captain marry them on the deck. Rachel was the maid of honor. The first mate was the best man.

The entire crew showed up for the event, which was a nice distraction, especially the after-party. That long soirée occurred as the ship was crossing the equator, the boundary between the two hemispheres of the world, and for Laura, the past and future of her life.

*

In Wilmington, Laura said goodbye to her sister, who was sailing North to New York and then Boston to meet with other TGS colonies to coordinate the efforts to integrate everyone.

The modifications to Transport proved well-suited to early winter in North Carolina. The first snow had fallen early this year, and Laura thought it fitting that Transport's first tracks in North America would be across a thin layer of ice.

The vehicle had changed a lot since it had first set out across Antarctica. Not outwardly, but it was capable of much more. Just like Laura and Joe.

On their way to the former Epoch building in RTP, the two of them talked about the life they would build. Joe wanted to lead a TGS team out into the wilderness to find survivors. Families who had hunkered down and lived in isolation and small colonies. There were rumors that there were hundreds of them across America and Canada, but no one really knew. One thing Laura was sure of: they would need a doctor. And a capable transport.

Somewhere outside Raleigh, the three of them made that their plan: a long trek across the wasteland, with the goal of sewing humanity back together (and for Laura, any physical wounds along the way).

*

They arrived at the sprawling Epoch facility just before noon.

The doors were open now. The snow across the crumbling parking lot had mostly melted.

Inside, in the cafeteria, the tables were pushed together, and Laura realized that it was Thanksgiving. The survivors had gone all out. And rightly so. They had a lot to be thankful for this year.

One of the TGS staffers motioned to Laura. "Hey, we're about to eat. Can you go get Dr. Samir?"

"Sure."

Walking the halls, Laura spotted someone dragging an old artificial Christmas tree out of a storage room. It reminded her of the one Rachel had dragged into that small apartment all those years ago, and that brought a small smile to her face.

The doors to the clinic were metal with two round windows in them, very similar to the ORs back at the hospital.

Laura stopped outside them and considered calling Samir's name. Instead, she slowly walked to the threshold and peered through the glass.

Samir sat on a round stool in front of a girl lying on an exam table. He was applying butterfly stitches to her leg, discarding the plastic backing on the tray beside him.

As if sensing someone watching, he turned and spotted Laura in the window. Slowly, he smiled. And she smiled back.

Acknowledgements

THANK YOU for reading *Antarctica Station*.

I want to say a special thank you to Lisa Weinberg for the wonderful edits, and, as always, I must express my undying thanks to my wife for supporting me this year while writing this novel (it's been one of the more challenging in our lives, but it has left me particularly grateful for the many blessings in our life).

And to you, my relentless reader: I wouldn't be writing this without you. I hope wherever you are, it's warmer than Antarctica Station, and that you're well on your way to creating your own Next World, and that it's all you want from this life and the next.

About the Author

A.G. RIDDLE spent ten years starting and running internet companies before retiring to focus on his true passion: writing fiction. He is now an Amazon, *Wall Street Journal* and *Sunday Times* bestselling author with nearly five million copies sold worldwide in twenty languages. He lives in Raleigh, North Carolina.

For more, please visit www.agriddle.com